ALONE AT LAST

Adrian took a step, as he had earlier. Only this time there was no one around to interrupt. Dru didn't back away from him, and he took heart from her open expression. Her lips parted as though to speak. He silenced them the best way he knew how.

Her lips, when he ___ ___ the softest of velvets ___ ___ shame. The delicate so___ ___ air around her. He g___ ___ and to his delight she ___

Her hand ___ his shoulders, and he was elated ___ closeness. His hands learned the shape of her as she nestled against him. Such a delight was one that could be repeated forever, and he doubted that he would ever tire of it—or her. . . .

Drusilla's Downfall

Emily Hendrickson

A SIGNET BOOK

SIGNET
Published by New American Library, a division of
Penguin Group (USA) Inc., 375 Hudson Street,
New York, New York 10014, U.S.A.
Penguin Books Ltd, 80 Strand,
London WC2R 0RL, England
Penguin Books Australia Ltd, 250 Camberwell Road,
Camberwell, Victoria 3124, Australia
Penguin Books Canada Ltd, 10 Alcorn Avenue,
Toronto, Ontario, Canada M4V 3B2
Penguin Books (N.Z.) Ltd, Cnr Rosedale and Airborne Roads,
Albany, Auckland 1310, New Zealand

Penguin Books Ltd, Registered Offices:
80 Strand, London WC2R 0RL, England

Published by Signet, an imprint of New American Library,
a division of Penguin Group (USA) Inc.

First Printing, July 2003
10 9 8 7 6 5 4 3 2 1

Prologue

*F*ate, Drusilla decided with rising anticipation, was being extremely kind. She listened to her mother read the contents of the letter from her old school friend. It seemed that Mama's connection from so long ago, now holding the impressive title of Marchioness of Brentford, was in need of a companion while she recovered from an illness.

They were seated in the cozy morning room, gathered before the fire. Drusilla perched on the wing chair, eagerly waiting to hear what came next.

"It seems you are needed, my dear," Mrs. Herbert said in surprised accents, staring at her fourth daughter in delight. "She recalled my mentioning you girls and hopes I should be able to spare *you*, Drusilla, for a time. Not just anyone would do, you see. I must have remarked on what an excellent manager you have become."

Drusilla tamped down her excitement when she faced reality. "But if I were to go, that would leave you with only Tabitha for company. Other than Father, of course." Papa was not around all that much; his duties as rector of the parish kept him much occupied when he wasn't composing learned treatises on some obscure point of religion.

"The other girls are bound to return home at one point or another. My, this has been an eventful March." Mrs. Herbert stared off into space a few moments before turning her attention to Drusilla, offering her a fond look.

Then Mrs. Herbert frowned, and Drusilla wondered what nasty thing was to interfere. Of course, this request was bound to be too good to be true. Her heart plunged to her toes with the thought that she had high hopes only to find them dashed.

"There is, of course, the matter of her ladyship's son," Mrs. Herbert said. "She has in past letters bemoaned his unwillingness to marry and the wild life he leads in London, pursuing women and in general appearing to think life is one long lark. Fortunately, he would not be apt to be at their country residence, so you would be safe from any attentions he might send your way."

Drusilla thought the prospect of attentions from a London buck to a prim girl from the rectory highly unlikely. Not wishing to disillusion her mother on this score, she kept silent about any prospects, scandalous or otherwise.

"Since your sister Nympha sent us that marvelous package of lace, we should be able to create some very nice gowns, quite suitable for life at Brentford Court."

"She sent us each money as well, Mama," Drusilla reminded. "I should be able to present myself in garments quite proper for a companion." She made a wry face at Tabitha. She knew her younger sister would sympathize with her yearnings for stylish dresses.

"As to that, I do not see why we must garb you in drab things. She was Lady Violet Greene when we were in school, and she adored wearing the latest styles. I doubt she has changed much." Mrs. Herbert rose from her chair. "I fancy the notion of sending you dressed in the height of fashion, my dear. I think it will be a credit to your father."

Tabitha smothered whatever she intended to retort to that comment with a hasty cough.

"Yes, indeed, Mama." Family pride was to come to Drusilla's rescue. All of a sudden life held excitement, the promise of unknown delights. True, she would be at the beck and call of an ailing woman the age of her mother. But if they were good friends, surely she must be a kind person?

"We will send an acceptance at once, then go into Tunbridge Wells to buy all the fabric you shall need for a complete wardrobe."

Drusilla exchanged a delighted look with Tabitha. Odd, they had just been musing about how dull it was in the village with their three older sisters gone from home. And then the letter came—the third astounding letter this month.

Garbed in modish attire, Drusilla would be able to venture forth, ready for any adventure that might occur. That it was highly unlikely she would encounter such while caring for an older lady in the seclusion of her country estate didn't bother Drusilla. Normally a practical girl, her daydreams were allowed to take form and bloom.

The letter agreeing to Drusilla's visit was sent off, and a suitably delighted reply came back including details of Drusilla's trip.

The local mantua maker obtained extra help, and before she could believe it, Drusilla had a wardrobe assembled. True, it was a modest one, but she had the sort of gowns she had yearned to possess for ever so long.

The day of departure found her garbed in a charming white muslin round gown under a blue silk pelisse trimmed in matching blue plush velvet. She wore a dashing bonnet of the same blue silk and velvet that had the dearest feather curling around the brim. Blue as well, of course. The color matched her eyes, and she knew it flattered her honey blond curls. A glance in her looking glass showed that excitement brought a becoming pink to her cheeks, and she curved her lips in happy anticipation.

The knowledge that in her trunk reposed any number of smart dresses and gowns, a stylish spencer, and more slippers than she had owned heretofore gave her confidence.

Placing a foot on the step of the carriage sent for her, she entered the first stage of her journey to Brentford Court in the distant country of Herefordshire.

Tabitha ran a finger over the crest on the carriage door. "Enjoy all you can," she urged quietly so Papa wouldn't hear. He expected Drusilla to work all the time.

"I shall, believe me." Drusilla waved to her parents and brother, sharing a special smile with Tabitha as the carriage set forth. She was off and away!

Chapter One

*T*he March wind whipped some stray papers along St. James's Street along with a gentleman's tall hat. The fellow chased it, catching hold as he cornered it by the entrance to the esteemed White's, considered the supreme London club for gentlemen. Donning the hat after a casual brushing off, he entered the club, depositing said hat with the porter. He went around the corner to the morning room, where he found the man he sought—Brentford.

"I say, old man, never had such a fine time as I did at your country place. At least," Lord Taylor amended, "not for some years." He looked to another man seated nearby for confirmation who nodded his agreement. "Your mother looks splendid, positively top-of-the-trees. Handsome woman, I must say. Certainly gave a fine party. Never know she had been ill." He smiled, a gleam lighting his eyes. "Why, she kept us all on our toes. The young lady who keeps her company was rather fetching as well, if I do say so. Comely lass, wouldn't you say, Osman? Sensible, too."

Adrian Richmond, the Marquess of Brentford, lounged back in one of the comfortable club chairs to be found in the morning room of White's. Not even his closest friend would have spotted his rising ire. He rubbed his jaw, listening with apparent pleasure to the accolades heaped on the beauty of his country home, his delightful and charming mother, and not the least of it, her companion—a companion he had known nothing about!

He had spent a productive morning with his tailor, deciding on a new coat of the finest Bath cloth in a muted mulberry, a superb cream Marcella waistcoat, and a pair of fine black pantaloons in a smooth wool. He had been in the best of spirits when he had strolled into White's, assured of his welcome. Now he brushed off a speck of dust from his pristine biscuit breeches, examined the shine of his Hessians, glanced at the sleeve of his corbeau coat from which the spotless linen cuff of his shirt extended the proper length. It was a means of calming his vexation.

"This young woman is a wonder, Brentford. I have been at your country estate in the past, but this mere slip of a girl has the place running on oiled wheels." His father's close friend and still friend to his mother, Lord Osman, peered at him not far from where Adrian sat in silence, at last broken by him.

"A most worthy young lady, I take it?" Adrian kept the sarcasm out of his voice with effort. One who knew him well would have taken note of the darkening of his brown eyes, flashing with rising ire. Why had he not been informed of this young woman? To learn his mother had hired a companion was not all that bad, but he should have been told.

"What do you mean by 'worthy,' dear boy? Hardly so. She is an enchantress. Why, were I twenty years younger—and not wed—I'd have tried to attract her myself. But then, surely you must have met her?" Lord Taylor queried.

"She truly sounds a paragon. Boring lot, paragons— eh, Ives?" Adrian exchanged a cynical glance with the man at his side, Reginald, Lord Ives, raising an eyebrow as he did. "I regret to say I've not met this jewel."

"I daresay there are occasional exceptions to the rule, Brentford." The gray eyes that returned his gaze held a measure of reserve, quite as though the owner knew personally of such a thing. Ives continued, "She actually may be all they claim."

Adrian stared at his good friend for a few moments, then rubbed his jaw again, deep in thought. At last he said in his low-pitched voice, "Perhaps it is time I paid my mother a visit. She wrote she is much better, but I'd see for myself."

"What? At the height of the season?" Lord Osman cried in dismay. "It is one thing for those of us of the older generation to jaunt off for a party, but were you to leave, all the hostesses of the *ton* would be desolate."

"I think you overestimate my attraction, Osman." He turned to his companion. "Perhaps you will join me?"

"Perhaps," Ives said with a considering frown. "However, I think it best were you to have time alone with your mother, without the distractions of others. Besides, I am obligated to a number of dinners and a few balls. I'd not care to raise the ire of any hostess by failing to appear!" Ives gave Adrian an ironic look.

"True. I have engagements as well." Adrian considered the matter in silence while Taylor and Osman chatted on about the delights found at Brentford Court. He did have obligations in London that must be met. No one of any character at all accepted a dinner invitation, then begged off at the last minute. It simply wasn't done. He listened with half an ear to the concluding remarks about his mother and her companion before the topic was changed at last.

The other wandered off at last to seek friends.

Adrian rose, bid Ives farewell for the time being, and headed for his London house still mulling over the matter of his mother and this worthy young miss who appeared to have taken over his country home. He would wager this clever chit was buttering up his mother in the hope she would bestow some of her generous income on her. He knew the sort—grasping females, the lot of them. He had encountered more than a few along the way. Perhaps there was time in which to prevent disaster? His mother was not likely to hand out sums of money on a whim. Surely he could take care of business in Town first?

Well, he would attend the promised dinners, look in on a few balls, then once free, he would head for Brentford Court. And he would send this young interloper packing.

Drusilla surveyed the bedroom with a near-professional eye. The bed was freshly made with lavender-scented sheets; all was in readiness for a guest. She believed in preparedness. There were a few books placed on the bedside table should the guest desire something to aid in sleep. She had put a fresh supply of paper, a nicely sharpened quill pen, and a full inkpot on the writing desk. The room had been well aired, too.

As she walked downstairs, she considered all that had occurred since she arrived at the Court in March. She had been welcomed warmly and made to feel completely at home.

The beautiful room she had been given was done in shades of blue and cream with a marvelously comfortable four-poster bed, and she was treated to life as she had never known it. The wardrobe was far larger than needed to hold her modest array of garments, but she refused the marchioness's kind offer to augment her selection. To have a chaise longue by the window overlooking the gardens to the rear of the house was treat enough. She could sit here in idle moments—which admittedly were few—to contemplate the gorgeous view.

The marchioness was a delight. Tall and a little too slim, likely a result of her illness, she had perfect posture and a regal presence, yet wasn't intimidating in the least. Her dark hair was streaked with gray, and there were fine lines by her sable-brown eyes, but those eyes saw everything of note. Best of all was her smile, which she bestowed on Drusilla often.

She bloomed with the tender care that Drusilla lavished on her. Poor darling, she must have been dreadfully lonely before, with little company to amuse her hours. Drusilla had quietly altered that.

She saw to it that the house was run with little bother to her ladyship, enlisting the help of Priddy and Mrs. Simpson. The butler and housekeeper, aging retainers who adored their mistress, were eager to do anything to make her life easier. So Drusilla had stepped in and, after first consulting with Mrs. Simpson, began doing many of the little tasks the housekeeper now found difficult.

The little party Drusilla dreamed up had turned out a wonderful success. The elderly gentlemen and ladies, while few in number, had entertained the marchioness splendidly. Drusilla, recalling the things her parents and others their age liked to do, set out to see the visitors were well amused. It had worked, too. Of course the marchioness had been cosseted and kept from overdoing, but she had enjoyed the small gathering so much.

It was time to cheer the marchioness with some music. It was pleasant that they both enjoyed the same composers and the same pieces.

"All is in readiness for your next influx of company, ma'am. We will not be caught unprepared." Drusilla offered a quick curtsy while giving an impish smile.

"Dear girl, what would I do without you," Lady Brentford said with a fond smile. "When I asked your mother if she might spare her daughter, I had no idea what a jewel I was to acquire."

Drusilla laughed lightly in amusement. "I am not so out of the ordinary, ma'am." She quickly sought the pianoforte and began to play the music she knew her ladyship enjoyed.

While playing the lively sonata by Mozart, she considered her present situation. She had no idea how long she might remain here, but it behooved her to make the best of things and do her duty by the lady who obviously needed someone to be with her. Of course she would have liked to be tending her own household, but fine gentlemen didn't grow on trees, particularly for a rector's daughter. Not that she was penniless. She merely had a modest portion, nothing to tempt a gentleman unless he had an abundance of his own. That she was a comely miss she dismissed, never having nurtured a high opinion of her looks. After all, she had four lovely sisters as well as a brother who took delight in puncturing any vanity.

She wondered about the son. Thankfully, he had not appeared on the scene. She hoped the attractions of London would be sufficient to hold his interest for months to come. Not that she had heard evil of him—in spite of the rumor that he disliked women—not trusting them, Mrs. Simpson had confided with relish. She'd hinted of a love gone wrong with a predatory woman of the wrong sort—whatever that might be.

Rather, it was that he rarely came here and never for long. How sad for the lonely lady who had endured her illness with such fortitude. Now she made excellent progress, no thanks to that neglectful offspring. If he did show up at the door, Drusilla had a mind to give him a scold for his dereliction of duty to his only living parent. She couldn't imagine treating her dear parents with such lack of care or consideration.

What the marchioness required was someone to take an interest in her well-being and urge her to improve. It was an enjoyable task, one that Drusilla had taken to with a will. She had efficiently instituted a number of comforts offering relief for her ladyship. What a joy it had been to see her improve. Dru concluded the Mozart.

"Now what would you like me to play for you?" Dru inquired, her voice and manner bright.

"Something soothing, I think. Do you believe I might have another party? I should like to invite Lord Osman again. Some younger people as well. Perhaps I may entice Adrian here. He comes so seldom, I fear it is too dull for his amusement." She frowned, looking a little sad.

What Drusilla thought of having to lure one's own son to visit was not uttered. She turned the pages of the music before her while she thought. "I do not see why such an entertainment could not be done. Is there anything more agreeable than a gathering of friends?"

"Oh, good." Her ladyship's face cleared, and she beamed a smile at Drusilla. "I hoped you would concur with me. I think it would be rather nice if there was a young gentleman about your age. These older men, while pleasant for me, are not the thing for you, my dear."

"Dear Ma'am, I am not here to find a husband!"

"I did not say you had to marry the chap, merely have company." The marchioness gave Drusilla such an innocent look, it was immediately suspect.

"And who else might you wish to invite?" Drusilla thought the matter of a gentleman to amuse her best ignored. How could she oversee a party if she had to entertain some man she didn't know—and probably didn't care two pins about?

"Well, Lady Felicia Tait is a charming young woman. I have long thought she would be an excellent wife for Adrian. She has a fine dowry and is a pretty behaved girl." She glanced at Drusilla before looking down at the needlework in her lap. "You shall write invitations to the list I will give you. Priddy will know where the addresses for them are—in the library desk, I believe."

"It will be my pleasure, ma'am." If this lonely lady wanted company, she would have it. And Drusilla would see to it that she did not overtax her strength or become overly stimulated.

Drusilla settled on a piece of music that she knew her ladyship found tranquil and began to play. She wasn't polished, but her playing had improved measurably while using the fine Broadwood grand pianoforte that stood in the corner of the drawing room. It was a far cry from the spinet housed at the rectory.

Later that afternoon while the marchioness took her nap, Drusilla spent some time in the library at the immense desk that took pride of place in the center of the far end of the room. Tall windows that opened out onto the terrace were behind the desk, providing extra light for the person seated there.

Priddy, that elderly but most efficient butler, found all the required addresses for the list of names. He handed them to Drusilla with a question in his eyes.

"Her ladyship desires another party, Priddy."

"I see his lordship's name on that list. Not likely that he will attend. A trifle dull, I should think, Miss Herbert. He's a top-of-the-trees London gentleman, if you follow my thinking. A party in the country at the height of the London Season would hardly appeal to him."

"Well, I shall make a point of urging him to come. Perhaps I can think of words that will entice him? Since Lady Felicia is on the list, he might be attracted with the promise of her company." She gave the butler a grin before settling down to hot-pressed paper, fine quality ink, and a good pen with one of those new steel nibs that truly made writing an enjoyment.

The directions for his lordship were in the Mayfair area of London, something she expected. His mother had said he had rented out the grand mansion built by his father years ago. It seemed that Lord Brentford found a small, neat house more to his liking.

Well, it would be sensible, she supposed, for a single man not to rattle around in the family mansion. Sad, though, in a way. He ought to be married with a clutch of grandchildren for her ladyship to enjoy.

Setting aside her vague dislike for the yet-to-be-met gentleman, she completed writing and addressing the invitations. She had a good hand, as did all the girls at the rectory. Their father had seen to that part of their education. He insisted every young lady should have a fine hand, able to write well so that her words could be easily read. She could do her sums as well, and calculate bills with ease.

When finished with the invitations, she handed the results to Priddy before going to gaze out of the window in the drawing room. Since it was on the ground floor, the gardens seemed close and inviting. It was a mild day with a sun shining down on the scene. She quite longed to stroll among the beds of flowers the marchioness had instructed the gardener to plant.

The tulips were bursting into bloom, as were anemones and primroses. The Brentford Court gardens were exceptionally beautiful now and likely to remain so all the year. The head gardener was devoted to her ladyship and exerted himself to please her. The extensive lawns were scythed to impeccable smoothness. The marchioness could stroll across to admire the blooms without fear of stumbling.

So, after her refreshing nap, they did just that. Leaving the house by one of the French windows, they wandered through the garden. The flower beds were praised, the colors sighed over, and the scent inhaled with delight. Drusilla picked a cluster of the blooms for her ladyship so she might sniff the scent, feel the satiny petals.

"I am so glad you are here with me, dear girl. I'd not likely meander along these flowers were I alone."

There was no self-pity in her ladyship's words. Rather she was matter-of-fact in her statement. She knew her limitations and attempted to stay within them. Drusilla coaxed her to try that little bit more, improve that tiny speck each day, extending those limits. They understood each other well, her ladyship going along with Drusilla's suggestions with a knowing smile. Time and again she remarked how like a daughter Drusilla had come to be.

"I suppose I cannot claim you here forever. Some handsome fellow will steal you away from me, I feel sure. But until then, I intend to enjoy your company." She gave Drusilla a sweet smile that held a merest hint of mischief.

When rain threatened, they hurried to the house and settled with a tea tray before a nicely blazing fire in the drawing room, Lady Brentford's favorite place on the ground floor. She applied herself to her needlework. Kitty, a plump silver-striped tabby, curled up by her feet, creating the perfect image of domesticity.

She glanced at Drusilla from her needlework to remark, "I do hope Adrian will come. I've not seen him for ages. Not that I am one of those mothers who ask for constant attention from a son, especially one as much in demand as Adrian. But it would be nice to see him."

Drusilla returned a stiff smile, thinking she would most definitely give his lofty lordship a piece of her mind should he deign to share his exalted company with them. The very idea that he should believe the paltry offerings of London more important than the health and well-being of his mother! Drusilla quite longed to give him a sound tongue-lashing.

At the Metcalf ball, Adrian bowed to the young woman before him, trying to recall her name. They had been introduced, he was certain, but her name had made no impression on him, nor had she. He sighed inwardly and swept her off to partake in a lively reel.

Really, the fulfillment of the obligations that remained before he could head down to Brentford Court were most trying. The dinner prior to the ball had been excellent. The company was boring. Or perhaps it was just himself?

At last the dance ended and Adrian wondered how soon he might leave without offending the couple who had invited him. Their son, Harry, was a particular friend of his.

"Nice do, eh, Brentford?" Gray eyes lit with laughter met his. Lord Ives said, "I know how you dote on balls and the like."

"Ives. Just when I was ready to do a flit. Are you about ready to leave all this?" Adrian gestured to the colorful throng now performing an elegant country-dance.

"I promised to follow you some while after you go. Perhaps this girl isn't what you suspect." Lord Ives bent his head, studying his polished patent dancing slippers with seeming interest. "She might be one of those rare creatures who enjoy helping others. Didn't your mother write that her father is a rector? I should think a girl from the rectory would be accustomed to doing good deeds."

"Good deeds, bah." Adrian smiled politely and bowed in the direction of one of the leading lights of Society.

"Pity you cannot put the past behind you." Then, likely knowing he had said more than he ought, Lord Ives began an amusing anecdote on a mutual friend that lightened the mood considerably.

Later, while enjoying the light supper offered at midnight, Adrian's thoughts returned to the remark his friend had made. Putting the past behind him was something he had not bothered to do, he supposed. Ives insisted it had turned him into a woman hater, a true misogynist. Adrian didn't think so. He still enjoyed a dance, a pretty dinner partner. He simply didn't trust them.

It was several days later that the missive arrived with his post. Adrian broke the seal, then unfolded the letter. It was an invitation to his own home! By Jove, this was the outside of enough! He took note of the date when it was hoped he could arrive, and decided he would go a day or two early. Nothing like catching the enemy off guard!

He knew the handwriting was not his mother's, so it must belong to the companion. She prettily begged him to join the small gathering in honor of his mother's birthday. He had forgotten that was coming up, the family not given to lavish displays for such events. But her words were couched in phrases designed to make him feel the veriest cad if he didn't appear. Lady Felicia Tait's delightful company was hinted at—if she accepted, and she would.

He would attend, all right. And he would send this calculating hussy back to the village where she belonged. She could jolly well tend the biddies there and leave his mother—and her fortune—safely behind.

He couldn't wait to meet her.

Chapter Two

$\mathcal{A}$drian found a suitable gift for his mother at Rundell, Bridge and Rundell's jewelry shop. She liked sapphires, so he bought an especially lovely brooch designed like a spray of delicate blue flowers with emeralds for leaves and diamonds sparkling as accents.

Returning to his house, he found himself drawn again to the invitation. He studied the precise handwriting, perfectly formed letters, and the words therein. Very prettily put, those words. They would squeeze tears from a stone. "Come to celebrate the birthday of your devoted mother," he read aloud.

Tossing the sheet of hot-pressed paper on his desk, he wandered to the window that looked out on the busy street below. How could he best prepare for this confrontation? That he intended to send the presumptuous chit packing, he had determined. But how to get around his mother? Could she have formed an attachment for this village girl? True, the gel wrote an excellent hand. Likely her father saw to that. But her education would be sadly lacking, not to mention her social graces. He very much doubted if she was so much as acquainted with proper use of a finger bowl.

Curious as to her family, he sought out a fellow he'd met who would possibly have some information. He had met the Archdeacon Pallant at one of the more elevated parties he'd attended this Season.

Surely he might be acquainted with the various rectors near London?

It didn't take long to find him—at White's of all places. He joined him, casually making his inquiry.

"Hmm, the Reverend Mr. Herbert, you say? I do know something of him. The family is an old one, goes back to the Conqueror's days, you know. He is the eldest son of Lord James Herbert, the second son of the Earl of Stanwell. Has six children but limited money. Wrote some excellent papers. Is that what you wished to know?" He cocked his head at Adrian, curiosity clear in his eyes.

"I believe that will do." Seeing that he needed to give some explanation, he added, "My mother has one of the Herbert girls staying with her as a companion."

The archdeacon nodded with supreme dignity. "Most appropriate. She is of good family and doubtless knows how to serve others. Most rectory children are taught from childhood to be caring people."

Adrian had the feeling that the archdeacon knew more but chose not to say it. While it piqued Adrian's interest, he had received the essential information he required and was content to let it be at that.

Adrian concluded the conversation while considering the intelligence given him. Caring? Oh, this chit was undoubtedly caring, and undoubtedly hoping for a fat plum to fall in her lap from his rich mother.

He had not expected the girl to be from a fine gentry family, however. The Reverend Mr. Herbert could use Esquire following his name if he chose, being the eldest son of the second son of a peer. This put a slightly different slant to the picture. The chit, this Miss Herbert, was not some nobody. She had connections. He must proceed with care. The Earl of Stanwell might be elderly and not mix in Society, but he was a man to be reckoned with. His grandson was everywhere in London, at all the best soirées and dinners. Adrian had to admit he was of the highest *ton*. He mulled over just how he ought to proceed until his thoughts were cut off when Lord Ives entered the room.

"Ives, good fellow! I am glad to see you." Adrian rose to his considerable height and crossed the room to grasp his friend's hand.

"I gather something has annoyed you. What ho?" They walked back to stand before the window slightly apart from the others in the room.

"A surprise. I talked with Archdeacon Pallant only to discover that the companion who clings to my mother is none other than the great-niece of the Earl of Stanwell. Her father is the eldest son of Lord James Herbert."

"That does put a different complexion on it. What will you do now? You can scarce claim she isn't fit to serve your mother as a companion, coming from gentry of that standing!" Ives took a seat near the window. Adrian joined him in a moment after taking two glasses of fine sherry from the summoned footman.

"I am not sure," Adrian admitted. "I suppose I will have to decide what approach is best once I get there."

"When do you plan to leave?"

Adrian gave his old friend an amused smile. "Several days before I am expected. The element of surprise ought to work in my favor, would you not agree?"

Lord Ives studied his longtime friend before replying. "I trust you know what you are doing. Somehow I doubt your mother is going to take kindly to your shipping her companion back to her village. What will you do if she objects?"

"My mother has never argued with me before. I have no doubt she will see the wisdom of my wishes in this instance." Adrian ignored the skeptical look Ives sent his way. That he might upset his mother was a thought he nudged aside. All he did was for her own good.

"If you say so. I intend to join you as soon as I can leave London. All of a sudden, I have the feeling that you are going to have a turbulent time. I'd like to see that." Ives's grin rankled just a bit.

Later, Adrian returned to his house before going to dine with friends. He paused in the hall, then entered his study to stare down at the crisp sheet of cream paper. A roguish smile lit his face. Sitting down, he pulled out a piece of his own writing paper to compose his acceptance.

Dipping his pen into the inkpot, he thought for a moment before beginning to write. When finished he read the words aloud, satisfied that they conveyed no more than he wished. He sealed it with a blob of red wax. It did not say precisely when he would arrive on his own doorstep. After all, his household was to be ready for him at any time.

That knotty problem solved, he went to his bedroom and, with the help of his valet, Colyer, he dressed for dinner. At the same time he informed Colyer that they would be removing to the country estate in a few days' time.

"Pack enough for a few weeks. I have no idea how long this business will take down there."

Never mind that the estate was north of London. One always spoke of London as being up and anywhere else as being down. It had been that way as long as he could remember, and likely would remain so.

He went off to his engagement in a high state of anticipation, his lips curved into a genuine smile of satisfaction. Not even the vapid conversation of the young woman who was his dinner partner dimmed his feeling of pleasure at his coming confrontation. He would succeed. That girl would go. He'd see to it.

Drusilla brought the post to her ladyship, where she was seated in her favorite chair by the drawing room fire.

"Here you are, dear ma'am. There looks to be acceptances to your birthday party."

"Hmm. I recognize Adrian's writing on this letter." She broke the seal, bits of red wax falling into her lap.

Drusilla waited while the older lady read. Then she thrust the letter into Drusilla's hands. "Read it and see what you make of it."

Drusilla did as instructed. "Mother, dear, I look forward to celebrating your birthday with you. I will contrive to arrive in good time."

Silence reigned for a few moments.

"Well, other than he says he is coming, we are given no date for his arrival."

Tapping the note against the arm of her chair, Drusilla considered his words. "I wonder if he thinks to catch us out? I believe I will go to his room at once to make certain all is in order. I'd not have him complaining that things are not done right."

Lady Brentford gave her a quizzical look, then nodded. "I suspect you have the right of it, my dear."

Drusilla checked to see her employer had all she wished before seeking out Mrs. Simpson.

"Lawks, if it wouldn't be just like his lordship to pop up when least expected. We had best air his room and see to the dusting. I'll send the maid up when she is finished with the dining room."

"I believe I shall inspect it for myself." Drusilla exchanged a significant look with the housekeeper. "Perhaps if all is not to his liking he will blame me, and I'd not have that!"

"As if anyone could find fault with you, Miss Drusilla. The things you do here!"

After offering a pleased smile, Drusilla left the housekeeper's room to find her way to the one designated as belonging to Lord Brentford.

Throwing open the door to the suite belonging to the marquess, she began a meticulous inspection. The writing desk was fine, she checked the fireplace, and made certain that the windows gleamed in the May sun. She could visualize a fine gentleman in here, relaxing before his fire, enjoying a glass of wine before going down to dinner.

At last, content the room was as it should be, she went to the adjacent bedroom. The four-poster was intimidating, very masculine in its cream and deep blue damask bed hangings. There was a crown atop the canopy, and she fancied it well became the lofty gentleman who had such regal notions.

The bed linen was reasonably fresh, lavender scent still lingering in it. She was able to report all was well when she returned to her mistress.

"I imagined it would be, my dear. Do not worry so. Adrian won't bite you." She smiled as she said this, but Drusilla noted that she seemed uneasy.

"No? I imagine you are right." The subject was changed and they went in to dinner in perfect amity.

It was but two days later that dust rising from the graveled avenue alerted them to approaching company.

So warned, Drusilla stationed herself in the entryway, urging Priddy to go forth to greet the guest.

Only, it wasn't a guest. His lordship had arrived.

"My valet will be along with the luggage shortly, Priddy. I trust all is well?"

Priddy, almost speechless with delight at the sight of the master, bowed and ushered him toward the drawing room. They were partway there when his lordship spied Drusilla.

"Good day, Lord Brentford. I hope you had a pleasant journey?" A woman stepped forward from the shadows.

The thought rushed through his mind that this young woman was not only self-possessed, she was very beautiful. Honey blond hair neatly bound back from her face allowed a man to enjoy her luminous blue eyes and creamy complexion, not to overlook her sweetly curved lips. Upon closer inspection, he observed, her eyes were the aqua-blue of the sea on a fine day. They sparkled like the sea as well, causing him to wonder what prompted that glitter. At his perusal a blush rose to tint her cheeks, creating a beauty beyond belief. However, there was no welcoming smile.

This was going to be difficult. Had she been ugly, it would have been a snap to dispose of her. Somehow, her loveliness changed matters, although he wasn't sure why.

"I gather you are Miss Herbert?" He strove for composure, not wishing her to think she impressed him.

"Indeed so. Miss Drusilla Herbert, companion to your lady mother. You will find her much improved. She is in the drawing room as usual at this time of day, at her needlework." She curtsied gracefully, thus affording him a good look at her figure. She had a fine bosom, he noticed, and she was slender, but not too thin.

When she straightened up, she looked at him and he was taken aback at the dislike he saw in her eyes. He was accustomed to fawning, flattering females, not a clear-spoken young woman who stared at him with her dislike—if it was no more than that—obvious.

"Excuse me, my lord. I have things to do." She bobbed a slight curtsy before whirling about to march up the stairs. As she went up, her hips swayed in a fetching way. Looking at her blond tresses, so neatly bound, he wondered how long they were and how they would look cascading down her back. He stared after her, feeling as though someone had punched him in the stomach.

"Ahem," Priddy said. "Her ladyship is anxious to see you, my lord."

"What? Oh. Yes, indeed." Feeling slightly off kilter, Adrian strolled into the drawing room to seek his mother.

"What happened, dear? You were a long time in the entryway. Did something nasty occur to your luggage?"

While something happened, it wasn't to his luggage.

"Not at all. I merely paused to greet your companion."

"You met Drusilla Herbert. Isn't she a lovely creature? And she is as good as she is pretty. I do not know how I would manage without her."

Adrian thought back to the young woman he had

seen in the entryway. "Pretty" was inadequate to describe such a breathtaking female. If she chanced to walk into an assembly in London garbed in the latest fashion, she would likely create a riot with all the men seeking her hand.

He gave himself a mental shake to dislodge the image of the beautiful Drusilla. Perhaps he might call her something else less evocative. Dru sounded brief, blurring the memory of those swaying hips, that tantalizing bosom, not to mention those eyes with the hint of the tempestuous sea in them. Indeed, he would call her Dru.

"Forget this young woman you allow to impose on you. I insist you cancel this foolishness, this birthday party. Surely you are not well enough to tolerate such nonsense!"

Lady Brentford dropped her needlework, ignoring its fall to the floor. She stared at her son as though he had just gone mad. "You surely do not mean that!"

"I do. I fancy it is the influence of this young woman that led you into such absurdity. You are barely on your feet, and now you plan a house *full* of guests to entertain. I forbid it." He had no doubt she wanted the party. The question was, would she survive it!

She sank back against her chair, her right hand clutching her throat while her left grabbed at the arm of the chair, as though she was about to faint. "I cannot deny you the right to cancel an event in what is, after all, your home. Although it was mine before you were born." She looked into the glowing fire a few moments before returning her gaze to him.

It was an anguished gaze, causing Adrian to waver in his determination. He truly loved his mother; he had never been very good at showing it. But he also knew what her doctor had told him, that she must lead a quiet life for some time to come, else her heart might be weakened.

"I thought you cared enough to permit me the company of a few friends," she declared in quiet accusation. "You are never here. I become lonely. It has been better since Drusilla came, but still . . ." She straightened in her chair, composing her hands in her lap and glaring at him in a defiance she'd not have done before that young woman came. Dru.

"The little affair you had here a few weeks ago did no harm?" He was weakening and he hated that. Once he set a course, he usually was determined to stay with it.

"No, no. I have been just fine. Drusilla took care of all the details for me. All I did was sit quietly and visit with friends, enjoy excellent meals, and listen to Drusilla entertain us with music in the evenings. She is a very accomplished musician."

"I am sure she is accomplished at a number of things," Adrian said dryly. "Nevertheless she must go, and you must forget about that party. Cancel it at once and send your regrets." He placed his hands behind his back, pacing before the fireplace while thinking furiously.

"Did I hear you correctly? You not only want me to cancel this party, but send Drusilla Herbert home?"

"Yes." He nodded at her comprehension.

"I cannot believe what I just heard." Tears rolled down her porcelain cheeks from eyes so like his. She found a handkerchief in her reticule and dabbed at her eyes, blowing her nose in a refined manner. "You do not know what this girl means to me. She is like a daughter. I thank heaven every day that my dear school chum was willing to share one of her five girls with me."

She had hit a vulnerable spot, for Adrian well knew how she had wished for a daughter.

"Nevertheless, she must go. I blame her for this party nonsense. You would not have thought of it on your own. Believe me, I only want what is best for you."

"Drusilla takes care of every concern. I'd not have been able to cope with all the details." She rose from her chair to confront her only son. "I shall see you later. I have no desire to look on your face at the moment, for I do *not* believe you care what is best for me." She went to the door, her skirts swishing about her slender form.

Adrian watched as she disappeared from his sight. He only wanted what was best for her.

The house was utterly silent.

Upstairs the silence was broken when Drusilla found her mistress weeping quietly as she walked to her bedroom.

"My dear ma'am, what has happened? I thought with your son here all would be well." Privately she thought Lady Brentford looked on the verge of a collapse.

Her ladyship halted. With a hurt expression she stared up at Drusilla. "He insists I must cancel my party. Worse yet, he demands I send you home. Heartless child! How can he be so cruel? Promise me you will defy him. I will not be denied your company to please some whim of his. That my own son could contemplate such a thing! It is insupportable!"

Drusilla placed a tender arm about her ladyship, walking with her to her room. She urged her to lie down on her chaise longue, draped a lovely shawl over her before begging her to close her eyes for a rest.

"You must not permit this to upset you unduly. I will go down to deal with your son. I cannot believe he would do such a thing without a reason."

The marchioness reached out to clasp one of Drusilla's hands. "Would you, my dear? I have never been able to reason with Adrian."

Drusilla's mouth firmed, and she thought of all she would like to say and do to his lordship. "I will gladly attempt to persuade him to see reason. You rest. I will return later."

Leaving the marchioness in her abigail's tender care, Drusilla first checked her appearance, then marched down to the drawing room with the air of a militant general. Moreover, it was a general determined to win a victory.

"Sir, if I may have a word with you?" She forced herself to be polite, seemingly meek and outwardly serene.

"Yes, yes. Indeed you may. I was wishful of speaking with you as well."

Drusilla hoped he was as ill at ease as she felt. "It regards your mother," she began.

Apparently realizing it might be better if they were seated, he gestured to a chair, the very one his mother favored. "Perhaps we could talk in comfort?"

Sitting in his mother's chair would give her strength. She nodded with deceptive docility and perched on the edge of the chair. She hoped she made him uncomfortable.

He lounged back in his chair, studying her with the reflective air of one about to buy an item. An expensive one, like a mare of sound stock.

"I just met your dear mother in the upstairs hall. She was frightfully distressed, in tears, and scarce able to reach her room without help. You"—Drusilla pointed a finger at the man she found quite as annoying as she had anticipated—"are the cause of her grief. How could you deny her the party she yearns to hold? She intends to invite a few younger people in the hope you might linger here and enjoy her country party as well. She so desperately longs for you to remain with her for a time. She misses you very much, yet she never complains to you about your absence. At least, to my knowledge she has not done so since I have been here."

"The gathering of which you speak is far too much for her to manage." His expression was hostile. Clearly he was not about to yield with any grace. He might not yield at all, come to think of it. She had no intention of mentioning her being sent home. The money she earned was not a soft plum. She worked hard for every pence. But she loved the marchioness and counted it worth every minute.

She gazed at the man across from her, absorbing his sherry brown eyes, the sculptured nose, somewhat thin mouth and the thick dark hair that slightly curled in a way reminiscent of a Greek statue. She had seen drawings taken from the Elgin Marbles, and that was the sort of look those images wore.

Drusilla gave him a patient look, the sort she realized her mother gave her father when he was being particularly obtuse. "That is why *I* am here," she explained in the way one might to a dense child. "I organize everything from the meals to the rooms, the entertainment, well—just everything. All your mother has to do is look pretty and enjoy herself." She thought a moment before adding, "She especially enjoyed Lord Osman's company and requested he be invited again."

"Osman!" Lord Brentford exploded, shooting up from his chair to pace back and forth before the fireplace. "That old gaffer?"

"I thought him most pleasant. He dotes on your mother. Come, did you think your mother past a taste of romance?" Handsome his lordship might be. Annoying he was.

"What?" He halted, staring down at her in plain disbelief. "I do not think I hear you aright."

Drusilla felt at a distinct disadvantage while perched on the chair, so she rose to meet him face-to-face.

"I think your mother ought to be amused. She is not so young, as you must be aware. Allow her to enjoy herself. I promise to do all I can."

"And that is another thing. You are dismissed as of now." He gave a dismissive wave of a hand in her direction. "You have disrupted this entire household, set things on end. This cannot be good for my mother."

She gave him a pitying look. "How would you know? You have not seen your mother in ages. I believe Christmas was the last time you drove down here, and that was for but a few days—most of which were spent out shooting."

"Not true. I came when she took ill."

He must have worn that expression when he was

called before the dean at school. "Well, she didn't
know it. By the time she was well enough to be aware
of things, you had returned to London."

"Young woman, you are impertinent!"

"I imagine I am," Drusilla said calmly. "It is so
tiresome to be meek and humble. I cannot think why
the meek are supposed to inherit the earth—they
wouldn't know what to do with it if they obtained it."

He coughed, as though something struck in his
throat.

"I should like to know what makes you think I have
turned the household upside down. Oh, I wish you
would turn around and go back to London instead.
Your mother might love you, but it is clear you truly
do not care a pin for her feelings or what is best for
her. I refuse to leave! You, sir"—she again pointed a
slender finger at him—"are a worthless son!"

"What?" He looked thunderstruck.

"Well," she said with caution, "no one is completely
worthless. You must have some redeeming qualities."

"What makes you think you are a judge of
character?"

She gave him a level stare. "Perhaps it comes from
living in the rectory?" She refused to back down, fix-
ing her gaze on him, challenging him.

He looked as though he might explode if she said
another word. Turning on his heel, he left the room
and was soon heard tromping up the stairs.

Chapter Three

Adrian stormed into his rooms with more wrath than he could ever recall knowing. The unmitigated gall of that girl—to say that he "must have some redeeming qualities" was the outside of enough. Never in his life had anyone spoken to him in such a manner! She must go!

Colyer entered the bedroom from where he had been stowing away Adrian's clothing in the vast wardrobe. "Is anything amiss, my lord?"

"Anything amiss?" He laughed, a harsh sound in the peace of the house. "Nothing I cannot handle. What have you learned so far?"

"I moused around a trifle, knowing you are concerned about the young lady. From all accounts she should be granted sainthood. Right proper good lady, she is. She has taken over the jobs Priddy and Mrs. Simpson find difficult. You must know they are getting on in years, yet neither of them would wish to be pensioned off quite yet. Supervises the house admirably, I gather. Do you wish to learn more?"

"By all means." The more he knew about her, the more ammunition he might have, although sainthood was scarcely a disqualifying trait. And how they could claim she was saintly when she spoke her mind in such a manner was beyond him. Being reared in a rectory must account for that.

He poured a glass of claret before crossing the room to stand by the windows. While staring out at the spring gardens beyond, so colorful and gay, the absurdity of it all hit him. That young woman—that mere chit—dared to scold him! It made no difference to her that he bore an ancient and respected title. She took him to task for ignoring his mother like he was a recalcitrant schoolboy.

How amusing! He had thought that once he reached the ripe old age of thirty, he was able to cut the leading strings that attached him to filial duties. Apparently this young woman believed those strings were never to be cut.

But the fact that she had the audacity to speak in such a manner to a member of the peerage was . . . Well, what was it, precisely? He did not consider himself to be sacrosanct. Indeed, he was far from perfect, even though all of the Season's women claimed he would be the perfect husband. But he was hardly a target of scorn.

He would tread warily with Miss Herbert. She was like a keg of gunpowder—and he didn't know what would set her off. And she refused to depart! He sensed this was not going to be the usual dull trip to the country. Not dull by a long shot.

Drusilla paced back and forth in her bedroom, feeling all kinds of fool. How dare she speak to his lordship with such a lack of respect? He would surely send her packing in spite of her refusal to leave. Father would not be pleased to have his daughter turned off for being disrespectful.

There was nothing to it. She must apologize to Lord Brentford. Much as it galled her to do so. True, he was not the one who paid her modest stipend, but he could find a means of dispatching her if he wished.

While changing for dinner she considered the various words she might say. Simply tell him she was sorry? But she wasn't and that was the problem. He had deserved every blessed word she had said to him. Perhaps she might apologize for stepping out of line? Or something like that?

The maid who helped her dress scratched on the

door and entered when bid. She capably assisted with buttons and tapes, smoothing down the back of the white muslin round gown. The fabric had the faintest blue stripe, and Dru thought her blue reticule went nicely with it. She tugged at the puffed sleeves, thinking they might have been a trifle longer. Yet they were stylish, and she did admire them very much. The modest ruffle around the hem added to her pleasure in her new gown. How delightful it was to possess an entire wardrobe of modish garments.

Thanking the maid for her help, Drusilla dismissed her, then debated on tucking a bit of sheer silk into the low neck of the dress. She draped the frothy length around her neck, arranging the silk just so, and was pleased with the result. Now if it would just stay in place while she ate her dinner. Somehow sticking pins into the silk didn't seem right—the silk might be ruined.

With one eye on the clock, she assembled her blue reticule, making sure she had a handkerchief in it. She might well have need of that before the evening was over.

Blue kid slippers made no sound when she left her room to check on the marchioness.

The darkened room made it difficult to see anything, let alone discern her ladyship.

"Drusilla? Is that you, dear? I do not feel the least like going to dinner. I shall eat something here. I simply cannot face Adrian at present. And to think he is my dearest son!" The voice came from a pile of pillows.

"Perhaps he will have a change of heart, ma'am. I shall do all in my power to attain your wishes." Drusilla advanced to the foot of the bed, frowning into the dim light. The marchioness seemed to have shrunk into an older woman, frail and unhappy.

"I know that you will. You might even succeed." With a dry chuckle, the older lady pushed herself up against her pillows. "What can you possibly say to him to attain that?"

"I am not certain—but I will try."

"You had better go down now. Adrian hates to be kept waiting, and it would be better for you to be early."

At once seeing the wisdom of this plan, Drusilla bid the marchioness good evening, promising to look in later.

And then it was time to walk down the carpeted stairs to the ground level and face Lord Brentford. She briefly wondered if this was something like those poor prisoners felt on their way to the guillotine. She might not have her head removed, but she felt in her bones that his lordship could be extremely cutting in his denunciation of her forwardness if he so chose.

The thing was to put her oar in before he might say a word. If she apologized at once, could he have reason to cut her to bits? She devoutly hoped not.

The ground floor reached, she made herself walk to the drawing room, where the marchioness and she always met prior to dinner. True, her footsteps dragged a trifle.

At the doorway she peered about the room and took a deep breath of satisfaction. She was here before he was. Hurrying to the fireplace, she absorbed the faint warmth of the fire while she continued to mull over what she knew she must say. She would not sleep this night if she did not make her amends.

"Miss Herbert."

Drusilla looked up to stare at the figure entering the room and swallowed with care. He looked cool, inflexible. Had she thought him quite splendid before, he was now the epitome of male elegance. He wore a dark blue coat over a cream Marcella waistcoat of exquisite weave. His gray pantaloons fit him superbly. He had trim, well-muscled legs, signifying he was not an indolent man. Like most men of the *ton,* he doubtlessly rode and drove, perhaps even sparred with a sword or at the place her brother called Gentleman Jackson's.

"Good evening." Her tongue wanted to stick to the roof of her mouth. Oh, for a glass of water.

He bowed, then went to pour two glasses of sherry. He handed one to her, lifting his glass in a toast.

"My lord," Drusilla began, "I must apologize . . ."

"Do not say another word, I beg you." His eyes mocked her solemn voice and face.

"What do you mean, not say another word?" Drusilla demanded to know, totally forgetting her intention of being meek and conciliatory. How dare he spurn her words of atonement? "I must speak! I was rude, unconscionably so. It is only proper that I beg your forgiveness."

"I fear you do not mean it, my dear girl."

"I am not your dear anything, my lord." She glared at the man, insufferable cad to make his dear mother so unhappy. "I was uncivil. That rudeness demands I apologize."

"Pity we couldn't cross swords. I have a feeling you would like nothing better than to plunge one into me."

She gave him a speaking look, sniffing a trifle as she did. What a detestable man! True, he was as handsome as may be and had a voice to melt stone, but nonetheless he was detestable.

"That is not true. I was angry with you because you would treat your dear mother in such a way. How anyone could deny that darling lady a small treat is quite beyond me. She adores you so—how can you behave like this?" Drusilla took a small gulp of her sherry and wished she hadn't. Naturally it went down the wrong way, and she coughed and wheezed fit to tie her in knots.

Lord Brentford grabbed her glass before she could spill a drop, and thumped her on her back in a most unkindly manner. It was, however, effective.

"Take another sip, it will help." He returned her glass to her hand. His fingers brushed hers as he did, and she was proud her hand remained still. Had he felt that spark shoot through him at their touch? Perhaps it was her imagination? This had been an eventful day and he didn't make it any easier.

Whatever he might have said next was to be lost. Priddy entered to announce dinner was on the table.

Since there was just the two of them, precedence did not permit her to escape his company for a moment. She placed her hand on his proffered arm, noting the solid muscles covered by his coat, and they walked to the dining room.

"Your mother dines in her room." Drusilla glanced up at him, wondering what he was thinking.

He ushered her to the table with the care lavished on a Society lady. "So I learned." His face gave no clue to his thoughts as he seated her next to him.

The dining room was on the other side of the entryway, a large, gracefully furnished room. Mahogany table and chairs from the workshop of Sheraton, a sideboard from the Hepplewhite shop, and the crystal chandelier from a fine London store brought elegance to the room, as did the draperies at the windows. The rich wine fabric picked up the wine-and-cream stripe of the chair coverings. The room positively reeked distinction.

Drusilla decided she truly didn't do the room justice in her simple white muslin dress that had the narrowest of blue stripes. "I ought to be wearing silk." She spoke her thoughts aloud before she realized it.

"Surely my mother would fill your wardrobe with silk gowns if you wished." He spooned up the mushroom soup with every evidence of pleasure. His eyes revealed no amusement. She suspected he would oppose any move by his mother to provide her with a wardrobe.

"I should say not. I brought an adequate collection of gowns with me. I merely save the silk ones for more formal occasions. I would never ask or even hint that your mother should buy me so much as a handkerchief. And if you think I would be such a mercenary nitwit, think again. I should hope I have more integrity than that!" Drusilla glared at him, setting her soupspoon in the bowl. Suddenly, she was no longer hungry.

"Ah, the rectory is speaking. I was told that rectory children tend to be very caring people. Is that so?"

She thought he asked idly, the sort of comment one makes for conversation. She answered in kind, ignoring the snide tone of his first remark. "I suppose so. I do care about people. And what about a marquess? I have heard that peers tend to do nothing important with their days. And that is a pity, you know. I should think the trouble with doing nothing is that you never know when you are done."

It was his turn to choke, sputtering into his crisp linen napkin.

Concerned, Drusilla pushed her chair back and whisked around to thump him on his back. "Are you all right?"

He took a sip of claret before replying in a somewhat strangled voice. "You do have a way with words, my dear."

She was going to remind him that she was anything but "his dear" when she caught his gaze on her. She decided it might be better to attend to her meal and forget about sparring words with him.

"Now, to return to the matter at hand," he began.

"What matter?" Drusilla queried, her head still full of her required apology.

"I was under the impression that my mother desired to have a few friends come down for a party." He gave her what she considered to be a rather sarcastic look. "Well?" he prompted.

"Yes, well, the invitations have been sent and a few acceptances have arrived. We had no idea you would disapprove when we hatched this plan, you see." Drusilla accepted a helping of turbot with lobster sauce, peas, and a mound of potatoes. With any luck she ought to be able to eat a portion of everything on her plate. If she didn't, she'd not sleep. And she would *not* go wandering about this house in the night with his lordship in residence! And the thought of being hungry in the night was not a welcoming one. She took a bite of the delicious food and hoped she'd be allowed to eat in peace.

"Who is invited? Besides Lord Osman, that is." He demanded, politely, but it was a demand she couldn't ignore if she wanted, and there was no reason to prevaricate.

Drusilla listed the older people first, sensing that would be wise. Then she mentioned Lady Felicia Tait and Lord Ives, which brought a smile to his lordship's lips.

"How very providential. I have already invited Ives to come down here for a time. You will like him, I know." He forked a morsel of turbot and cast her a searching regard that made her curious as to what was in his mind.

Drusilla wondered how he knew that she would like Lord Ives, and took note that he said nothing about her liking Lady Felicia Tait. It seemed to her that he was going to permit the party to proceed. "Your mother will be very pleased with your decision. When I looked in on her before dinner, she was half buried under pillows and a throw, looking as though she had lost her last friend."

"She is indeed intent upon this party." He paused in his eating to study Drusilla. "I thought I could persuade her otherwise. It seems not."

"Even if she wrote you, you might not understand. Letters rarely convey what the person wishes them to, do they?" She watched him carefully, thinking if a gentleman might squirm, that was what he was doing now.

He ate for a time, then fixed his gaze on her. "You, Miss Herbert, are a very unsettling young woman."

"Oh, pooh. You make me sound like an interfering busybody. I truly am not the slightest meddlesome by nature. Only—I do like to see things done properly."

"This party is proper?" He sounded a trifle goaded.

"Well, of course it is. I promise you that I will do

all I can to make it a success. You'll see. Your dearest mother will not have to lift a finger."

"I doubt she would anyway."

"That isn't what Mrs. Simpson says," Drusilla snapped.

"And what does Mrs. Simpson know about it anyway?"

"She related that your mother was used to planning all her parties to the last detail. Everything from menus to entertainment, the bedrooms seen to, the flowers arranged. That is what I shall do for her. Bless her heart, the dear lady will have nothing to do but visit with her friends."

"And Lord Osman? Will he amuse her as well?"

Drusilla shrugged, and the frail silk scarf eased from inside her bodice. "He has accepted. She was so pleased. They do get along very well, you know. Would it anger you were your mother to marry again?"

"Marry!" He leaned back in his chair to stare at Drusilla, as though she had just sprouted a second head.

"People do, you know. Particularly lonely widows. I trust you have taken care of her finances so she will be protected no matter what?"

"Miss Herbert, it is scarcely any of your business what I do in regard to my mother's finances."

"Don't look at me like that. I am aware that there are gentlemen who are not always gentlemanly in their actions. For all I know, Lord Osman—although a delightful man—could be courting your mother for her money. It does happen."

"I doubt if I have ever in my life partaken of a conversation like this," he observed in what sounded like a choked voice.

"It is eminently practical, my lord."

He took a deep breath and began to eat again. Drusilla did as well.

She was well on her way to finishing the delectable meal when he spoke again.

"When do you expect these people to arrive? Are there provisions for them? Rooms made up and so forth?" He placed his fork and knife on his plate, signaling the footman to take them away. Since it was a simple meal, the next course would have the pudding Drusilla had discussed with Mrs. Simpson along with a bowl of stewed fruit.

"You must have a dreadful opinion of my efforts, sir. Thankfully, we expect them in a few days. Provisions and menus are set. The room are made up, only lacking flowers to make them welcoming." She gave him a severe frown.

He bestowed a somewhat grudging look of respect on her. At least it appeared so. "You have done well, Miss Herbert. I can see why my mother claims you a treasure."

"Your mother, my lord, is the treasure. A sweeter lady I have yet to meet." Drusilla flashed him a reproving look. What was she supposed to say to such a fulsome tribute?

Priddy set the pudding and bowl of stewed fruit on the table, inquired if there was anything else either of them wished, then exited the room, taking the footman with him.

Drusilla took another sip of her wine. It had flowed rather more freely this evening than usual, and his lordship had been careful to keep her glass filled. Why? To show her what an excellent host he was? She suspected he had forgotten more about manners and rules of Society than she would ever learn! Although her parents had been strict, insisting upon proper manners for the children. Yet, there was a difference. He grew up in the upper strata of Society and moved among the very elite.

In her haste to leave Lord Brentford to his port, she nibbled her lemon pudding cake before easing her chair back from the table. "If you will excuse me, sir, I will check on your mother."

"Have your tea in the drawing room first. I doubt

my mother needs you instantly," he drawled with a derisive note in his voice.

She gave him an uncertain look, then fled. In the drawing room she sipped the tea Priddy brought her while contemplating several weeks of living in the same house as Lord Brentford. She rose from her chair to pace back and forth before the fireplace while she pondered her situation over the warmth of her China tea.

It was unsettling when she caught sight of herself in the looking glass with the wisp of silk hanging any old way about her neck. His lordship must have consigned her to the ranks of the unrefined rustic. She set down her cup to rectify her disorder, first removing her gloves. What must he think!

Adrian remained at the dining table, poured a glass of port, then considered Miss Herbert, or Dru, as he was more and more coming to think of her.

She was an original, without a doubt. Her forthright speech was something he rarely encountered, particularly among women. Most women flattered and cajoled, quite prettily as a rule. Dru would have none of that. He was coming to see what about her appealed to his mother.

Naturally, she wasn't the sort of woman he preferred. When he married, and he knew he must someday, it would be to someone proper, socially aware, not like this young woman, who was more inclined to be pot valiant!

Then it occurred to him that it was dashed peculiar that he would think of her at the same moment he considered marriage to anyone. Nonsense. Utter rubbish. The girl might be beautiful, but she was a managing female!

Unsettled, he rose from the table with his glass of port in hand. Strolling across the entry hall, he paused in the doorway to the drawing room. She was still there. Her cooling cup of tea sat on the table near the fireplace while she attempted to tuck that wisp of silk into her low-cut bodice.

"Why do you bother?"

She glanced up to see his reflection in the looking glass. "I am not accustomed to low-cut gowns."

"Were you in London, it would be deemed most fashionable. I cannot believe you obtained it from a mere village mantua maker. The cut and fit are excellent, as is the quality of workmanship." He strolled closer to her, enjoying the delicate rose that crept into her cheeks.

"The country seamstress receives fashion plates from London, my lord. And fabric is fabric. We are not *that* far from Town. Tunbridge Wells has fine shops, and our local seamstress does excellent work. My sister convinced me that this neckline would be agreeable. However, *I* do not agree."

"Well, accept that it looks becoming on you. That wisp of silk isn't required." He walked over to pull it from her hands, ignoring her gasp of outrage. He dropped the silk on the nearby chair with her discarded gloves.

"You have a fine figure. Accept it." Adrian wondered at himself. It was not like him to be so forthcoming to a young woman, even one sharing a roof, as it were.

"That is very plain speaking, sirrah." She flashed him another one of her disapproving looks.

He shrugged, bored with the topic of a sudden. He was not allowed to touch—which was a shame, for she had a superb figure. He guessed her fluttering hand longed to cover up that décolletage that tantalized his eyes.

"Finish your tea before it is cold." Odd, he couldn't recall being so tempted at the sight of low-cut bodices before. Why did the view of this particular woman, the luscious hint of cleavage, entice him so? He turned away to place his empty glass on a table. Then he rang for Priddy to bring a pot of hot tea. Perhaps something like tea would help to settle him?

Tea was fetched and a plate of tiny ratafia biscuits with it. Priddy set it down with a flourish, offering the faintest of smiles at Miss Herbert.

"Pour, would you?" Adrian requested as nicely as possible. It wouldn't do to put her back up unnecessarily. She might qualify for sainthood as far as the servants were concerned, but he had yet to make up his mind.

"You have made up your mind to agree to the party your mother wants?" Her eyes challenged him briefly before she dropped her gaze to the teapot. She poured the tea with a grace that surprised him, although he didn't know why it should. With the servants as well as his mother praising her to the heavens, he should expect her to walk on water!

"Er, well . . ." He capitulated. Her hopeful expression won. "If you can assure me that my mother will have nothing to do but enjoy the party, I suppose it is acceptable." He was unprepared for the brilliance of her smile. It was like having the sun burst forth after a dark, cloudy day.

"Oh, good. She will be so pleased." The radiance in her eyes was enough to light up a room, he mused.

Adrian wondered how pleased he would be. Then he recalled that Lady Felicia Tait would be attending as well as his friend Ives. Perhaps it would be agreeable after all. Ives would approve of Miss Herbert.

"Has anyone ever called you Dru?" he suddenly inquired.

She colored up slightly. "Indeed, sir. My sisters all call me Dru. It is tiresome to constantly be using a long name. Priscilla gets tagged Pru on occasion as well. It is a pity our parents thought to give us names that are so similar, but once we go our separate ways, it will be simple."

"Your sister is away?"

"She is in London with our aunt. And I do hope she is having a splendid time."

He stared at her with curiosity. "You do not envy her the chance to mingle with the *ton*? You have no wish to shine in Society?"

"None. Priscilla is the dearest girl and deserves the best that comes her way. I wish I knew what she is doing, where she is going. Letters are so slow!"

He agreed with that observation. They were able to converse for a time without crossing verbal swords.

When at last she rose to go to her room, Adrian moved to her side. He picked up her hand, brought it to his mouth, and kissed it. It was a simple gesture, one he had performed countless times. Yet had he ever felt skin so satiny and scented with lavender before? Or had it ever effected him to this degree?

He raised his gaze to search her face, wondering what on earth was the matter with him.

Drusilla drifted from the room in a muddle of emotions. Having her hand kissed was a new experience for her. She supposed it meant nothing to Lord Brentford. As to what it might mean to her was beyond speculation.

She did learn one thing. Her thoughts proved she was anything but saintly.

Chapter Four

"*H*e has agreed, dear ma'am. We will not have to send out cancellations." Drusilla gazed at the marchioness with glee. She suspected that her ladyship would sleep better with the matter of her house party settled to her liking.

"However did you manage to do that, child? Usually once Adrian has made up his mind, that is it! Well, I shall know what to do next time I wish to persuade a certain stubborn person!" She gave Drusilla a penetrating stare, not unkindly but definitely curious.

Drusilla smiled as likely intended. She still did not feel easy in regard to Lord Brentford. She could sense his dislike of her. Although why he had kissed her hand as he had was totally beyond her understanding. To say it had unsettled her was putting it far too mildly.

"Now, have you the menus? And where did we put Lord Osman?" Her ladyship leaned back against her bed pillows to peruse the lists as Drusilla handed them to her.

"Here are the menus. And this is the list of which rooms are assigned and to whom. Lord Osman is in the green room. Mrs. Twywhitt is in the yellow room. Sir Bertram Quimby is in the blue room. I thought Miss Knight could be in the coral room and perhaps Lord Somers will find the Chinese room to his liking?"

"Arthur will adore the Chinese room."

"And the others? It is acceptable?" Drusilla had worked with Mrs. Simpson and one of the maids to make certain those particular rooms were in readiness.

"What about Lady Felicia? And Lord Ives? I know Adrian will want something extra nice for them."

"Perhaps if Lady Felicia has the pink Adam's room and Lord Ives the gold room next to Lord Brentford's room, that might be agreeable?"

Her ladyship gave Drusilla an anxious look. "I had not seen how frail Mrs. Simpson has become until you assumed some of her duties. I should not wish to replace her."

"Perhaps an assistant for her? I will not be here always, and she does need someone."

"Do not speak of leaving me." Lady Brentford gave Drusilla an impish smile, quite as though she had something up her sleeve. Recognizing it for what it might be, Drusilla sighed inwardly and gathered up the papers her ladyship had strewn about on her bed.

After bidding a good night, Drusilla left the room to head for her own bed. Closing her door behind her, she placed the sheets of paper on her desk, then changed to her nightdress. Surely Lady Brentford didn't have a spot of matchmaking on her mind?

Of course, Drusilla was aware of her hopes for Lord Brentford and Lady Felicia. What other prospect did she nurture? And alliance for Dru? The only unattached gentleman would be Lord Ives—at least of her age. The other men might be single, but far too elderly for Dru to consider. She was not quite yet past her prayers. As to Lord Ives, she would just have to see.

Crawling between the sheets, she considered the evening. She had not expected Lord Brentford to capitulate. Not when he had been so adamant against the party. The thing that perplexed her the most was his good night, kissing her hand as he had. Surely gentlemen didn't go about kissing hands in that intimate manner anymore? Her brother had remarked that such salutes were old-fashioned. Well, out-of-date or not, she thought the gesture vastly romantic. And what a pity it had to be Lord Brentford—the most *un*romantic man she could bring to mind.

Upon that depressing thought she slipped into sleep, a deep, dreamless sleep from which she awoke with her usual zest for living, having put aside the troublesome thoughts of Lord Brentford.

Adrain wandered about his library, wondering if he was in the process of losing his mind—what little there was left of it. What in the world had possessed him to kiss Dru's hand in such a way? He was lucky she hadn't taken a poker and applied it to his head.

It would be better once the house filled up with people; he could more easily ignore the young woman who was so tempting and persisted upon infringing on his mind.

Ten guests—as house parties went that was not a large number. He could take the gentlemen out shooting one day. There would be the inevitable games of cards. He thought the older gentlemen might enjoy billiards. One never knew about the weather; it could rain. Perhaps they might persuade Miss Herbert— Dru—to entertain them with music?

Whether he liked it or not, he was the host of this affair. His thoughts returned to Dru. Perhaps his friend Ives might find her appealing? Something argued against that, but he ignored the flitting twinge. She was beautiful—he had to admit so obvious a plus. She appeared to be a thoughtful, caring person. However, appearances could be deceptive, as he well knew. She certainly was proficient. Witness the lists she had mentioned.

She was amusing. He had to smile when he recalled her remark about the people who did nothing. Worse yet, it was too true. If you were doing nothing, how would you ever know when you were done? Although the chaps he knew who were famous idlers wouldn't have understood the notion in the slightest. However, he suspected she had intended the sly allusion for himself. Like many, she was probably convinced that peers did nothing all day. He smiled at that. Even those highly social had some time to devote to estate business. Only a fool would ignore his patrimony.

But the young lady was too outspoken for his tastes. If he had to select traits for a wife, it would never include that!

He settled on a chair before the diminished fire to cogitate on the subject of desirable ladies until he glanced at the clock. Time he was in bed. He wanted to rise betimes. It wasn't that he did not trust Miss Herbert. He wished to be around to see what she might be up to next. One way or another, she bore watching. That watching her was not in the slightest way onerous, he disregarded.

Dru entered the breakfast room with her sheaf of papers in hand, intent upon conferring with Mrs. Simpson as soon as she finished consuming a light breakfast. When she saw who occupied the chair at the head of the table, she stopped at once.

"Oh! Lord Brentford! I did not expect to see you this early." Dru curtsied, careful not to dislodge her papers.

"Do you need a helping hand?" An odd expression crossed his face as though he wondered what had prompted him to almost offer to help her. She doubted if he had ever in his life had to assist with party arrangements.

"No, thank you. I feel capable of handling what remains to be done. With the rooms assigned and menus approved, the rest is up to the staff."

"You had better eat something to keep up your strength. From what you said last night, I gather planning is more effort than I had believed."

Placing the sheaf of papers close to where she intended to sit, Dru selected a light meal. He was right, of course. While she wouldn't explain to him all that was involved, she had a great deal to see to this day. Tomorrow would likely see the first of the guests arrive.

"That wouldn't sustain a mouse." His lordship gave her plate of toast and buttered eggs a dismissive glance.

"I have quite enough, thank you."

Mrs. Simpson bustled into the room at that moment, sparing Drusilla any additional comments.

"Miss Herbert, when you have finished I hoped you would do the flowers."

Casting an amused look at his surprised lordship, Drusilla nodded agreement. "Of course. With a riot of spring blooms abounding, I should have some pretty vases done in no time. Her ladyship approved our menus." She exchanged a look with the house-keeper that said volumes. "And here is the list of which rooms will be in use. I shall be up later on to check them if you wish."

Although the housekeeper was in charge of arrange-ments, Drusilla knew full well that running up and down the stairs and inspection of the rooms would be difficult for her and she'd not trust a maid.

Lord Brentford remained blessedly silent until Mrs. Simpson had gathered up the papers and left the room.

"I will go with you while you pick the flowers. Or do you leave that to the head gardener?" The narrow-eyed look he slanted at her was only a bit unnerving.

"He has more than enough to keep him busy. I have a fair notion of what I want. I made a duplicate list of the rooms to be in use and will select flowers to go with the decor of each. But if you like, you may carry a trug for me. I could have a footman assist." She issued her challenge not only with her eyes but also with her words. Surely he would consider a job like toting a gardening trug to be beneath him? She figured she would be free to roam the gardens at will, enjoying the fragrance without his disturbing presence.

A smile twisted his firm mouth, quite as though he saw through her ploy. "I would deem it a pleasure. Even though this party is not of my making, I can surely add my mite?"

Dru choked on a bite of toast. She hastily swallowed some tea and in a moment was her usual self.

"So be it." She made her words brisk. She fully intended to continue thus, mostly to keep him at a distance. She wasn't sure why that was needed, but needed it was.

Adrian studied the down bent head. Her honey blond hair was twisted into an elegant knot. What would that length of honey blond look like hanging down about her shoulders? Spread across a pillow? Tangled on a man's chest? The image stirred him.

She wore a simple lilac-sprigged muslin gown of tasteful design. With her charm and beauty, quality clothes and exquisite taste, what was she doing serving as a companion to an elderly woman? Surely she didn't need such a position?

He still wondered about her clothes. In his experience the daughter of a rector did not possess such fine quality. He might not know a great deal about costs, but he knew that the lace trim on her gown was expensive.

She rose from the table. "I will fetch my spencer and bonnet to be ready for the garden outing in a trice . . . if you are still of a mind to go with me?" Her voice dared him to accept.

"Oh, I will go with you, my dear." Adrian was going to see if he could trip her into admitting his mother had bought her stylish clothes. It simply didn't stand to reason that her father could afford them. She looked too virtuous to be under some fellow's protection—had she the time to arrange such a matter. Or the inclination.

He was walking slowly about the entryway when she came running lightly down the stairs. Bonnet neatly tied under her chin and a pair of sensible gloves on her hands; she looked far too pretty to be performing tasks for the household.

Or was that what she intended? To charmingly work her way into his mother's graces in order to reap whatever benefit might be bestowed on her?

Under Priddy's benevolent gaze, they left the house to aim for the gardens to the rear.

"That is an attractive gown, Miss Herbert. Seems almost too nice to wear for picking flowers." Adrian cast an admiring look to make his point.

"It is the lace that does it, my lord. My older sister sent us a large packet of lace from Nottingham, where she is with our great-aunt. Mama thinks that Nymph might possibly be made our great-aunt's heiress. That would be very nice, indeed." She spoke without a trace of envy in her voice.

"Indeed." Adrian wondered if there might be more money in the family than he had suspected. If the Reverend Mr. Herbert was nephew to the Earl of Stanwell, it ought to obtain him some manner of preferment. Still, that was neither here nor there as far as Miss Dru was concerned.

She gave him a quizzical look, then picked up the secateurs from the trug. She chose with care. Soon colorful blooms of Persian irises, anemones, and polyanthuses were neatly piled in the trug. They found tulips in the special cutting garden, planted solely for the purpose of flower arrangements in the house. She obtained fragrant stock from the greenhouse.

The sun-warmed earth gave off a pungent odor to mingle with the stock to create a heady aroma. Each of the flowers had its own particular scent, but none so potent as the lavender that clung to Miss Herbert's skin and clothes. Off in the distance the country charm of leafing trees and newly sprouted fields formed an appealing backdrop for her beauty.

She paused for a few moments, staring off into the distance, then bent to her self-appointed task once again.

Adrian was fascinated with her selection of flowers. She added sprays of greenery in various shades of green from yellowish to gray. It would be interesting to see what she did with these.

"There," she said with a note of finality. "There are

so many arrangements to create. Most of them are dainty—for the bedrooms, you see, plus a few others."

"You will really have a job on your hands, Miss Herbert, one you will no doubt do well." He noted the puzzled look she gave him and smiled. He fully intended to keep Dru on her toes. It was the best way to deal with an opponent. And he definitely considered Drusilla Herbert an opponent—until he was proven wrong about her.

The other feeling he had would be tamped down, buried. There was no place in his life for an outspoken, managing female! Even if she was beautiful. Like now, with that aqua-blue spencer reflecting the glorious color of her eyes, he admitted she looked delightful.

It was a pity, really. She was beautiful, well-spoken, graceful, and considerate of his mother. Therein was the problem. She cared just a little too much and he did not trust that.

Carrying the trug, now loaded with colorful blooms, he strolled at her side until they reached the kitchen entry.

"We had best part ways here, my lord. I shall be going to a small room next to the scullery to arrange the flowers."

Adrian almost smiled. She looked anxious to be away from him, like she escaped from an ogre. He wasn't a vain man, but he knew his worth. Never before in his life had he experienced such behavior, accustomed to the opposite. He confessed it nettled him a trifle. And to have it come from a country rector's daughter made it all the more vexing. Surely she knew his position in Society? A marquess? Well, her greatuncle was an earl, so she should have some idea.

Aware she was waiting, looking at him with that perplexed expression again, Adrian hastily handed her the flower-laden trug. "I shall see you at luncheon, I fancy." Without waiting to see what she did, he turned, briskly walking off around the opposite side of the house.

Drusilla stood where she was a few moments, trying to guess what she might make of his behavior. At last, called to her tasks when the kitchen cat wound its way around her ankles, she went into the room with a briskness that matched his lordship's stride.

She placed completed arrangements on the wooden tray used for this purpose, then went up the back stairs to put them in the various rooms. Once the bedrooms were done, she returned to the ground floor by the central staircase.

Priddy opened the front door just as she reached the final few steps. She frankly stared as a very handsome gentleman entered, handing his tall hat to Priddy to reveal a neat head of brown hair, only faintly wind-blown. He was of medium height and perfectly groomed in excellent, if subdued, taste. A gray coat over a dove-gray waistcoat blended with dark gray breeches. His black books had a shine to equal that of the boots Lord Brentford wore.

She met his gaze in a fluster of confusion. That she could stare so at a stranger embarrassed her. His gray eyes seemed kind. Perhaps he was accustomed to young women ogling him in an utterly shameless manner? She took another step, intent upon escaping.

"Welcome, Lord Ives," Priddy intoned at his most starchy fashion.

Having handed Priddy a copy of the room arrangements, she knew that Lord Ives would be placed in the gold room. She hoped he liked the small arrangement of yellow tulips, polyanthus, and a few bluebells for contrast that she had just set on a bedside table. Then she inwardly grinned. How silly. Gentlemen rarely noticed flowers in a room.

At that moment Lord Brentford emerged from his library to walk smartly along to the entry hall.

"Ives! Good fellow! I hoped you might arrive before the rest of the group. Welcome!" The two men shook hands with more animation than a frozen-in-place Drusilla would have expected.

"Come, you must meet my mother's companion."

He drew his friend along to where Drusilla still stood and performed the introduction smoothly, with the ease of long practice.

Drusilla felt herself inspected most thoughtfully, as if they had discussed her previously and now this stranger was weighing her up—which had to be utter nonsense. Why would her name occur in any conversation between these two friends? Unless . . . but that was absurd. Why would Lord Brentford even mention her? She was no more than a companion to his mother.

"How pleasant you could join Lord Brentford in the celebration for his mother's birthday. I trust you will enjoy yourself." Drusilla hastily excused herself, then hurried of to the tiny room where she arranged the flowers. There were still the large arrangements for the entry hall and the drawing room to complete.

Adrian glanced after the departing Dru Herbert before returning his gaze to his friend. He nodded ever so slightly before ushering Ives to the library for a welcoming drink.

"*That* is your mother's companion?" Ives inquired in a quiet but surprised tone. "She is not at all what I anticipated, old friend. Where is the harpy, the conniving, money-grubbing female out to steal from your parent? You must see that she in an incomparable!"

"Yes, well," Adrian sputtered. Really, he would have to check any reaction he might feel toward Dru Herbert while others were in the house. Ives always did see too much. "I suppose she is what might be expected from a rectory. Do recall she is great-niece to the Earl of Stanwell."

"You say that as though it is some sort of excuse. Does she, then, rely on her connection?" Gray eyes assessed Adrian in a way that made him somewhat uncomfortable.

"Never." Adrian felt compelled to correct any impression he might have given regarding Dru Herbert. "She appears to be a caring, thoughtful young woman. Capable and modest as well . . . and very outspoken," he concluded reluctantly. Were he to interest Ives in Dru, he had to be honest. Otherwise Ives would catch her out and be quite annoyed.

"Tell me, are rectory girls always of such beauty?" Ives spoke over his shoulder as he strolled across the vast expanse of the library to gaze out of the window at the scene beyond.

"I wouldn't know." Adrian hoped that Lady Felicia would arrive before long. Unless he could convince Ives to discuss something else, he would probably worm more from his host than wanted.

"I always have to admire your grounds, Brentford. If I could, I would spirit your heard gardener away from you."

"Try," Adrian said with a smile that concealed his relief at the change of topic. "He is well paid and devoted to my mother." He thought a moment, then added with a note of surprise, "And he seems to have taken to Miss Herbert, too. I cannot recall when he has permitted anyone the freedom to cut as they please in his garden."

"So she is a charmer as well?"

Adrian struggled with being honest and concealing his pleasure in her company. He might not fully trust her, but she was a tempting young woman. "It would seem so."

Apparently his reluctance to discuss Miss Herbert was not missed. Ives adroitly changed the topic. "Who else joins us this week?"

"Lady Felicia Tait, plus Mrs. Twywhitt, Miss Cordelia Knight, Lord Osman, Sir Bertram Quimby, and Lord Somers."

"If I guess rightly, your mother means to pair you with Lady Felicia. That would place me in the company of the beautiful Miss Herbert! Well, well. How nice of your mother."

Adrian agreed in part. While he was aware of his parent's desire to see him suitably wed, he was not certain that Lady Felicia was the one he would choose.

"It should be interesting. Lord Osman is definitely

interested in your mother. Naturally you have secured her fortune." Ives studied Adrian with an inscrutable gaze.

Adrian smarted at the memory of Miss Herbert asking him the same thing. "Naturally. Mother may be as clever as can be, but finances are not a strong point with her."

"Few women are clever with numbers. I suppose the valuable Miss Herbert can manage a household account in her stride?" There was a hint of irony in his voice.

Adrian shook his head, determined not to sound disgruntled. "I suspect that Miss Herbert can do anything she sets her mind to doing. She is a remarkable woman."

Ives set down his empty glass before turning the conversation to people they both knew in Town. London was in the height of the Season; much was going on. To be away even for a few days meant there would be gossip to hear.

"I bumped into Harry Metcalf and his friend Gregory Vane before I left. They wondered where I was headed. Harry said something about looking in on you some vague date in the future."

"Harry is a good chap. Always enjoy his company. I do not know Vane as well." Adrian allowed his curiosity to color his voice, making his remark a query.

"Nice chap, perhaps a bit more reserved than Harry. I expect they will pop in when you least expect them."

Adrian shared a grin with Ives. "Just as long as they don't appear during my mother's house party."

Dru busied herself with the flowers, creating an arrangement of surpassing beauty for the entry hall. Arranging flowers was an art she had enjoyed for years. Her family knew how much pleasure she derived from her gift, and the job was always hers at home. It allowed her thoughts free rein.

Lord Ives was certainly a surprise, handsome with

manners just as polished as his boots. She wondered about Lady Felicia. Most likely she would be a gorgeous creature.

Then she reflected on the numbers and realized that if Lady Brentford intended Lady Felicia for her son, she intended Lord Ives to partner Drusilla. Now *that* was absurd. She ought to have invited a young lady for Lord Ives as well. Perhaps there might be someone suitable to be found in the local area? It would be wise to take note when in church next Sunday.

Drusilla reminded herself that she was not here to find a husband. Ridiculous, the very thought of catching a gentleman who would be a guest in this house! Only the premier members of the *ton* would be invited to visit here at any time. She must remember her place. While she was of acceptable gentry, she was employed. Here. As a companion. Nothing more.

Her arrangement completed, she carried it into the hall toward the drawing room. As she approached the library, she noticed that the door was partly open. Hurrying her steps, for she had no intention of listening to anything that might be said therein, she faltered when she heard the words "capable and modest as well . . . and very outspoken" said by Lord Brentford.

She couldn't imagine who he meant if he didn't refer to her. He had told her she was outspoken. And now he said it as though it were much to her detriment.

Her soft footsteps were lost in the vastness of the entry hall, with its thick Turkey carpet to give color and warmth. Once in the drawing room, she wondered why those words hurt so much. Capable and modest were faint praise at best, and outspoken was damning at worst. Why should it matter what he thought of her? He made her sound dreary and dull, quite right for a rectory miss.

Chapter Five

*T*he flurry of activity the following day made Drusilla long for the peace of the gardens. Even the bustle of the rectory was more agreeable. On the other hand, this all was rather exciting, if taxing.

The guests began arriving in early afternoon. First, Lord Osman entered the house with a hearty greeting for Lord Brentford and a warm one for Drusilla.

Remembering him well from when he had captivated Lady Brentford on the previous visit, Drusilla responded with unguarded pleasure. "Lord Osman, so good to see you again. I trust you had a tolerable trip?"

The elderly gentleman took her proffered hand in both of his, exclaiming, "My dear girl, I can see you are in blooming health. As to my trip—it was barely tolerable. Roads are a disaster as usual. Perhaps someday they will find a proper means of draining off the water after a rain so that we can escape the ruts."

Only when she turned away to remind Priddy which room was assigned to Lord Osman did she catch sight of Lord Brentford's expression. He stared at her with eyes full of cynicism. She did *not* know why he was so suspicious of her. What had she ever done to him? Although, when she considered the direction of his remarks, she wondered if he thought perhaps she hoped to gain more than employment from his mother. Dismissing that notion as unworthy of a marquess, she decided to ponder it later.

Her enjoyment dimmed, she nonetheless went about her task with brisk capability. Close on Lord Osman's heels came Miss Knight, followed almost at once by Mrs. Twywhitt.

Miss Knight had a little dog with her, a King Charles spaniel. Drusilla, recalling a neighbor's nasty King Charles spaniel that had a habit of nipping ankles, kept her distance from it.

"Don't be afraid of my Binky," Miss Knight cried. "He is a dear little lamb. He loves everyone. I have never had him nip at a soul, bless his little heart."

"Cordelia, you spoil the beast." Mrs. Twywhitt smiled at Drusilla, adding, "I will admit he is a good little dog and is very quiet. You needn't fear him barking at all hours of the day."

Miss Knight held her pet out so Drusilla might pat the little creature. With more caution than anything, Dru gave it a tentative stroke on the head to be rewarded with a lick on her hand. Just so he left her ankles alone, all would be well.

From the top of the stairs, Kitty surveyed the arrival and disappeared into Lady Brentford's room, likely intending not to be seen until her enemy departed!

Since Priddy was busy answering Lord Osman's queries, Drusilla took it upon herself to escort the ladies to their rooms. Fortunately, the pair knew each other well, and what was even better, appeared to like one another. Drusilla was glad she had put them in adjacent rooms. Their maids followed to learn which of the rooms had been assigned to their mistresses, then disappeared to supervise luggage.

At the other end of the long hall, Lord Osman chatted with Lord Brentford, who had kindly walked with him to his room, leaving Priddy to oversee baggage, footmen, maids, Lord Osman's valet, and any guest arriving in the interim.

Just as she feared might happen, Drusilla met Lord Brentford at the top of the stairs. She was aware she had done something to displease him, but hadn't the vaguest notion of what that might be. She plunged into conversation. "I am so glad those two ladies are friends. It makes things so much more pleasant if people at a party like one another." She paused, then continued at his silence. "I hope that dog behaves."

He gave Drusilla a cool look she was sure she didn't deserve. "Was it necessary to be quite so exuberant with Lord Osman?"

"I like the gentleman," she replied with her customary directness. "I liked him when he was here before and see nothing to alter my opinion as yet. He is your mother's favorite, and as such it behooves me to be especially kind to him." She flashed an annoyed glance at Lord Brentford, taking care not to stumble on the steps. The last thing she needed was a twisted ankle or worse.

"There is kind and there is kind. No need to gush."

"Well, of all the things to say! I was not gushing. If you wish me to really gush over someone, do let me know and I will oblige you!" Drusilla snapped at him. What on earth was the matter with the man?

"Just remember that the very wealthy Lord Osman is here to visit my mother."

"Of all the ideas!" Drusilla stopped at the bottom of the stairs to glare at the handsome gentleman at her side. Why he couldn't have a squint or be as bald as a mushroom she didn't know. If she had to be on her guard with anyone, it was Lord Brentford. Since he had kissed her hand, she viewed him in quite a different manner. She must be wary of him. For all she knew he was attempting to trap her into an indiscretion so she might be fired!

"You are angry." He looked faintly amused.

"Quite so! I am furious that you would consider me the sort of woman who would flirt with a gentleman who is old enough to be my father merely for financial gain." She placed her hands on her hips and gave him a tight-lipped, narrow-eyed stare.

He looked away first, then gave her a rueful smile. "If I apologize, will you cease your glowering?"

"Naturally, I must. But do not attribute motives . . ."

What else she meant to tell him was lost forever when Priddy opened the vast front door to usher in the most exquisite lady Drusilla had been privileged to see. She was a vision of pink-and-white loveliness with dark curly hair entrancingly framing her face beneath a modish pink velvet bonnet with white plumes. Her dark eyes had a pixyish tilt to them, and her mouth looked as though it had been designed for smiling. Possibly kissing, as well.

"Lady Felicia, welcome to my house." Lord Brentford bowed, taking her hand while giving her a pleased look.

Drusilla was introduced and ignored by the lady. It was curious that while he had kissed Dru's hand, he didn't kiss Lady Felicia's. It was an oddly comforting thought.

The pair walked away utterly engrossed in each other, with Lady Felicia chattering away about mutual friends. Priddy and Drusilla were left to deal with a mountain of luggage, as well as the maid and groom who had come with the vision.

Well, Drusilla decided, she had wondered about Lady Felicia, and she need wonder no more. Lord Brentford looked to be entranced, as well he might. His mother would be thrilled. Drusilla kept her opinion to herself.

Lady Brentford came downstairs to join Lord Osman and the two older ladies. They were strolling to the drawing room when the remaining guests arrived. Sir Bertram Quimby was a tall, thin fellow who possessed a pair of twinkling blue eyes. Lord Somers was short and stout, but looked agreeable even if he wasn't smiling.

Drusilla arranged for tea and wine, along with seed cake and ratafia biscuits for them. After which she settled the valets and luggage where they belonged. How Mrs. Simpson might have coped with all the ups and downs was beyond Drusilla. She would likely have crawled into bed to emerge a week later. Even Dru felt her stamina tested.

Lord Ives came running lightly down the stairs, just missing Drusilla as she contemplated the remaining stack of baggage and took a step backward. He put a hand on her arm to steady them both. "How does it go? It would seem to me that you have taken over from Mrs. Simpson. A bit frayed, are you?"

Drusilla resented being told she looked a hag, but then, she probably did. A glimpse in the looking glass convinced her that Lord Ives spoke only the truth.

"Only a little frayed."

"Come with me—play truant for a bit. Priddy will see to everything now that the rooms are settled. Mrs. Simpson can see to the maids and valets without your assistance."

"How did you know that is what I am doing? I tried to be unobtrusive." She patted her hair into place, thinking it would be fun to take a respite from her assumed duties.

"Easy." He took her arm to guide her out to the terrace off the dining room. "Mrs. Simpson wasn't here."

Drusilla had to smile at the truism. They walked along the terrace admiring the view, particularly of the distant flower beds. At the far end they encountered Lord Brentford and Lady Felicia.

Lord Ives did not appear pleased at what he saw. Drusilla could feel his arm muscles tighten, and he seemed to retreat even if he didn't move. "Lady Felicia." Oh, he was polite, bowing with impeccable grace, but he was cool.

Lady Felicia, on the other hand, was bubbling friendliness. "How lovely to see you again, Lord Ives." She shifted her gaze to Drusilla and frowned. "I saw you when I came in. Miss Herbert—the companion."

"She is my mother's right hand, most competent." Lord Brentford nodded slightly at Dru.

"Do you have a sister named Priscilla?" At Dru's nod Lady Felicia explained, "I met her before I left London. She captured the regard of Earl Latimer. You look alike."

"How interesting," was all Drusilla managed to say at this startling bit of family news. She observed that Lord Brentford appeared almost as surprised as she did regarding Priscilla's beau. He had glanced at Dru with a brief frown.

Lord Ives edged closer to Dru, causing her to send him an uncertain glance. Now what?

"There is plenty of time remaining before dinner. Unless you wish to change or refresh yourself, why don't we enjoy a stroll in the gardens?" Lord Brentford urged.

Lady Felicia agreed, laughing. "I ought to change now, but I will wait. Adrian doesn't mind me as I am."

"You always look delightful, my dear."

Lord Ives took Drusilla firmly by the arm and walked her back along the terrace until they reached the few steps that led to the garden path.

She took a hasty breath. "I gather there is some hurry? Dinner will be"—and she checked the tiny watch pinned to her dress—"in three hours. Perhaps you would like something to drink?"

"Nothing. Nothing at all." He proceeded to ignore the others and discussed the various flowers at great and knowledgeable length with Drusilla.

Somewhat bewildered, she joined in the discussion, while wondering what prompted his behavior.

Every time she took a peek back at the other pair, she encountered Lord Brentford's frowning gaze. Perhaps he disapproved of her being with Lord Ives. The baron was all that was charming, and handsome to boot. If she had no problem with the arrangement and the baron seemed pleased, she didn't know why Lord Brentford should complain. But then, there were some people you simply couldn't satisfy.

At last they sauntered in the direction of the house. When she had the opportunity, she was going to demand that Lord Brentford explain his antagonism to her friendship with Lord Ives. She doubted if the baron had anything more in mind than a mild flirtation, if that. He was being warmly polite.

"La," Lady Felicia exclaimed, "I must go to my room. It will take me hours to change and be ready for dinner. Traveling takes such a toll on one." That she looked as fresh as the flowers in the garden made no difference.

Dru smiled and offered to show her to her room.

"How kind of you. I should like that." The two young women headed into the house and up the stairs at once.

Adrian watched the pair disappear through the terrace door leading into the dining room, then turned to his friend. "You seem pleased with Miss Herbert's company. She can be shockingly frank at times."

Ives looked amused. "I found her charming and surprisingly well-informed on gardening matters."

"That is likely because my mother dotes on her garden, and Drusilla tries to please her."

"You seem quite taken with Lady Felicia. She is a beautiful girl, should you like short, dark-haired sprites with a temper. Miss Herbert is tall and regal. I wonder how long that gorgeous blond hair is?" he mused.

Since Adrian had wondered the same thing, he was of no help, although it annoyed him that Ives should contemplate the matter. They strolled along the terrace in silence for a time. Adrian wondered how he could convince Ives that Miss Herbert would be a proper wife and why he wasn't more enthusiastic about the idea.

"Dru?" Adrian responded without thinking. It was not the done thing to use a nickname for a woman you hardly knew. Although with a friend it should be acceptable.

"You call her Dru?" Ives queried in surprise.

"I think of her that way. If I called her that to her face, I would probably receive a lecture on propriety. The rectory, you know."

"Ah, yes. I wonder if her sister in London is as lovely. Latimer is not known for pursuing plain women."

"Likely beauty runs in the family. Lady Felicia has two handsome brothers."

Eventually they entered the house and went up to their respective rooms to change for dinner.

Adrian admitted he enjoyed seeing Lady Felicia again. He had a strong hunch why his mother had invited her. His dear mother made no secret she wanted to see him wed with grandchildren for her to spoil. Well—he would become better acquainted with the lady and see what developed. She was charming, beautiful, and possessed great poise. She also had an enormous dowry.

Would Dru take an interest in Ives? He had shown an odd reaction to Lady Felicia, behaving in a manner so unlike his normally genial self that Adrian had almost said something. A close look at his face told Adrian to remain silent. It was too much to think Ives might be jealous!

Garbed in proper clothes for the evening, he left his room only to encounter Drusilla slipping from hers to hurry down the hall toward the servant's back stairs.

He stopped her. "What in the world are you doing?"

Her look could only be described as vexed. "I must see if Mrs. Simpson requires my assistance."

"I should think she can manage a mere dinner. She has Priddy, the maids, and the footmen to help. You're a companion, not a servant. Cook isn't giving her trouble, is he?"

"Not that I know of." She appeared to gather courage. "Why were you frowning at me while we walked in the garden? I do not think I was doing anything wrong. Or was I?"

"No. No, you were fine. You enjoy Ives's company?" He couldn't have explained just why he had frowned at her. He wasn't certain himself.

"It is difficult to dislike a gentleman who is handsome and pleasant, and who offers no insult."

"Who offers you insult?" Adrian took hold of her

elbow and guided her to the top of the stairs, then down.

"No one at the moment, sir." Her mouth firmed, and she looked as though given a chance she would sniff in disdain.

He would have pursued the matter if they hadn't reached the bottom of the stairs and joined the others in the drawing room.

All the ladies had changed for dinner. In their silks and satins they formed a colorful grouping, chatting with the men. Osman wore a green velvet coat that went nicely with Adrian's mother's delicate foam-green gown. She might have been buried in the country, but she still had modish gowns. Mrs. Twywhitt wore rose while Cordelia Knight had on a gown of salmon jaconet that gave her a nice color.

Once Ives and Lady Felicia—wearing ice pink and fragile lace—joined them, it was a short time before Priddy announced that dinner was served.

Dinner turned out to be far more pleasant than Drusilla expected. She had decided to use the Wedgwood china with the scenes of classical ruins and the crystal finger bowls that looked so well with it. The marchioness had declared that whatever set of china that Drusilla wished to use was fine with her. The less she had to do, the better, in her sight.

The food was delectable, particularly the roasted turkey. The delicate silver epergne Priddy had polished with such loving care held a luscious-looking pineapple on the top portion with the lower shelves holding various small fruits destined for the sweet course. Cook had made a splendid trifle that was decadently rich.

Lord Somers was on her right, while Lord Ives sat to her left. Both gentlemen were charming. Brought up in the rectory where company was common, Drusilla had early on learned the facility of agreeable conversation suitable for the dining table.

"Brentford told me that you play the pianoforte. Do I dare hope you will entertain us this evening? I enjoy music. I promise to turn pages for you if you will."

Drusilla glanced at Lord Brentford, then to her ladyship seated close enough to have heard what Lord Ives said. "Of course, if Lady Brentford would wish."

"Lady Brentford does wish," that lady said with a winsome smile. "There is something so congenial about fine music following dinner."

At the foot of the table, Lady Felicia could be observed in animated conversation with Lord Brentford. At the change of courses, she paid scant attention to poor Sir Bertram, then returned her sparkling laugh and beaming gaze back to Lord Brentford.

Drusilla had no doubt that nothing would be said to *that* young lady regarding her high spirits! A lady of her rank could speak as she pleased without censure. Her reflection on the manners of those of rank came to an end when Lord Ives queried her about her sister in London.

"Priscilla went to stay with our aunt, Miss Mercy Herbert. I gather she has been busy, for there has been little news. At least," she amended, "nothing has been passed along to me. I confess I was pleased to learn she has caught the eye of a fine gentleman, as I gather Lord Latimer is. She deserves something good."

"It is nice to hear a young woman so happy for her sister. And you? Are you planning to marry?"

"Like any young woman I wish to marry, but it does not always happen, does it? Some of us are destined to be spinsters, whether we wish it or not."

"Somehow, my dear, I doubt it is your destiny to remain in spinsterhood."

He said no more, to Drusilla's disappointment. She smiled politely at Lord Ives, changing the topic to gardening, something she knew he enjoyed.

In spite of the delicious food, Drusilla was glad when the dinner reached the stage where the marchioness nodded to the women. They rose to leave the room to the gentlemen and their port. Lady Felicia and Miss Knight followed, with Drusilla trailing behind. Sir Bertram had risen to bow the ladies from the room. He firmly shut the door behind them.

"Did I hear that you play the pianoforte?" Lady Felicia inquired in her high-fluting voice.

"I do my humble best. It has been a joy to practice on the fine Broadwood in the drawing room."

"It is nice to have a worthy instrument. Later on, you shall play and I shall sing. You can accompany me?"

Drusilla gave her a rueful smile. "That depends on what music you select. Would you care to look over what is available here?" She guided the exquisite lady to the stack of music reposed on a table by the pianoforte. It took some minutes to find something suitable.

The time without the gentlemen was usually a dreary interval, and it was no different tonight.

Priddy brought in a large silver tray with the fine china, silver teapot on a spirit stand, with creamer and sugar bowl, and dainty cakes in a silver cake stand. There was also a bowl filled with candied nutmeats. The marchioness summoned Drusilla to pour.

Drusilla poured out the fragrant, well-brewed tea into the fragile cups. A footman carefully offered them to the other women. Lady Felicia flounced over to the sofa, accepting her cup of tea and a tiny cake with a bored expression on her face. When she caught Lady Brentford watching her, she swiftly became the same animated woman who had sat next to Lord Brentford at the dining table.

Well, well, Drusilla mused. It would seem at second sight that the young lady was not all she appeared to be.

Miss Knight sent for her little spaniel, explaining, "He gets so lonesome in my room, I hate to leave him there for long periods of time."

There was time for gentle chatter before the gentlemen joined them. Lord Osman was the first one through the door, with Sir Bertram right behind him.

"Ah, our fair ones. I trust you have missed us!" Sir Bertram cried, his blue eyes sparkling with pleasure.

"If I know you, there will be a demand for a game of whist immediately," the marchioness said with amusement.

Not wishing to play cards, for she was an indifferent player at best, Drusilla rose to go to the pianoforte. She now knew the marchioness liked to have soft music while she indulged in her card playing. Drusilla was only too happy to oblige.

"I promised I would turn pages for you, and I shall keep that word," Lord Ives said quietly so not to disturb the four who were setting up a table of whist.

Miss Knight stood by the door, obviously waiting for her pet to be brought to her. Lord Osman and Sir Bertram joined Mrs. Twywhitt and Lady Brentford at one card table while Lord Brentford, Lord Somers, and Lady Felicia patiently waited for Miss Knight to take her place.

At last the dog arrived and that foursome began their game. All would have been well but for the little dog that kept growling at Lady Felicia.

Poor Miss Knight, who had been exclaiming about what a docile creature he was, turned red at the dog's behavior. "He always loves everyone," she said weakly as Binky issued another low growl. She patted the dog in a comforting way, stroking the silky fur and soothing it as best she could.

Drusilla exchanged a look with Lord Ives. "A neighbor of ours has a dog like that. Bites my ankles at every chance, the little beast." She spoke softly out of deference to poor Miss Knight, but she devoutly hoped the animal would not be turned loose.

"Dogs are sensitive creatures. They know who likes them and who doesn't." Lord Ives stood at her side, waiting to turn the page of the Mozart sonata she played.

"I had never thought of a dog as needing to get on the better side of one, but I suppose it makes sense in a way." She glanced at him, then concentrated on her music. It was better that way. He looked very handsome this evening. She thought him ideal company; a pleasant voice, excellent manners, and above all no desire to scold her for anything. It was a pity that try as she could, the face that kept popping up in her mind's eye was that of Lord Brentford!

At least two games had been played when Lady Brentford announced it was time for refreshments. "My poor brain needs the stimulant of a cup of tea."

"Do not, I beg of you, forget those ratafia biscuits," Lord Osman declared.

Sir Bertram added, "I must confess a partiality to your cook's seed cake."

"We shall have both. And, Cordelia, do something about Binky, dear. Perhaps the dog wishes to go out?"

Miss Knight, who had relaxed her hold on her pet, smiled and was about to comment, when the animal leaped from her lap and dove under the table to attack Lady Felicia's ankles.

Lady Felicia screamed and kicked out. "Nasty beast!"

The terrified dog dashed madly across the room, where she spotted someone she knew. Drusilla. She immediately jumped up to what she expected would be an accepting lap.

Drusilla froze, her hands in midair. Liquid sable-brown eyes beseeched her.

"What can I do?" Dru whispered to Lord Ives. She carefully placed a hand on the dog, stroking it to calm it and trusting Miss Knight would shortly rescue her.

The dog smiled—she would swear it did—and settled down in her lap as though anticipating a snooze.

"Binky, you bad puppy!" Miss Knight cried as she hurried across the room, only to halt at the sight of the dog draped on Drusilla's lap.

"Here she is," Dru said quietly, hoping not to disturb the animal. She had no wish for nipped ankles. She offered Miss Knight an encouraging smile.

"Look, he likes Miss Herbert! I have never seen

him take to someone like this! My dear girl, it is truly marvelous.'' Miss Knight eased her little dog up in her arms, earning a lick on the cheek for her efforts.

"I think I need a cup of tea as well.'' Mozart forgotten, she rose from the piano to be joined by Lord Ives. The hot tea was more than welcome.

Miss Knight handed Binky to one of the footmen to be taken for a walk. She apologized profusely to Lady Felicia, who returned a strained smile while rubbing her ankle.

"I do hope I am able to walk without difficulty. My skin is so tender. I am not accustomed to such things.''

Since Drusilla had endured nipped ankles, she couldn't censure Lady Felicia too much. She thought she might have been just a bit more stoic about it. One thing was clear—Lady Felicia had a temper, and she didn't like dogs.

Chapter Six

"*S*he is a lovely creature, is she not?" Lady Brentford declared in ringing tones once Drusilla had escorted her to her room and helped her ladyship arrange things to her liking.

"Indeed, ma'am. Lady Felicia is pink-and-white perfection." Dru made no comment on the temper and the kicks at the little dog. After all, she on occasion had a flare of temper, and she certainly wasn't fond of the neighbor's spaniel. But she hadn't booted it.

"She assuredly is," Lady Brentford said in the fondest of manners. "Although, I must say, she shouldn't have kicked little Binky." She frowned, as though mildly vexed.

"Well, as to that, nibbling on her ankle likely did not endear the dog to her." But Lady Felicia could have simply shooed the pup away using her hands. It wasn't necessary to kick the animal.

Dismissed for the night, Drusilla made her weary way to her room. While this job was not difficult, it was very tiring, particularly since Lord Brentford arrived. He had a way of making Dru feel uneasy. Or something. She preferred not to consider the feelings he stirred in her.

She went into her room and walked across to the dressing table, where she proceeded to take down her hair. She was brushing out the tangles when she heard a snuffle. Whirling about, her brush in hand, she stared at her bed.

"Binky! What a fright you gave me." Dru replaced her hairbrush on the table and stared at the small spaniel. "What are you doing on my bed? And how did you enter?"

Soulful brown eyes stared unblinkingly back. Not so much as a woof was offered. The dog's expression would have melted a heart of stone. Dru's sensitive organ felt pity for the poor dog, doted to death by Miss Knight. He probably had escaped one way or another.

Dru uneasily searched around the room. "Well, if I make no mistake, Miss Knight will want you in her room immediately. I don't want to think of the hue and cry raised should she realize you are gone missing."

She scooped the dog up in her arms and opened the door with difficulty. Edging around it, she pattered over to Miss Knight's room. She rapped on the door while coping with the wiggling spaniel.

"Binky! Whatever are you doing out there?" her owner demanded softly.

"I have no idea how he found his way into my room, but when I came in, there he was, cozily ensconced on my pillow." Dru scratched under Binky's chin. The pup clearly enjoyed the attention.

Miss Knight frowned in puzzlement, then accepted the little dog from Drusilla. "Thank you, my dear. I do not understand Binky at all. He never trails after someone else, nor does he fix his attentions on another."

"He is in a strange house. Perhaps he became mixed up?" Dru backed away from Miss Knight, intent upon returning to her room before someone saw her.

"Of course, that must be it. Good night." Miss Knight, her precious spaniel once again in her care, firmly shut her door at once, leaving Drusilla standing in the hall.

Turning about to retrace her footsteps, she froze when Lord Brentford appeared at the top of the stairs. "Oh," she breathed, "please don't let him look this way." Deciding that animals had a good notion with remaining utterly still when a predator came into view, she turned into a statue.

Not that she was improperly garbed. She still wore the simple white muslin gown. But a lady, her mother had drummed into her, did not appear before a gentleman with her hair down and tangled about her shoulders. There was a bedroom intimacy implied in such display!

Of course he spotted her. "Ah, Miss Herbert. Is there a problem?" He paused before strolling down the hall.

Dru curtsied and began backing toward the door to her room. "No. I found Binky in my room and returned him to Miss Knight."

He frowned. "How did the dog come to be in your room?"

"Perhaps he slipped inside when the maid went in to turn back my bedcovers and see to the fire?" She spun around, intent upon reaching her room and her bed as soon as possible. She was too tired to battle wits with his lordship this evening.

"You were preparing for bed when you found the dog? Where was it?"

Dru halted in her retreat to look back at him over her shoulder. What difference did it make? Or was he the sort of man who needed every detail? "He was on my pillow."

"I see." He gave her an arrested look.

What might be unusual about a little dog curling up on a pillow was beyond Dru at the best of times, and this was not one of them. Suddenly aware that her hair must seem dreadfully untidy to the impeccably groomed gentleman standing a trifle too close to her, Dru swallowed with care, then offered a tentative smile. "Excuse me. My hair is all a tangle. I was brushing it when I discovered I had a visitor—Binky." She hastily gathered the long blond tresses together, twisting them into a soft rope.

"I had no idea your hair was this long." He reached

out as though to touch it, then drew his hand back instantly. Probably recalled it wasn't proper to go about running hands in someone else's hair. Dru wasn't certain she would welcome his touch.

"Perhaps I ought to have it cut. It is a bother to care for, you see." She was babbling. She hated babbling. She backed toward her door, groping for the knob.

"Allow me—I promise I don't bite." He reached around her to open the door and thrust it ajar. "And, my dear girl, whatever you do, do *not* cut your hair."

Dru looked up at the rather stern face and nodded much like one pacifies a child about to have a tantrum. The tangy scent of bay rum teased her nose, and that rich voice of his made her think of the decadent trifle she had eaten. "Ah . . . I wouldn't dream of it."

He nodded, then backed away from where she clutched the doorknob like a lifeline.

Within a moment Dru whisked herself around the door and into the safety of her room. "Whew!" Although why she ought to feel like that she wasn't sure. All she knew was that he had a powerful effect on her that try as she could, she couldn't dismiss.

If only he wasn't quite so perfect, so utterly handsome and beautifully groomed in the best of taste at all times. What a pity she couldn't find something to dislike about the man! She couldn't even fault him for the attention he paid to Lady Felicia. How could an unattached male *not* fall in love with such a beautiful creature? Somehow long blond hair didn't compare too well with pink-and-white perfection. Dru admired the dark hair that curled about a winsome face with eyes that possessed an entrancing tilt to them. She was magical. Pity that Dru couldn't like her. But, then, one couldn't like everyone.

And then Dru recalled that Lord Brentford had wanted to oust her, send her packing. He had only come down to the country in order to vet her, and apparently he had found her wanting—hence the desire to dispatch her at once.

It was amazing, truly, that she was still here when she considered it. Perhaps he thought her useful? Although he had scolded her when she was tired, said she wasn't a servant. No? Well, she certainly felt like one, waiting on her ladyship all day without respite. She hadn't asked about time off. She doubted she would receive any, Lady Brentford being as absent-minded as she could be at times, especially if it was something she didn't want to bother about. Those few snatched minutes in the Garden with Lord Ives might well be the most free time she would have!

Adrian entered his room with mixed feelings. While he should have been contemplating the delights offered by Lady Felicia, he found himself meditating on the golden charm of Miss Herbert's long hair. Good grief, he had never seen anything like it—spun gold, almost molten, flowing down her back and over that one shoulder like a cape of precious metal. She was a siren in a demure gown, with wary eyes and a kissable mouth, garbed in a cloak of golden innocence.

He had almost touched her hair. It wasn't the done thing, to run fingers through a woman's hair, a woman not so much as betrothed much less married to you. But he had wanted to do that very much. His fingers had longed to thread themselves through the strands of pure gold. An aura of lavender lingered about her. He would wager her hair held the same scent. He liked the smell of lavender, a clean, sharp aroma. It was not like the almost cloying odor of French violet that Lady Felicia wore.

Drusilla Herbert was a distinct challenge. Lady Felicia made her availability all too plain. Reflecting on it, Adrian thought he rather preferred a challenge. It made life far more interesting. Yet he knew full well what his mother expected of him and what was due to his title. That complicated things a bit. He was not free to choose as he pleased. And yet . . .

Well, tomorrow was another day, and it behooved him to entertain the guests his mother had invited. It would not be difficult to please Lady Felicia. Ives would be delighted to spend time with Dru Herbert. He had behaved oddly to Lady Felicia. Adrian had never before seen him act as he had today.

As Adrian slid into bed his thoughts turned to Dru Herbert, the enchantress with her wealth of golden hair. He didn't know quite how he felt about her, but he was certain she was not right for Ives, nor was he right for Dru, even if his mother had thought to pair them together. To tell the truth he didn't know what sort of chap would suit Dru Herbert. She was such a beautiful creature. Pity she did not come from a family of higher standing. Yet she was of sufficient gentry status that she would never consider being some man's mistress.

With thoughts of those golden tresses spread across the pillow for his pleasure, Adrian slept.

When Adrian entered the breakfast room, he found Miss Herbert demurely seated at the table conversing with Lord Ives in a quite acceptable manner. It annoyed Adrian, though, and he wasn't sure why. What a dog he was becoming.

"We were just commenting on the weather," Ives said.

Adrian succeeded in banishing the scowl he wore. "Yes, well, it appears as though we will have a fine May day." He helped himself to a substantial breakfast, then seated himself between Miss Herbert of the golden hair and Ives.

"What shall we plan for the day?" Ives inquired, glancing at the door as though expecting someone to enter.

"Lord Osman said something about a picnic. Surely we might all enjoy that?" Dru Herbert offered in her pleasing voice. "The weather is unusually fine."

Adrian had noticed yesterday how well-bred her tones were. Not that he made a point of studying how a woman spoke, but it was a matter he had observed and tucked away in the back of his mind.

"I say, that ought to occupy a few hours." Ives poured another cup of coffee and leaned back in his chair.

"When I am finished with my breakfast, I will speak to Mrs. Simpson. I feel certain that Cook can arrange a splendid picnic luncheon for us." Miss Herbert took a bite of her roll, then a sip of tea.

"No footmen, I beg," Ives inserted. "I went on a picnic at the Hathertons'. We could have just as well remained in the dining room, for all the feeling of an alfresco affair." He turned to Miss Herbert to add, "There was a table covered in crisp white linen and all the crockery you can imagine, complete with an epergne laden with fruit. Why bother?"

"I agree with you, but will my mother?" Adrian asked.

"If you like, I could ask her?" Miss Herbert said with timidity unusual for her. Adrian thought she might have barged in to place the suggestion. Upon reflection he realized he wronged her. She would diffidently submit the notion and let his mother assume it was hers from the start—which is how he dealt with his mother.

"No, no, you deal with Mrs. Simpson and Cook while I propose the outing to Mother. If Lord Osman said he would enjoy it, she will be only too happy to oblige." He made a wry face at Ives, who responded with a rich chuckle.

"It looks to me as though you are going to be parent to your mother, my friend."

Adrian grimaced. "The very thought terrifies me."

In short order the three left the breakfast room, each headed in a different direction. Lord Ives wandered off in the direction of the library. Adrian went upstairs. Drusilla headed for the kitchens.

Adrian soon found himself permitted to speak with his mother, who reclined on her chaise longue by the window.

"A picnic you say? How quaint."

"Lord Osman expressed a desire to commune with nature in an alfresco meal." He watched his mother react to this bit of news. She looked thoughtful, mulling it over.

"I see. In that event we must please our guests."

"Miss Herbert is talking to Mrs. Simpson and Cook. She promised a feast to please the most fussy taste."

"How thoughtful of her. Really, Adrian, she is utterly indispensable. However will I do without her?" She gave her son an imploring look before turning to face the view from her window.

"I was not aware she was leaving us. Surely you can persuade her to remain? Pay her more." Adrian felt a strange reluctance to see the last of the woman he had intended to send away at once when he arrived.

"I do not want her leave, nor has she indicated she might. But a girl of her beauty cannot be left to spinsterhood. Do you suppose your friend Ives has taken an interest in her? I thought he kept rather close to her side last evening. It would be a nice thing for her to marry the baron. Imagine her a titled lady." Lady Brentford sighed.

Adrian wondered if Ives was prepared to settle down to married bliss anytime soon. "Then you have no objection if we proceed? I will have carriages arranged and all else necessary. If you can enlighten your guests regarding the treat you have in store for them . . ." He trailed off as his mother rose from the chaise longue.

"Dear boy, how like your father you are. Incredibly thoughtful when you wish. I will have everyone assembled in two hours' time. Is that agreeable?"

"Fine." He was aware she had paid him her highest compliment in likening him to his father. Adrian and his other parent had never been close. He had only learned to know his mother somewhat after his father's death when he perforce found it necessary to be present at the estate. And that had been less and less in the past two years.

When Adrian ran lightly down the stairs, he found Dru Herbert marching along the hall coming from the kitchen.

"Well?" she inquired, caution coloring her voice.

"All is well. We have two hours, possibly more if I know my mother at all, to have the party ready to move. I wonder where we ought to go?"

"Adrian, *chérie!*" the high-fluting voice floated down the stairs as Lady Felicia daintily skipped her way to meet the pair who stood not far from the bottom of the steps.

She gave Dru a glance, then smiled. "What is going forth? Plans for the day?"

Adrian took it upon himself to reply. "Indeed. We are going on a picnic. I trust you can be ready in about two hours?"

"Only two hours! Horrors! Perhaps, if I apply myself at once, I shall be prepared to embark on a picnic." She gave Dru a suspicious look. "Whose idea was this?"

"Actually Lord Osman said he would dearly like to go on a country picnic. I hope he will not be disappointed."

Lady Felicia's face relaxed. "I shall be ready, I promise."

Dru watched the elegant young woman drift up the stairs. She had looked complete to a shade. Whatever might be needed was beyond Dru. A change of dress? Was there something special one wore to a picnic? She glanced down at the simple lilac-sprigged muslin she wore and grimaced. She was taken aback when Lord Brentford touched her chin, raising it so she must meet his gaze or close her eyes.

"You look very charming. I fear Lady Felicia thinks she must present herself as though at a Venetian breakfast. Not so. I cannot imagine a more appropriate gown for a picnic than the one you wear. All you need is a pretty bonnet to shade your face."

Dru wondered what he was buttering her up for—something unpleasant, undoubtedly. She brushed his hand from her chin, giving him a doubtful look. She quite ignored the effect his touch on her chin had on her nerves.

"Well, is everything set?"

Lord Ives broke the odd silence that had crept up between Dru and Lord Brentford. She was strangely disappointed that Lord Ives appeared. Pasting a smile on her lips, she turned to face him.

"We are to leave in two hours. I do *not* know how we are to persuade all our elderlies to be ready in that short a time." She gave the ambitious Lord Brentford a dark look.

"The thing to do is summon what maids are around and send them to the various rooms with the news of the departure in one-and-a-half hours from now."

"But Mother promised two," Lord Brentford objected.

Ives chuckled. "Always give them a shorter time if you want to leave promptly."

Dru exchanged a look with Lord Brentford, thinking of Lady Felicia. They had told her two hours, and she would doubtless use use every bit of it.

"Trouble?" Lord Ives inquired.

"We just informed Lady Felicia that she had two hours." Lord Brentford grinned at his friend's horrified reaction. "Well, *you* tell her it is less."

Lord Ives gave Lord Brentford a sidelong glance, then began to walk up the stairs.

"Where are you going? Surely not to her room!"

"If you do not hear from me shortly, send a footman after me to pick up the pieces."

Dru supposed he was joking, but she thought Lady Felicia quite capable of reducing a gentleman to ribbons if she pleased.

"He's mad, you know," Lord Brentford confided. "To insist a lady of quality hurry her preparations for the day is tantamount to committing suicide." He gave a dramatic shudder, causing Dru to chuckle.

"I am thankful that I am as ready as need be. Now, to hunt out the rugs and other things we shall need."

"You speak as one who has gone on numerous picnics." He fell in beside her as they walked to the cupboard where Dru knew such odds and ends might be found.

"Oh, I have. When all of us were home we often took off on an impromptu picnic in a neighboring field—one where no bull was likely to be found."

"There is the crux of the matter. Where can we go? I should have liked more time to have the spot groomed."

"Well, it would remove all spontaneity from what is supposed to be a spur-of-the-moment lunch in the fresh country air." Dru opened the cupboard and pulled forth several soft rugs perfect for reposing on grassy knolls. Dumping them to one side, she probed until she found some pillows. She held one up. "Most necessary. I shouldn't be surprised if your mama wants a few chairs along as well. Oftentimes older people balk at sitting on the ground."

"I *can* see that you are a wealth of information." He paused, then went on hesitantly, "I trust you slept well? Did you figure out how the dog entered your room?"

"I slept very well, thank you. And I think it was as I said. Binky came in when the maid had the door open. *Why* it popped into my room is another matter. I don't fuss over the creature at all." Dru gave him a confused regard.

"And what do you dote on, Dru, that is, Miss Herbert?"

Dru gave him a startled look at the use of her nickname, then she smiled. "Strawberries, my Lord. I do adore strawberries."

The look he returned created odd little fluttery sensations in her stomach, the sort one experienced when beginning a new venture or going into strange company.

"I shall order strawberries in that event. I am certain the gardener will find some for me . . . and you."

Throwing caution to the winds, Dru clasped a pillow

in her arms, facing him squarely. "If you are flirting with me, I think it most inappropriate, sir. Wouldn't it be better to order the carriages?"

She barely refrained from smiling at his look of stunned affront. Relief was swift when he chuckled. She had risked her position, and they both knew it.

"Indeed, ma'am, I go at once." He turned, then paused. "But you shall have strawberries. And you will have to do something to reward me. I don't know what at this point, but I will think of something later."

Dru stared at his departing figure with dismay. What had she done!

Adrian grinned as he walked to the stables. What would he insist Miss Dru Herbert do for her strawberries out of season? He paused at the sight of his head gardener to request the needed berries be brought at once to the kitchen. All that could be found. The old fellow wasn't pleased to see his precious berries taken away, but that was hardly Adrian's problem.

Whistling a merry tune, he continued until he located his head coachman. He could have simply ordered a number of vehicles brought around to the front, but he considered that since Ben Coachman had lived here all his life, he might know of a likely spot for a picnic.

Ben scratched his head a few moments, then offered a suggestion. "There be a fine bit of meadow down by the stream. Iffen you recall, you once had a swing there. Nice sunny spot, if that's what you seek."

"That will do well. We shall need transport for the food and drink. Perhaps three carriages will do. There are ten of us."

Ben nodded his head, then set about ordering the necessary vehicles.

Adrian paused at the door, adding, "Have them in front in an hour and a half if possible."

The older man shook his head in dismay, but Adrian knew it was possible. The vehicles were always kept in top condition and with the help in the stables, three carriages should be ready to roll well within the time limit.

The fourgon would be sent to the rear of the house so the provisions could be easily and quickly stowed aboard.

Adrian entered the house by the back entrance through the kitchens. He glanced about to see the preparations for the picnic well advanced.

"Aye, my lord, and busy you make us!" Cook declared. "But there will be one of my hams and pork pies, plenty of other foods, ye won't be going hungry."

"And do not, I beg of you, forget the strawberries that Jim Gardener will bring in shortly. Perhaps a bit of cream as well?"

His eyes gave him a shrewd look. "Indeed, I will."

Adrian quitted the kitchen, knowing he disturbed the order of the place by his presence. He found Ives in the hallway and motioned him along. "Come on."

In the central hall he found his mother surrounded by Lord Osman, Mrs. Twywhitt, Sir Bertram, and Lord Somers. Only Lady Felicia and Miss Knight were missing. And, of course, Miss Dru Herbert.

"Am I in time?" The high-fluting voice floated over the assembled guests like Gabriel's trumpet.

Adrian altered his position so he could receive the full benefit of Lady Felicia's apparel.

She swung a pink parasol about, narrowly missing a statue much favored by the marchioness, whose indrawn breath could be clearly heard. Dressed most inappropriately in pink silk with a deluge of lace trim here and there, she looked to be off to a tea rather than a picnic.

Lord Ives walked over to take charge of the wayward parasol. "Allow me, my dear. You ought not be encumbered by so mundane a thing as a parasol."

Lady Felicia fluttered her lashes at the gentleman who was doing what Adrian knew was properly his job. He had enough on his hands without a temperamental young lady who sought to impress one and all with her stylish dress.

He began to urge the others to head out to where the carriages now awaited them. They all had just left the entry hall when Dru Herbert came dashing down the stairs with Binky in her arms, followed more sedately by Miss Knight carrying her parasol and a number of other articles.

"Binky would hide under my bed," Dru whispered to Adrian as she came close, looking frustrated with her bonnet in disarray, strands of golden hair in wisps around her face.

"I cannot understand what has come over that dog," Miss Knight complained.

"I trust you have a lead for him so he won't run off?" Adrian inquired with a hint of firmness.

"Oh, Binky never runs away. He is always so good." Which remark in view of recent antics seemed silly.

Chapter Seven

They set off in a gay mood, with Adrian whistling a happy tune. The other men shortly joined in, much to Lady Brentford's displeasure.

"Gentlemen," she said with a sniff, "do not whistle."

"Do not spoil it, Mama. Enjoy your party." Adrian rode beside the carriage, the better to check on things.

She gave him a thoughtful look and said no more.

Miss Knight had handed Binky to Dru as they entered the carriage. It was odd. Miss Knight usually had the little dog clutched in her arms. Perhaps that was why it sought to escape from time to time? Well, all Dru might do is hope for the best. She intended to be free for a little bit if the marchioness permitted. With Lord Osman to hover over her, Dru doubted she would be needed every minute.

The meadow proved to be a perfect site. A little stream wandered at the far end, not far from where a giant oak stood in splendid majesty. A footman was testing a rope that hung from a broad bough. There was a board at his feet, looking much weathered but still sturdy.

It was evident that cattle had frequented the meadow as the grass had been nipped close, almost as well as if it had been scythed. Other signs of their presence had been swiftly taken away so as not to annoy her ladyship's guests. Patches of wildflowers could be seen tucked here and there by trees and near the stream. It was bucolic England at its finest.

Servants were setting forth a proper picnic under the shade of yet another vast oak. A humble trestle table—no starched linen in sight—had a simple checkered cloth atop it with dishes holding the roast ham and pork pies, as well as all the other delicacies promised. In one especially pretty china bowl, a heap of bright red strawberries could be seen with a pitcher of cream next to it.

Dru was so happy she could have floated rather than merely walked. The sun was shining, spring flowers peeped from here and there, the little stream gurgled on its way to who knew where. Sheer heaven.

Drusilla saw to Lady Brentfort's comfort with pillows and cushions and rugs underneath. Lord Osman remained close to her side while Sir Bertram and Mrs. Twywhitt strolled about the meadow exclaiming over pretty wildflowers and discussing the various birds they spotted.

Miss Knight and Lord Somers threw a ball for Binky to chase. The dog was off its leash and behaving nicely. Dru cast a wary eye at the spaniel. She didn't quite trust the gleam in those little brown eyes.

"Well, what do you think? Is it a proper picnic?" Lord Brentford said when he unexpectedly popped up at her side.

"Indeed. It is beyond words marvelous. How you managed to conjure all this," and she swept her arm to encompass the meadow, "in such a brief time is amazing. I am impressed, my lord."

"Good. I was hoping you might be." He took her hand in his to lead her across to the table, directly to the bowl of strawberries. He took a fine ripe one, popped it into her mouth, and stood looking like a magician.

Dru cast him a reproving look, munched the berry, and then said, "That was delightful. But I believe there is another lady who would enjoy such attentions." She glanced at Lady Felicia, who was happily chattering to Lord Ives. Yet Dru had the distinct feeling her ladyship was well aware of Lord Brentford's whereabouts.

"Leave her to Ives. Come, I would show you my swing." Again he took her hand in his to lead her across the meadow to the great oak from which dangled the stout rope. "I had this when I was a lad."

"I haven't tried a swing for ever so long," Dru said, with a laughing glance at his lordship. What a strange mood he was in—particularly for a man whose mother fully intended he should wed the pink-and-white beauty strolling along the little stream with his good friend. Dru wondered what caused *his* change of heart regarding the beauty. His initial coolness had changed to warm regard.

"Take off your bonnet, lest it fly away." He looked ready to do it himself if she delayed, so she did as requested. He took the straw bonnet from her and tossed it to a shady spot before motioning her to sit on the weathered wood seat.

"This would not be kind to pink silk, I believe," Drusilla said consideringly as she positioned herself squarely on the swing.

He made no reply to her remark, rather drew her back to let her swing forth.

She had forgotten what a heavenly feeling it was to soar up into the trees, then rush downward again, only to be thrust up higher yet when pushed. Scented spring air rushed past, young leaves teased her with their nearness. Only strong arms could send her so high, and she had observed before that Lord Brentford was far from being a weakling. Oh, such delight, such pure pleasure!

Her skirts flew about her ankles, and she suspected that Lord Brentford saw far too much of them to be proper. But for once she didn't care. Swinging was like being transported to another world, almost like flying, as if one could be a bird for a few moments.

She could peer down into the stream as it meandered beneath her. There was a small trout, a lot of minnows, plus a fat toad sitting on a rock. Tall grasses grew along the stream, thrusting their verdant spires in the air with impudence. A chaffinch swooped past, and she made a face at it, thinking she was near to flying herself.

Wisps of her hair floated about her face, and she cared not a whit. She would be proper when she returned to earth. And return to earth, she would in more ways than one. She'd think about that later.

Adrian pushed her higher again, noting with satisfaction that her hair was coming loose. Oh, he was a rogue for doing this, but he wanted to see that golden drift of silken hair again, and there were few means of doing so. She was always so properly garbed. He appreciated Ives keeping Lady Felicia occupied some distance away. He wanted nothing to interfere with this.

Then the golden shower he had hoped to see occurred. The pins holding Dru's hair lost their hold, and her hair, all that lovely molten gold, came cascading down her back.

"Oh!" Her cry came with an attempt to halt. Rather than cause damage to her leather slippers, Adrian gallantly stopped the swing, bringing her almost into his arms.

"I'm sorry," he said quite without an ounce of truth. "Let me help. It is the least I can do." Without waiting for a reply, he gathered her hair in his hands, twisting it around into a rope as he had seen her do before. Her hair was all he had expected; like finest silk, scented with lavender, and as wondrous as he had desired. He deliberately fumbled, allowing the silken length to slide through his fingers in what had to be the most erotic sensation he could recall. He had never dreamed of doing anything like this, but here he was, enthralled with a web of golden enchantment. What would it be like to be alone with her, to see that golden length spread over his pillow?

"Allow me," she commanded quietly, obviously not

wishing to draw attention to her *deshabille*. She bent over, gathering up what pins she could find. Adrian did the same, finding almost as many as she did.

He held the pins in his hand, watching as she caught the strands of hair up, pinning them neatly in place to his sorrow. To his way of thinking, her hair was a treasure to be admired. Then he realized he was selfish enough to desire it all for himself. And wasn't that a fine kettle of fish?

"Adrian! Whatever are you doing? Come here. You must see this dear little flower I have found." The high-fluting voice floated across the meadow, its annoyed accents clear.

Adrian knew that Felicia would never understand why any man would ignore her and pay attention to a companion.

"You had best go," Miss Herbert urged. "I do not think she will be pleased to see you playing lady's maid for me."

"But I like playing lady's maid for you."

Her eyes looked shocked, although she said nothing more, only shooing him away. Ah, well, he'd had a brief glimpse of heaven. He could always scheme for another.

Dru watched Lord Brentford walk across to where Lady Felicia stood waiting for him. Whatever the little flower was that she had found couldn't have come close to what Dru had discovered. She very much feared that rather than disliking his lordship, she was becoming far too fond of him. It was a frightening sensation, like a dip in the road that you didn't anticipate and your stomach felt as though it would sink to your toes.

She recalled her sister Tabitha reading out a poem by Ben Jonson called *The Dreame*. One line in particular she remembered, *"I am undone tonight, love in a subtle dream disguised hath both my heart and me surprised."* She did not claim to be in love, but she certainly had a surprised heart. It would never do to allow her foolish fancies to be evident. That she was attracted to him she could not deny, try as she might fight it. What a dilemma!

She suspected he might toy with her for some absurd reason of his own. His eyes had looked amused, their rich brown depths having golden sparks in them she had not noticed before.

Once she had finished pinning up her hair, she plopped her bonnet on again and walked to where Lady Brentford rested among her pillows. She had a pretty rose tint to her cheeks and was as unlike the pallid woman who had first greeted Dru as could be.

Lord Osman rose to greet her with his usual gallantry.

"Is there anything I might do for you, ma'am?" Dru wanted to be kept busy, really busy. She would think later, not now with the sight of Lady Felicia clinging to Lord Brentford's arm. From the corner of her eye, she could see them slowly walk to where the others were clustered not far from the laden table. His head bent close to hers, listening to her chatter. Lord Ives walked close behind, looking none too pleased.

"I see you survived the swing." Lady Brentford gave a nostalgic sigh. "My, how Adrian loved to swing as a child. I had forgotten it was here."

"Indeed, he showed me how pleasant it is." Dru managed a tight smile, hoping she looked somewhat her usual self.

"As long as no one is hurt."

"Now, my dear lady, as you can plainly see, Miss Herbert looks in fine fettle." Lord Osman said nothing about rosy cheeks or flustered mien. He assisted her ladyship to her feet, and they wandered over to the table, where they selected an ample assortment of delicacies.

Dru looked after them, then bent to straighten the rugs and pillows, thinking it was a bit too late to worry about someone being hurt. She feared that had already happened.

"My dear, you simply must try the ham," Lady Felicia caroled in Dru's direction. It reminded Dru of someone tossing a bone to a dog.

Rather than raise a question as to why she wasn't hungry out in the fresh air and activity, Dru nodded. It took but a few minutes to select a bit of ham, a roll, and some of Cook's best salad.

"I promised you strawberries, and have managed to gather up the finest. Enjoy them." Lord Brentford cast a glance back to where Lady Felicia debated between a roll and a scone. He thrust the little dish into Dru's hand, ignoring the small plate of food held in her other hand. Then he strolled back to join the others, giving no sign he had left them even for a moment.

Somehow Dru managed to sit down on one of the pillows while balancing her plate and the dish of fat, succulent strawberries. And cream, as well. He had thought of everything—except how his actions might affect her.

She wondered if Lady Felicia had observed Lord Brentford's attentions? For some reason, she suspected that she had. It wouldn't surprise Dru in the least if there were a reprisal of some sort. But then, perhaps she was being too mistrustful. She might have imagined those sly glances darted her way. And pigs might fly.

The food on the plate quickly consumed, Dru savored each red strawberry in the dish, licking the juice from her lips, enjoying the taste of the berries with a dash of cream. What a marvelous treat!

"Binky! Come back here, you naughty dog!" Miss Knight struggled to her feet, only to trip on a rug. There would have been a dreadful tangle had not Lord Somers saved the lady from disaster by catching her. Unfortunately, he couldn't catch Binky, the little dog being far too quick for the stout lord.

Having finished the last of her berry treat, Drusilla set aside her dishes and dashed after the dog. "Binky! Stop! Come back here!"

No one else appeared to be concerned with the pet's

dash for freedom. Lord Brentford merely raised his head, a questioning frown on his brow. Miss Knight was close to fainting and demanding her own share of attention.

The spaniel was enjoying more freedom than it had ever known and was off like a shot, with Dru in hot pursuit. "Stop at once, you mangy mutt," she muttered as she ducked under a low branch, then got hit with a smaller, more wicked limb. Her leather slipper came off, and she had to pause to stuff it back on. By that time it was almost impossible to catch the dratted dog.

But she did keep it in view. It was headed in the direction of a fence that had a hedge alongside it. She could only pray that the dog wouldn't figure out how to go through it—or around as the case might be.

It appeared that Binky had never encountered a hedge or a fence, for that matter. The spaniel stopped, stared, and seemed to puzzle out that here was something he hadn't expected to find in his delirious dash.

The pause gave Dru just enough time to dive into the long grasses to grab the dog in her arms. She held the little wiggling body tight against her, regardless of damage to one of her favorite dresses. She wearily returned to the open meadow and Miss Knight. It was an unrewarding experience.

"Poor little Binky! Did that naughty lady chase you through the weeds?" She gave Dru a scathing look. "Really, my dear, Binky is such a sensitive little creature. How could you chase him in such a way."

"How strange, madam! I was under the obviously wrong impression that you wished him to be fetched back to you." Dru was utterly furious. Not only had her bonnet fallen down her back, held by mere wisps of riband, but her hair also had partly come undone. Portions of the long strands straggled over her shoulder in a most unflattering way. When she looked down at her dress to brush it off, she discovered grass stains down the front and a few tiny tears. It was enough to make the most dauntless woman weep.

"My dear girl," the marchioness cried. "What has happened to you?" She marched up, looking shocked. Of course her words carried across the meadow to where the others perched on cushions under a beech tree.

"I thought to collect Binky for Miss Knight, when the little dog ran away. It seems I need not have bothered." Dru knew her bitterness could be heard in her voice, but there was no way she could keep from revealing it.

The marchioness gave her friend an annoyed look. "Cordelia, put the lead on your pet and keep him at your side, please do. Just look at the damage to dear Miss Herbert."

All Dru could think of at that moment was to go somewhere and have a lovely cry. That dratted dog had ruined her beautiful day.

"I am sorry, Miss Herbert," offered a chagrined Miss Knight.

Dru nodded, quite unable to utter a word. She turned away to accept help from one of the maids who apparently had ambitions to work as a lady's maid. She removed the tattered bonnet, smoothed Dru's hair into its usual shining arrangement. She brushed down the mussed dress, tutting at the green stains.

"I think this can be removed, ma'am," the girl said hesitantly. "Mrs. Simpson will know just the thing."

"I hope so," Dru said with resignation that her dress would never look quite the same anymore. It was all of a part with her day. Her heart would never be the same again, either.

But the afternoon was not done. Lady Felicia, with laughing demands that a thin cushion be placed on the board of the swing, kept Lord Brentford busy pushing her. Dru observed that he did not push her as high. Of course her bonnet did not come off, nor her short dark curls become disarranged.

"What was that sigh for, pray tell?" Lord Ives inquired with warm sympathy in his voice.

"Oh, many things." Not wanting to sound like a complainer, Dru forced a laugh. "It has been a mixed day."

"Most days are. Come stroll along the stream with me. I shall show you where the trout is hiding."

She suspected her smile was a trifle wan. She already knew where the trout hid, but she appreciated his attempts to cheer her. "Fine."

They walked along the stream. The water was so clear you could see every little pebble in spite of the ripples over the surface. Minnows darted here and there, unending in a quest for food. The toad still sat on the rock, his long tongue ever so often darting out to catch a tasty dragonfly or bug.

Soon Lord Ives motioned her to stop, pointing out the small trout motionless in the depths of the water. Only little side fins kept it stable and in position. It was a pretty sight and she said so.

"You like nature?" He tucked her arm in his and continued to saunter by the stream.

"Indeed, I do. Very much. The country suits me."

"You wouldn't like to live in Town?"

"As others have said, it would be a fascinating place to visit but a dreadful place to live." Although Dru admitted to herself that she would be happy to live anywhere with the man she loved.

Across the meadow she glimpsed Lady Felicia clinging to one of Lord Brentford's arms, smiling coquettishly and laughing a bit too loud, although she seemed conscious of Lord Ives.

"You always know where she is," Lord Ives commented.

"True. I'd not thought of that." Dru smiled.

Lady Felicia summoned Dru and Lord Ives to join them where they lingered under the great oak. "I think we ought to have a contest."

"What sort of contest?" Dru was wary of the young woman. She might look like a sugared plum, that didn't mean she was sweet.

Lord Brentford gave her a roguish look. "She wants

to see if Ives can push you as high as I did. And she thinks I ought to push her higher."

Relieved it was no worse than that, Dru nodded. "Shall you go first, Lady Felicia?"

Apparently it had never occurred to that young woman that she would ever be second at anything. She gave Lord Brentford a demure smile, then after insisting the little cushion be replaced for her, she allowed Lord Brentford to assist her onto the swing.

Dru watched with puzzled eyes. What the purpose of this so-called contest might be was beyond her. Silly, that is what it was. She glanced back to check on the elderlies. The six of them reclined on cushions and rugs, talking with more animation than she would have believed possible. She was free for the moment.

She wondered if Lord Brentford had pushed her as high in the air as Lady Felicia. How could they prove it one way or the other? "Can you pull off a leaf, my lady?"

The swing wobbled when she made a grab at the closest leaf. She screamed theatrically, clutching the ropes with a frantic grip. "Oh, that is impossible."

Dru could see that Lady Felicia was not high enough to grab a leaf, even if she did try.

Eventually the swing slowed to a stop, and the haughty piece left it to again cling to Lord Brentford's arm.

"I doubt if Lord Ives can match that exhibition."

Dru met his gaze with an amused glance. "We can but try our humble best."

"I do not know about you, my dear girl, but I am never humble." Lord Ives waited for Dru to position herself on the swing, taking care to use the same cushion her ladyship had used. There would be no talk of unfair advantage because of a lighter weight.

Dru sailed forth into the sky, soaring higher than ever before. If this was a contest, she liked it. The leaves were tantalizingly close. After several sweeps into the air, she was able to stretch out her arm and with ease pluck a branchlet from the tree. True, the swing wobbled a smidgen, but that was simple to manage. No screaming for her. She could have swung for an hour without tiring, but she feared Lord Ives was already wearied with the game.

She waved her little branch of leaves, a signal for him to cease his pushing. It was a good thing the maid had tied Dru's bonnet on firmly, and there was no problem of falling hair this time. Aside from her grass-stained dress, she looked reasonably presentable when she slowly swung to a halt. "Here it is." She waved her leaves in the air.

Lord Ives took it from her to hold over her head. "We are the winners, I declare. Now, what will be my reward?"

The others looked at him with varying expressions. Dru was leery of the glee in his eyes. A glance at Lord Brentford showed he was not pleased. Lady Felicia looked downright angry, spots of pink burning on her cheeks.

"I shall claim a kiss from my partner. Surely that is within bounds?" Before anyone could reply, he drew Drusilla up in his arms.

Within moments she found herself well and truly kissed. It was brief, but most certainly not unpleasant. She pulled away, but smiled up at him to show she was not displeased with his action.

"Well," Lady Felicia exclaimed, "I never!"

"You really should," Dru said sweetly. "It is quite lovely." She tucked her arm close to Lord Ives, as it had been before all the foolishness of a contest. "Why don't we pick wildflowers, sir? There should still be a number of them remaining."

A peek at Lord Brentford almost made her laugh. He looked like a thunderstorm had settled over his brow.

Lady Felicia still looked angry, too. And why that should be when she had Lord Brentford at her beck and call was beyond Dru. But then some people were never satisfied with what they had, always yearning for what was just beyond them. Or did she care for Lord Ives?

"Adrian," Lady Felicia said just loud enough for it to carry to Dru's ears, "are you going to permit your mother's companion to speak to me like that!"

"I saw nothing amiss with her remark."

That was obviously the wrong thing to say, for she looked about ready to explode.

Dru and Lord Ives turned away from the stormy couple. Within moments they were discussing the flowers to be found and wondering how many birds Mrs. Twywhitt and Sir Bertram had been able to name. That led to other topics.

Dru found that Lord Ives was very good company, and she liked his pleasant good nature. His gray eyes seemed to see a great deal more than one would think.

"You mustn't allow Lady Felicia to rile you. She is a rather spoiled young woman. She has always been catered to and allowed her way. She needs someone strong to take her in hand." He led Dru to the trestle table, where lemonade and scones still sat.

"Do you think Lord Brentford aspires to that position?" Dru inquired daringly. It was not a question she ought to ask, but she dearly wished to know.

He poured a glass of lemonade for her. "No, in spite of what his mother wants, I have reached the conclusion that he has his own plans."

Dru knew better than to ask what they might be. Even if Lord Ives knew, he would hardly confide these to Dru.

"My, you are far too serious for a picnic," Lady Felicia cried much closer to them than Dru had believed.

Had either Lord Brentford or Lady Felicia overheard her query? She hoped not. She set her glass on the table.

"Let's have a race," Lady Felicia demanded. "I shall pair with Miss Herbert. We shall run from here to the stream." She grabbed Dru's hand, a hard clutch from which Dru couldn't possibly extricate herself.

"Really, I don't think that is a good idea." Dru spoke quietly, not wishing to create a scene.

"It's a bit of fun. Come!" She dragged Dru with her.

There was little point in protest. Dru decided she might as well go along with the peculiar demand. They ran across the meadow, Lady Felicia pulling faster and faster.

Dru saw the stream nearing and was thankful the ordeal would soon be over. All of a sudden Dru found herself tumbling into the cold waters of the stream.

She came up sputtering, knowing her bonnet must be a sopping ruin, her grass-stained dress even worse, and her pretty leather slippers a total loss. She closed her eyes, not wanting to see the looks of disdain on various faces.

"Oh, dear," Lady Felicia cried, "I fear I was carried away in my enthusiasm. I am sorry, my dear." Dru thought she had been pushed, but couldn't be positive.

Lord Brentford removed his coat. He helped Dru from the water, allowed the little maid who had assisted before to blot some of the water off with a few napkins, then put his coat around Dru's shoulders in a surprisingly protective manner. He untied her bonnet, tossing it aside in a bedraggled heap, as it quite deserved. "What a shame that you had to fall like that. You must have tripped."

Lord Ives stepped up to escort Lady Felicia away. Dru would thank him later, for she had been very close to pushing Lady Felicia into the stream as well, considering that she probably had propelled Dru into the water. And that would have surely put paid to Dru's employment.

"I would like to go home." What she must look like with her gown plastered to her body, clinging to every curve and hollow, she didn't wish to consider.

His instant agreement was not balm to her spirit.

Chapter Eight

*D*ru stood silently by the carriage, too humiliated to move. The little maid who had come to her aid before stationed herself beside Dru, murmuring comforting sounds.

Lord Brentford's fine coat was probably ruined, and Dru felt even more dreadful about that, were such a thing possible. She wrapped it more closely about her, taking comfort in the brush of fine wool against her cheek and the scent of costmary. It was almost like having his arms about her to offer comfort.

She dropped her gaze to the ground, not wishing to see any condemnation in his eyes—or worse yet, amusement at her predicament. She must present a very droll picture. She risked a peep at him to find that he stared at her. She couldn't have felt more miserable with her hair in tangles, her soaking dress clinging limply to her form, and her bonnet consigned to the meadow. No doubt the cattle might find it tasty.

His sheer shirt was crisply white, his cravat a wonder of clever simplicity, and his waistcoat of white Marcella quite, quite beautiful, if one said such things about a waistcoat. The contrast between them was pitiful.

Lord Brentford turned aside to Lord Osman. "Take charge of things here while I convey Miss Herbert home."

The older gentleman agreed, looking concerned.

Lord Brentford assisted her into the vehicle, and

they commenced a silent ride to the Court. The maid, now sitting mute as a fish, had clambered in beside Dru.

Once at the Court he turned to the little maid as he handed Dru from the carriage. "Look after her from now on. See that Miss Herbert has a hot bath and a glass of port."

"Yes, your lordship." The maid bobbed a curtsy.

The two women hurried up the stairs to Dru's room, where in short order a steaming bath was arranged for her.

"Your name?" Dru wondered as the girl assisted her.

"Mary, Miss Herbert. I gather I'm to see to you, iffen his lordship meant that I'm to see after you from now on. I will take good care of you, too." She nodded emphatically.

In spite of her misery, Dru had to smile. "Very well, Mary. I surely could use some help. I fancy this dress is best consigned to the dustbin?" She plucked at the sodden muslin with a listless finger.

"Perhaps all is not lost. Mrs. Simpson will work her magic on it, you'll see." Mary offered a look of comfort.

"I wish I had your confidence. Mrs. Simpson has a great deal to do with all the company in the house. I doubt she will have time to fuss over the dress belonging to a mere companion." She didn't have all that many dresses with her. The ruin of a favorite would be a sad loss indeed.

"No, miss, there you are wrong. Mrs. Simpson would do anything for you. Thinks the world of you, she does. You help her, you see. Now she will help you."

When Mrs. Simpson entered to see what was amiss, she was horrified at the story Mary poured forth for her ears.

"I will see to it that this poor dress of yours looks as good as I can make it." Mrs. Simpson studied the sprigged muslin, shaking her head.

Dru stammered her thanks. She sank done into the blissfully warm water and allowed Mary to wash her hair with fine lavender-scented soap.

A tray bearing the glass of port was brought up with biscuits as well. Dru thought the port lovely but wondered what her father would have said to it. She sipped while Mary rubbed her hair dry, then brushed it to a fine silk.

Once Dru set the empty glass on the tray, she crawled between the sheets, permitting Mary to fuss over her. Did Lord Brentford know what a comfort it was to have someone to care about her? To tuck her in, see to her things?

Mary bustled about the room, ushered James and another footman in to remove the slipper bath. This was done with such dispatch, Dru was scarcely aware they had come and gone. The port had made her drowsy, and she willingly let sleep overtake her. A short nap would help restore her self-possession, which was a trifle lacking at the moment.

Adrian watched the two women go up the stairs. The plunge into the stream had likely placed a dampening effect on the rest of the picnic group. His mother would gather her friends to return at once. Knowing the servants would take care of everything else, he waited patiently for the group to return to the Court. His surmise was correct. Within a brief time he heard the carriages rumble up the avenue to the house. He flicked a glance at Lady Felicia, who was flirting with Ives and he seemed to enjoy it.

"I am sorry our outing had to end so precipitately." He spoke to the group in general, but turned to Felicia.

"Well, if your mother's companion wasn't so clumsy, we could still be enjoying ourselves." Lady Felicia preened a bit, aware she looked entirely delightful in her pink-and-white ensemble. "She had to spoil everything."

She twirled her parasol, batting her eyelashes at him

as she did. Adrian wondered why his mother was so bent on his marrying this self-centered pea-goose. It was possible that the foolish run across the meadow was all an accident. He couldn't believe a woman as beautiful as Felicia would stoop to such behavior. She didn't need to put any other woman out of her way. Yet—in his eyes—she had tried.

"I wouldn't have put it quite that way," he said dryly. He was host and had better remember that. She was a lady who knew what was due her station. Ives . . . thank heavens Ives was here. He exchanged a look with his friend, who assisted Lady Felicia from the carriage with care.

When they entered the hall Adrian caught sight of the lilac sprigged muslin over Mrs. Simpson's arm as she turned from the stairs to go to the kitchen. Leaving Ives and Lady Felicia to saunter on to the drawing room, he went to the housekeeper.

"Do you think you will be able to restore that poor gown to any sort of wear?"

She shrugged. "I'll do my best. The poor dear has so few clothes, she can ill afford to lose one." She glanced after the departing figure of Lady Felicia. "Not like some others who have more than enough."

"Is there some way the dress can be replaced? Could the local mantua maker copy it?" He frowned, doubting it would be possible.

"Deary me! I fancy she might at that. Would you be wishing me to have her see to it?" If the housekeeper was curious as to why her master was so concerned about a mere companion, she gave not the slightest indication.

"Please. And in the meanwhile, say nothing to Miss Herbert in the event the task cannot be done."

"Nary a word, you may be sure, my lord." She continued on her way to the kitchen, the sad dress dangling from her capable arm.

Adrian was about to follow Ives and Lady Felicia to the drawing room when he heard a carriage draw up before the house. Motioning to Priddy to open the door, he went out to see who had arrived. He wasn't expecting anyone, but it might be a neighbor.

Two fashionable gentlemen garbed in the very latest attire stepped from the traveling carriage.

Adrian extended his hands in welcome. "Vane! Metcalf! Well met. You are come to join our little party?"

"Didn't know you had one, Brentford." Harry Metcalf eyed Adrian with a speculative gaze, as though to gauge just how welcome their company might be.

"Well, we do—to celebrate my mother's birthday. Ives is here—as is Lady Felicia Tait. Miss Drusilla Herbert is also in residence." He didn't explain Dru was a mere companion. The very words stuck in his throat for some reason. How could any woman as gloriously beautiful be relegated to the status given a companion? He'd not have it.

Gregory Vane joined Harry to walk up the short flight of steps to where Adrian shook hands, making it clear they were welcome. He ushered them into the house, pausing to give instructions to Priddy regarding luggage and rooms.

"On a little repairing lease, are you? Thought you had won that large sum from Pickering?" he asked Metcalf.

"Oh, I won, all right. Only now every chap in Town wants to play cards with me in hope of winning it all away. I've a notion to hang on to such a lovely bit of money for a time." He grinned to take away the impression of fervor from his words.

Adrian gave him a knowing look. Harry was a good chap, but inclined to be a bit devil-may-care. Adrian turned to Gregory Vane. "And you just came along to keep Metcalf company?"

"London was a bit dull." He grinned.

"Be sure to mention that to Lady Felicia. I have no doubt she thinks she is missing everything of interest."

"Why do I doubt that?" Vane's expression grew cynical.

Adrian gave Vane a puzzled look before leading the

two men into the drawing room to make them known
to his mother and her guests. The men already knew
Ives and Lady Felicia. Felicia greeted them warmly.

His mother welcomed the new guests with her customary graciousness. She rose, saying she must see
Mrs. Simpson.

He watched her leave, then set himself to entertaining the others. If he wondered how Dru was faring,
he did not permit this to show on his face or in
conversation.

Lady Brentford did not go to the housekeeper's
room, but rather to Drusilla's. She tapped on the door
and went in when she heard an "enter."

"How are you, my dear girl? I was worried about
you."

"Your son insisted I have a glass of port after my
hot bath. I took a little nap and now feel splendid."

"And your poor dress. We shall have to do something about that." She crossed to the window to stare
out a moment, then pivoted to face Dru. "We have
more guests. Where shall we place two gentlemen?"

Dru thought a few moments. "Those two rooms at
the end of this corridor are still vacant. 'Tis fortunate
that you are blessed with a goodly amount of space."

"Fine. Could you direct the maids?"

Mary entered the room just then. She paused, ready
to retreat.

"Mary—you understand that his lordship wishes
you to look after Miss Herbert?"

"Indeed, ma'am. It will be a pleasure."

Lady Brentford walked to the door, halting a moment. "You will be able to join us for dinner, I trust?"

Before Dru could say no, Mary interjected, "I will
have her looking fine as five pence, my lady. She will
be there."

With that assurance, Lady Brentford sailed from the
room, leaving a mildly indignant Dru.

"I intended to remain up here." Dru was reluctant
to face Lady Felicia again.

Mary began to brush out the tangles from the

wealth of blond hair that cascaded over Dru's shoulder. "As to that, miss, there are now four single gentlemen below. I am sure that lady would like them all to herself. I expect it would be a shame to spoil the cluster about her ladyship. As it is, she's the only hen in the coop."

Dru smiled in spite of how she felt regarding Lady Felicia. "You have convinced me. Work what magic you can. I shall have need of it!"

One of the younger maids came to the room to receive her instructions regarding the rooms to be prepared for the new guests. All this while, Mary continued to ply her brush and comb. At last she finished.

When Dru checked the looking glass, she was astounded to see her reflection. A stylish, young lady stared back at her. "Amazing! You are a miracle worker. Thank you." Dru allowed Mary to select a gown for the evening, bemused by the change in her appearance. It was doubtful there would be any likelihood of hair tumbling down this evening. Mary had concocted a complicated hairstyle that looked nailed to Dru's head.

A gown of pale blue silk with dainty puffed sleeves and trimmed with delicate white silk roses around the hem gave her confidence. She had no jewelry to wear other than her simple gold and amber cross, a gift from her parents.

She pulled on her gloves, then before going down to the drawing room, she checked with the young maid regarding the rooms prepared for the new guests.

"Of course, miss. Their valets are in there now, arranging things to their liking."

Dru thanked the maid, then slowly walked down the stairs. The house was quiet now, with most everyone dressing for dinner.

"Ah, Miss Herbert I venture?"

Dru was taken aback by the appearance of a tall blond gentleman appearing from seemingly nowhere. His blue eyes had a kindly gleam in them that quite disarmed her.

"You have the advantage of me, sir, but indeed, I am Miss Herbert." She let a question linger in her voice, although she dare not ask his name.

"Since Brentford isn't here to perform his duty, allow me . . . I am Gregory Vane at your service." He bowed low before her, keeping a proper distance.

"Mr. Vane, how pleasant to make your acquaintance. Your room is satisfactory? You have all you need?" When he looked puzzled, she continued, "I am Lady Brentford's companion, but I also oversee a few other details."

Before he could comment on her status, another stranger ran down the stairs behind Dru to join them. He promptly introduced himself.

"Harry Metcalf, fair lady. I had no idea there would be two diamonds of the first water present. Vane, we are in luck." The three strolled along to the drawing room.

Recognizing his flattery for what it was, Dru merely smiled, thereupon suggesting the gentlemen avail themselves of beverages offered by the footman.

Moments later Lord Brentford came in, followed almost at once by Lord Ives. In minutes the older men followed.

"The ladies always take a bit longer, don't you know," Sir Bertram said with a wink.

Dru noticed that Gregory Vane had edged closer to her, whereas Harry Metcalf wandered restlessly about the room.

"Harry—you will wear out the carpet," Lord Ives joked.

"I am here, Adrian." Lady Felicia sailed into the room, a confection of pink with huge pink silk flowers in a diagonal line from hem to bodice. She wore pink silk roses in her hair. It was as though an entire rose bed had settled on the lady.

"Others are as well, dear girl," Lord Brentford said with a dry note in his voice.

Lady Felicia spun around with a patently false start of surprise. "I vow, it is vastly amusing to be the only lady with so many eligible gentlemen." She gave Dru a glance, adding, "Oh, dear me, I mustn't forget Lady Brentford's companion. You look very nice, dear."

Dru thought that had her tone been just a little more patronizing, hitting her over the head with a vase of flowers would have been fully justified. "You do as well, Lady Felicia." Dru had been taught to turn the other cheek, but in this case both cheeks had been used. Pushing Dru into the stream this afternoon had about wiped out Dru's patience and taken nearly all her store of polite nothings, not to mention her charity.

"If this is what the current crop of companions are like, I must urge my mother to obtain one," Harry Metcalf said with a laugh, a teasing note in his voice.

Then the older ladies, along with Lady Brentford, entered the room, chatting with the ease of old friends.

"Good, I see everyone knows everyone else. Drusilla, darling girl, you are feeling all right?" To the two newcomers Lady Brentford added, "Dear Miss Herbert had an accident this afternoon. She somehow fell into a stream and took a dreadful wetting." Lady Brentford's darted glance at Lady Felicia was missed by Mr. Metcalf, but not by Mr. Vane.

Dru murmured a soft reply that could have been anything. Mr. Vane met her eyes and shook his head. Why, she didn't know.

Priddy saved the day as far as Dru was concerned by announcing that dinner was served.

Lord Brentford escorted Lady Felicia while Lady Brentford took Lord Osman's arm. Mrs. Twywhitt and Sir Bertram followed, with Miss Knight and Lord Somers close behind. Harry Metcalf yielded to Gregory Vane for the honor of ushering Dru into the dining room.

Looking down the table to the foot where Lady Felicia made a fuss about sitting next to Lord Brentford, Dru thought back to recent comments. Lady Felicia seemed so certain of her place here. Could it be true?

Not for a moment did Dru forget Adrian's respect for his mother. He may not have been here often in the past months, but it was now obvious that he cared for his only living parent. He was merely casual about it.

Once the delicious soup had been served and the fish removed, they began the first course.

Dru sat between Lord Ives and Gregory Vane. Of all the people assembled, these two were likely the kindest. Neither had looked down his nose at a mere companion. She thought her father would approve of either one of them.

By the time dinner wound down to the point where the ladies left the gentlemen to their port, Dru wished the evening at an end. She had run out of small talk. She left the dining room with the thought of excusing herself. Her room was preferable to being around Lady Felicia and her flirting. She flirted with Lord Ives, as well as her host.

"Drusilla, my dear," Lady Brentford said after pulling Dru aside at the drawing room doorway, "would you be so kind as to play for us? I find I am not in the mood for singing this evening—so piercing, you know."

Dru agreed at once. If this kind lady wished music, it would be a pleasure to play for her.

When the gentlemen entered the drawing room, following their port and the gossip they exchanged after the women departed the dining room, it was to find the three older ladies enjoying their tea and listening to Drusilla play the pianoforte. Lady Felicia restlessly roamed the drawing room. There was no gentleman around for flirtation.

Lord Brentford broke off what he had been saying to Lord Ives to make his way to Dru at the pianoforte.

"You play well. The events of the afternoon did not upset you too much, then?" He sounded truly concerned, although Dru wondered how he could be. He was so cordial to Lady Felicia. Perhaps he believed the fall in the stream was an accident, nothing more.

"A simple wetting is nothing, my lord. I am far too healthy to be bothered by so little a thing." She continued to play, not wishing to draw attention to herself by stopping. That was the trouble with music intended to be the backdrop for conversation—if it was removed, everyone noticed at once.

He studied her a few moments, then apparently satisfied with the truth of her reply, he wandered away to chat with Gregory Vane.

With two more gentlemen around, two more women would be enormously helpful. Dru thought over the young women she had met at the village church. There were two she admired, lovely local girls. When she had a moment later on she would suggest the plan to Lady Brentford. •

"I notice you do not sing this evening, Lady Felicia. I am devastated." Harry Metcalf bowed over her delicately gloved hand. Apparently he enjoyed being close to one drenched in French violet. Dru thought it cloying, but likely she was peevish. There was not one thing that woman could do that would meet with Dru's approval. Except go.

Lord Osman persuaded Lady Brentford, Mrs. Twywhitt, and Sir Bertram to play whist. Miss Knight and Lord Somers were deep in a discussion about traveling in Europe.

Lord Brentford looked around at his friends, who were exchanging tales of London parties. Dru was surprised to find him at her side once again. She glanced up before concentrating on her music again.

"We have a problem."

Dru nodded. She didn't think he intended to pronounce the problem to be Lady Felicia. So she waited.

"We need two more women. Have you had the opportunity to meet any locally? Can you think of anyone who might do?"

"Might do?" she echoed. "Well, let me see. I met two girls at church. Miss Belinda Oaks—she's the daughter of Lord Swithin, and Lydia Percy, the squire's daughter. They are both well mannered"—

she couldn't resist a glance at Lady Felicia, "very pretty, and I should think would be flattered to be invited to anything here. Do you go shooting in the morning?" At his nod, she went on, "I could call on them to see if they are agreeable. I should imagine your mother will be busy with her guests."

"Excellent. I knew I could count on you for a solution. We must find things to amuse them all. The weather is likely to come on rain." He glanced to where Lady Felicia flirted with Lord Ives and Harry Metcalf. Gregory Vane strolled over to join Dru and Lord Brentford by the pianoforte.

"Ah, Vane, I mentioned to Miss Herbert that we are in need of more feminine company. She has a solution I think may please us all. Two local beauties."

"All?" The tall blond gentleman raised his brows and cast a glance back at Lady Felicia. "I know one who would be quite happy to leave things as they are."

Dru peeked at Lord Brentford quickly. Concentrating on her music again, she repressed a grin. That gentleman did not look the slightest bit happy. She wondered what annoyed him the most.

Dru was exhausted when at least she excused herself to head for her room. Lord Brentford stopped her at the bottom of the stairs.

"Thank you for your music this evening. I feel sure you would have far preferred to go to your room and enjoy an early night."

"True," she admitted. If he was surprised at her frankness, he gave no indication. "It has been a trying day—or ought I say tiring?"

"I should think both might apply." He hesitated slightly. "I am sorry your picnic was spoiled. For what it is worth, mine was as well." He studied her a moment. "Your maid—she suits you?"

"Indeed, she does. I had not expected such a comfort as my own maid. She is clever and a dab hand with hair."

"She did very well if your hair this evening is anything to go by—it's unlikely to come down. Very well, she shall stay with you. If Mrs. Simpson feels the necessity of hiring on a few more maids for the duration of this party, by all means tell her to do so."

"Yes, sir. And thank you for your regard. I appreciate it." Dru curtsied politely. She hurried up the stairs to find Mary waiting in her room.

"Mary you are a wonder worker! My hair stayed as it should all evening. I cannot begin to tell you how many times before I have had to retire to fix it during an evening." Dru pulled off the gloves she had put back on when she finished with the pianoforte.

Mary assisted her to undress, then slipped a nightgown over her head before helping her into bed. "I'll bring you a hot posset to help you sleep. 'Tis no doubt you have had a busy day and then some."

The maid left the room, ignoring Dru's murmurs that her posset wasn't necessary. How lovely to be pampered a little. She knew it was Lord Brentford's doing.

She was slipping off to sleep, the hot posset having a good effect on her nerves, when she wondered if Belinda and Lydia would take kindly to a late invitation. Well, it would be incumbent upon Dru to make it seem as though the young ladies were doing the marchioness an enormous favor.

And then there was the matter of an amusement for them all in the event of rain. She prayed earnestly for dry weather.

Chapter Nine

The following morning Drusilla ran lightly down to the breakfast room, intent upon eating her meal before the others came to intrude. Save for the soft voices and footsteps of cautious servants, the house was quiet.

The room was empty; however, the sideboard was laden with an abundance of breads and meats, cheese and jams. Drusilla filled her plate, then began contemplating what she ought to say to Lady Swithin to persuade her to let Belinda attend the perfectly respectable party at the Court. The matter of Lydia Percy was a simple one. If Lady Swithin agreed, Mrs. Percy was certain to follow her lead. At least, that is what Mrs. Simpson indicated.

"You are up and about early." Gregory Vane paused at the doorway before entering, as though unsure of a welcome.

"Come in, do. I am about finished, so will leave you to eat in peace. Priddy will fetch you an egg if you wish." Dru half rose from her chair only to be waved back.

"I beg you, keep me company for a time—unless you have something pressing that must be done?" He walked to the sideboard to help himself to bread and meat. He sat opposite Dru. She had decided he was a pleasant gentleman. She thought he was an unlikely companion for Harry Metcalf. That gentleman struck her as a typical London beau.

"I have a task to perform for Lady Brentford this morning that must not be delayed," Dru explained. "However, I can spare a few minutes." She glanced at the timepiece she wore pinned to her dress, wondering how early she dare appear at the Swithin front door.

"The weather looks to hold for the day at any rate. I gather all the men are going shooting?" He carved up his gammon with a deft hand while glancing up at her.

"So I understand." She knew Cook would welcome any and all birds taken this day. With so many in residence, extra fowls were gladly received.

"And you will entertain Lady Felicia?" He paused in his consumption of bread to stare at Dru, looked amused.

"I doubt it. Even if she is a guest, I have obligations to fulfill." Dru could not imagine what it would be like to be required to dance attendance on the conceited Lady Felicia. "I doubt if Lady Felicia would welcome my company—a mere companion."

"I would hazard those are welcome obligations on your part." His blue eyes had an amused light in them, and she smiled in return.

"I am not displeased to perform my tasks, sir. No matter what our station in life, we all have certain obligations. It is our attitude that makes the difference, I should think." Mary told her that Mr. Vane's valet had said that the gentleman was heir to a viscount and well liked in London.

She glanced at her timepiece again and rose from her chair. She could hear footsteps in the hall directly outside the breakfast room. She wanted to be gone before anyone else entered the room or tried to engage her in conversation. "I really must go. I wish you well in your shooting."

"It will be interesting, I feel sure." His voice held a dry note that indicated to her that he was dubious.

Dru collided with Harry Metcalf when she whirled around the door frame.

"Ah, the blond beauty of a companion. And what other talents do you have, my dear?" He grinned at her.

"Not many," she said with a grin, thinking him harmless. "Excuse me, I have things to do for Lady Brentford." She sped down the passage and up the stairs to her room.

"You look as though you be in a hurry," the maid observed.

"Mary, I must go to see Lady Swithin. I trust it is not too early?" Was she correctly garbed for her calls?

"I should think you might have a go at Lady Swithin now. By the time you take the gig out and reach the Swithin place, they will be up and about."

"I would like to have both girls in residence before the men come home. And, if possible, it would be wonderful to settle them in before Lady Felicia rouses."

"I understand her ladyship has no intention of rising early, what with all the gentlemen gone for the day."

"Somehow, that does not surprise me greatly." Dru exchanged a look with Mary before gathering her reticule and gloves. "Oh, I nearly forgot—would you pass along the request that the remaining two bedrooms be prepared for the girls? They are small rooms, but rather pretty. I doubt they will mind overmuch."

"Not likely," Mary said with a grin. "They will be happy to be here, I'm thinking."

The house remained fairly quiet, with only a male rumble emanating from the direction of the breakfast room, where the gentlemen assembled prior to their day of shooting.

Dru gave Priddy her request that the gig be brought around as soon as possible. She waited in the hallway.

"There you are. I feared you had already left." Lord Brentford entered the room with a brisk step.

Dru stood quietly, waiting to learn what brought him searching for her.

"No aftereffects of the tumble into the stream?"

"None at all. I have always been disgustingly healthy." She gauged the distance between her and the door, intent upon leaving as soon as she might. To spend time with him was asking for trouble. He stirred things within her that she did not comprehend at all.

"I still do not understand quite how that happened.

What do you remember?" He was positioned so that it would be awkward to go around him.

Dru thought back to the unpleasant occurrence. There was no way she could tell him that Lady Felicia had on purpose pushed her into the stream. "I couldn't say for certain. Most likely I tripped on a patch of rough grass."

"Hmm." His eyes held a suspicious look in them. She met his gaze squarely, unwilling to say a word against the woman his mother wanted him to marry. That she would be horribly wrong for him was beside the point. So many marriages in the *ton* were arranged and little more than a marriage of convenience for dynastic purposes.

"Well, if that is your end of the story, I must let it be. Not that I totally believe you, but as a rector's daughter you are given to telling the truth."

She gave him an amused smile. "I am no saint, sir. I can bend the truth if absolutely necessary."

"You look poised to dash like a rabbit released from a snare. Am I keeping you from an errand? Of course, you are dressed to go out and are waiting for a carriage to be brought around to the front." He stepped closer.

As though on cue, Priddy announced, "The gig is waiting, Miss Herbert."

"You are driving the gig?" He touched her arm lightly as though to keep her from going. A tremor shot through her at the contact.

She tilted her chin a trifle. "I am used to driving at home, sir." She swished past him, her skirts brushing against his boots in her haste to leave.

"Do your best to persuade the ladies we need them."

Dru made no reply, thinking it unnecessary. Within minutes she was out of the house and had the reins in hand, tooling down the avenue in the direction of the Swithin place. It took several minutes for her senses to calm.

Lady Swithin was home to the early call from Miss

Herbert come on an errand for Lady Brentford. Her curiosity was evident when Dru entered the morning room, where Lady Swithin received her.

Dru came right to the point. "I am on an errand of mercy, dear lady. I am hoping you can help us."

Her ladyship preened slightly.

"Lady Brentford is having a small birthday celebration, and several of her London friends are in residence as well as Lady Felicia Tait and Lord Ives. Then yesterday we unexpectedly received more company, Mr. Gregory Vane, heir to a viscount, I believe, and Mr. Harry Metcalf. He is a particular friend of Lord Brentford's. I fear the gentlemen outnumber the women. I was hoping you would allow Belinda to join the party. Her ladyship would be so pleased."

Dru could almost see Lady Swithin's mind at work. Several wealthy peers, premier gentlemen of the sort rarely seen outside London were near to hand, and it wouldn't cost her a cent to send her yet-to-be-presented daughter over to Brentford Court. "That would be lovely. How soon would you wish Belinda to join you?"

"The gentlemen are out shooting today, so I was thinking it would be excellent for her to come over as soon as might be. She could be all settled before they return."

"A fait accompli?" Lady Swithin was thinking rapidly.

"Precisely."

"She could come in short order. And if there is anything she requires, it can be sent over in a trice. By the bye, how is Lady Brentford?"

"She is improved," Dru replied with caution. "She still tires easily. Fortunately, her old friends understand and retire for naps or quiet intervals."

"Well, it is important to see these unexpected guests are kept amused. How tiresome for you."

Surprised at the sudden sympathy, Dru smiled. "I do my best to assist her ladyship, you may be sure. She is such a very dear lady."

Dru left shortly after that with Lady Swithin's assurances ringing in her ears that Belinda would present herself at the Court as soon as she was dressed and packed.

The drive to the Percy house took a little time, but the day was mild, with sun shining and only a little wind to ruffle Dru's gown as she tooled along the lane.

Mrs. Percy was all agog to receive a caller from Brentford Court. When Dru explained her mission and the interesting fact that Belinda Oaks would be taken over as soon as she was packed, Mrs. Percy nodded, waiting.

"Could Lydia join us, please? I have been impressed with what a charming young woman she is and I feel certain she will blend in with the group very well." Dru went on to explain all who were there.

Obviously not wishing to be too eager, Mrs. Percy appeared to cogitate a few moments before beaming a smile at Dru. "It will be our pleasure to send Lydia to join you. It will give her a chance to pick up a bit of polish."

"Indeed." Relieved, Dru rose from her chair to depart.

Lydia hovered in the central hall, eyes wide with curiosity.

"You have been invited to join the party at Brentford Court. Tell your maid to pack up appropriate garments for you." Mrs. Percy smiled fondly at her eldest daughter.

Eyes wide, an ecstatic smile on her pretty face, the girl bobbed a hasty curtsy, then dashed up the stairs with unseemly dispatch.

Mrs. Percy exchanged a resigned look with Dru and thanked her for coming. She watched from the portico as Dru climbed into the gig to drive back to the Court.

The house was empty and silent when Dru entered the front door. She made her way to the kitchen to see how matters went with Mrs. Simpson and Cook.

"As long as I don't have to climb those dratted stairs, I do fine enough," Mrs. Simpson said with a sigh.

Dru turned to Cook. "And you?"

"Bless your heart, all be fine here."

"Miss Oaks and Miss Percy will arrive shortly. I suspect it will be the fastest that either of them has been packed and bundled out of the door in their lives." Dru walked to the door, pausing to add, "I will go up to check on their rooms. Has Lady Felicia appeared as yet?"

"No, miss. All is quiet from that room." Mrs. Simpson gave Dru a significant look, before returning to her work in the stillroom creating sweets for dinner.

With more guests, the dining table would require extra attention. Dru paused to check the epergne, noting what would be needed. Mrs. Simpson apparently had everything well in hand on the main floor.

The two bedrooms allocated for the girls were truly charming. Dru made a mental note to bring up a few flowers.

The door to Lady Felicia's room opened after Dru had passed. She hurried on, not wanting a confrontation with that lady if it could be avoided. Rather than linger in the house, she sought refuge in the garden, thinking to gather a few flowers while avoiding that lady.

"Good heavens, you are in a pique. Those poor flowers are under attack!"

Amused at the remark, Dru glanced around to see Lord Ives leaning against the pergola close by. "I thought you were out shooting."

"I became tired of it. The beaters flush out the birds, and we take aim and fire. There is little sport in such occupation."

"But it is what is done." Her smile warmed.

"Somehow, I believe that basking in your smile is more to my liking."

Lord Ives was flirting with her! Dru was taken aback. Not that she was annoyed, she was surprised. While Lady Brentford might have invited him, Dru doubted anything was intended between Dru and Lord Ives. Hadn't Lord Ives flirted with Lady Felicia quite fulsomely, and she with him? Dru wondered what Lord Brentford thought of that.

She inadvertently glanced up at the house. Lady

Felicia's room overlooked this garden. Had there been a white blur of a face in her window just now? Or was it merely a curtain?

She checked the watch she had pinned to her dress, thinking it was close to the time when the two girls ought to arrive.

"Do not tell me you have a schedule to keep! I'll not believe it."

"There are two guests due to arrive soon. I had best take these flowers in so I can be nearby when they come."

"Am I apt to know them?"

Dru laughed. "Hardly. Two local girls are obliging us by balancing numbers. It did not seem fair for the gentlemen to have no one but Lady Felicia to amuse them. These are two very pretty young ladies."

"Felicia won't like that. She prefers to have all the attention." He exchanged a knowing look with her that she judiciously ignored. "And two *pretty* young ladies? Not kind, dear lady, not kind at all."

Dru wisely gave him no reply to that comment. She turned just as the lady in question came around the corner.

"Ah, just in time to amuse me, Reginald. Take me for a drive, or a walk, or something. This is a very dreary party with no one around." She clasped his arm, sending Dru a triumphant little smile. It shifted to a more intimate look as she turned her gaze to Lord Ives.

He merely laughed and strolled off in the direction of the stables, with her clinging to his arm and chattering loudly about something absurd. Again, Dru wondered what had happened to alter his opinion of Lady Felicia. Or had he been miffed to see her making a dead set at Lord Brentford?

Dru made quick work of the flowers. She had just returned to the entry hall when Priddy opened the front door to Miss Belinda Oaks.

Dru was amused. Had she become so old that she could spot the anxiety of the very young? The desire to fit in, to be accepted and please could be read on Belinda's pretty face. By the time she had her come-out in London, all that would be replaced by an ennui such as required in young ladies making their bow to Society.

"Welcome, Miss Oaks." Dru shook her hand, then glanced up as Priddy went to the door once again.

Within minutes Lydia Percy entered the house in a burst of enthusiasm. "Oh, what a smashing thing to happen. I never thought to be one of a party at the Court! Thank you, Miss Herbert, for thinking of me—and Belinda as well."

Dru chuckled. "I am very glad to see you, and I suspect the gentlemen will be happy to see two pretty faces at dinner this evening. Why do we not go up to your rooms so you may settle in? Dinner is at country hours presently. Won't it be delightful to surprise everyone?"

And wouldn't Lady Felicia have her nose out of joint when she encountered these two adorable fresh young women? They were out of the schoolroom, but not out yet in Society. However, Dru had observed them following church and thought them to be nicely mannered as well as pretty.

Lydia chattered all the way up the stairs while Belinda kept a reserved silence, darting looks at everything around her, no doubt committing to memory all she saw.

The girls were delighted with their rooms. Dru hoped their chatter wouldn't reach Lady Felicia once she returned to her room. Inspired, she gathered them close to her.

"Why do we not surprise everyone this evening? Keep very quiet, and when I think it best for you to come down, I will send my maid for you."

"You have your own maid?" an awed Lydia cried. "Mama said you are a companion to Lady Brentford. I never knew companions had maids."

"Well, I suppose most don't. Lord and Lady Brentford are gracious and kind people."

The two girls exchanged looks. Dru decided it was as well she hadn't put the two of them in together to share a room. They would chatter half the night.

Two maids came from the servant's stairway, edging into the rooms behind their mistresses.

"I can see you will be ready in time now that your maids are here. What shall you wear?" Dru was only mildly interested. She stalled for time because she intended to keep out of Lady Felicia's path if possible. Lord Ives couldn't entertain her forever. Or could he?

The girls chatted on, relating what gowns they had and going so far as to seek Dru's advice. She was touched, and surveyed the gowns with a kind eye.

Eventually she decided she could no longer hide away and neglect her duties such as they were. Surely Lady Brentford was downstairs with her friends by now.

Leaving the two young women to make final decisions, Dru braced herself for a possible encounter with Lady Felicia and returned to the ground floor. She would look in on Lady Brentford to see how she fared.

Her fortitude wasn't tested, as no sign of Lady Felicia could be seen. Perhaps Lord Ives took her on a drive to a nearby village? Dru, in spite of liking his company, devoutly hoped so, and that her ladyship would be agreeably tired, sufficiently so that she would not pick on Lydia and Belinda out of pique. She suspected Lady Felicia could be nice if not competing for the attention of a gentleman.

"Drusilla, my dear, have Belinda Oaks and Lydia Percy arrived?" Lady Brentford said from where she had been chatting with her friends.

"Indeed, they have, my lady. Is there anything you wish?"

Before the marchioness could reply, voices rang out in the entryway. The fluting tones of Lady Felicia soared over the subdued bass of Lord Ives. There was a brief silence, then within minutes the pair entered the drawing room.

Lord Ives looked bemused. He studied the woman

at his side, as though he didn't know quite what to make of her.

Lady Felicia shot Dru a triumphant glance. "We have had a perfectly lovely drive. What a charming village you have nearby. Quite picturesque! What a pity you are tied to your duties, Miss Herbert. You must long be out and about in this pleasing countryside."

"Actually, I was out this morning." At the doubting stare from Lady Felicia, Dru added, "I took the gig for a short drive. I suspect you were still abed." Dru gave Lady Felicia a pitying look before turning to Lady Brentford. "I shall check the dining room for you, then see how Mrs. Simpson does."

"Very well. I trust you to handle everything."

It was amusing to see how that simple remark appeared to vex Lady Felicia.

In the entry hall Dru found the gentlemen returning from a day's shooting.

Lord Brentford immediately came to her side. "The young ladies were able to come? They are here?"

"Indeed, their mothers were pleased to come to our aid. Belinda and Lydia are in their rooms, changing for dinner."

"Ah, indeed, I expect we had all best do the same thing." He had addressed the men as a whole.

Dru wondered at the curious expression on Mr. Metcalf's face. He had watched Lord Brentford as he spoke with her, then kept an eye on her while she replied. He wasn't close enough to hear what had been said, but why the curiosity?

"Have you thought of a clever means of entertaining them?" He stepped close to her as he had done this morning.

And again she felt a quiver shoot through her. It played havoc with her thinking. "Not exactly. We always play games, silly ones that children love. Adults can find them equally hilarious. Snip-Snap-Snorem is much enjoyed. My brother likes a game of Brag. I imagine Lady Felicia would enjoy a game of Matrimony." Dru gave him an innocent look.

"What a devious girl you are." He took another step, almost touching her. She felt as though she was suffocating, finding it difficult to breathe. Her heart was beating much too fast. She searched his eyes, wondering what he was thinking.

The other men had all gone to their rooms, and Dru was alone with his lordship in the entry hall.

"I like a joke now and again," she said in a whisper. From the look in his eye, she wondered if he was about to kiss her. Again, he lightly touched her on her arm.

"Well, what have we here?" Lady Felicia drawled. "Amusing yourself with the help, Adrian?"

His face revealed nothing. He stepped away from Dru, turning to the other woman with a respectful bow. "We were discussing what manner of amusements you all might like. Do you have a suggestion?"

Dru admired his politeness in view of Lady Felicia's behavior. How he could tolerate the thought of marriage to this creature was beyond Dru. He deserved better.

"Why not attitudes?" She struck a pose that Dru imagined had something to do with mythology. It certainly showed her figure to advantage.

"Miss Herbert, any other pastimes you know?" he asked.

"What about a play? You have several books of them in the library. Perhaps a light comedy? We could copy out the various parts and read them—no need to memorize or anything so tedious." She looked pointedly at Lady Felicia. She did not give that lady high marks for mental ability.

He cleared his throat, covering his mouth with his hand.

"A play?" Lady Felicia gave a tinkling laugh. "I must admit that is a clever notion. I had no idea you could think, Miss Herbert."

"Perhaps it is as well you don't know what I think, Lady Felicia." Dru smiled.

Lord Brentford took Dru by the arm. "Felicia, per-

haps you wish to dress for dinner and stun us all with
your beauty."

"What a dear you are," the lady exclaimed. "I shall
at once. Perfection is not achieved in a moment, you
know." She whirled about and lightly went up the
stairs.

"Come, we shall locate the book you mentioned."
Dru found herself steered into the library. Once there,
he shut the door and collapsed against it, laughing.
"Remind me never to fall into a battle of words with
you, my dear. I would never win." He recovered his
usual mien and guided Dru to the area where plays
were shelved.

"This is a comedy. I think something light might be
suitable, all things considered." She pulled out one
book.

He nodded agreement. "*The Delusion.* There are so
many ways one could take that."

"Indeed. I fancy it is rather easy to be deluded.
Particularly if there is one who is gifted at such
things." She fixed her gaze on him, allowing him to
see her skepticism.

"I trust you to keep a level head on your shoulders."

"Naturally. I always do." Which wasn't quite the
case when it came to him. She had silly delusions, but
nothing serious. She did not dislike him anymore. As
to how she did feel about him, she refused to consider
the matter. There was too much else to do.

Priddy rapped on the door, then nudged it open.
"Your mother wishes to speak with you, my lord."

He nodded, stuffing the book into Dru's hands before leaving the library.

She studied the little book, wondering what would
happen when they read out the parts. It wouldn't be
dull, that was certain. Nor, her heart replied, would
she likely be spared Lady Felicia's ire.

Chapter Ten

*D*inner, by anyone's standard, was a rousing success.

There were a few moments when Drusilla doubted the wisdom of inviting Lydia and Belinda to join the party. Lady Felicia took one look, and sweetly queried both girls on their backgrounds. When she discovered they were no more than green girls, quite in awe of her sophistication, and far from being competition in her eyes—she relaxed. Everyone else was able to as well.

Lady Brentford had not missed the assessment of her local beauties. Dru caught her frowning as she listened to the politely edged questions casually tossed out by Lady Felicia. None were rude, but most bordered on intrusive.

Lady Brentford fixed her gaze on Dru, and she wondered what was to come next.

"Adrian tells me you selected a play for our amusement. Have you decided who is to take part in it?"

Before Dru could reply, Lord Brentford spoke up. "No, Mother, we haven't had time. Perhaps, following dinner, I might meet with the—ahem—coproducer? Miss Herbert?"

This pronouncement met with general laughter, as he likely intended. Dru didn't miss the darted glance from Lady Felicia. Did she perhaps think Dru would attempt to capture Lord Brentford? What utter nonsense!

Harry Metcalf was in his element, impressing Lydia with his knowledge of London Society. Dru caught a skeptical look in the girl's eyes and was thankful the chit wasn't gullible, as well as refreshingly sweet.

Gregory Vane sat to one side of Dru, with Belinda on his other side. At the removal of the first course, when there was that inevitable lapse while dishes were removed and the second course brought forth, he turned to Dru.

"May I applaud you on your excellent choices for augmenting our group? They are delightful, unaffected girls."

"Oh, do you think so? I had the same feeling."

"And they are no threat to the beauty." He grinned.

"True," she replied with a smile. The footmen were placing the second course on the table. Once that was consumed, those dishes and the finger bowls were removed. The sweets were then offered, as well as the contents of the epergne, the nuts, dried fruits, and the hothouse offerings.

When the women left the room, there was a feeling of anticipation in the air. Dru hoped Lady Felicia would not demand the starring role. Although from what she had scanned, it was not easy at first glance to determine just who was the leading lady.

Lydia and Belinda offered to play and sing, which they did with commendable charm.

"Ah, youth," muttered Lady Felicia, "such enthusiasm."

"I am certain you have not lost all of yours," Dru remarked with charity.

"How kind!" her ladyship said with surprise.

Dru merely looked meek and hoped that was sufficient.

"The gentlemen join us," Lady Brentford declared. "I propose a game of cards." She motioned to her friends to join her. Harry Metcalf and Gregory Vane immediately sought Belinda and Lydia. With a suspicious look at Lord Brentford, Lady Felicia queried his meeting with Dru, remarking, "I expect you won't be long?" She said nothing more, but the look she cast at Dru held doubt.

"Not long at all." Adrian beckoned to Miss Herbert to join him in the library. She came, but seemed wary of him, quite as though she didn't trust him—or was it herself she failed to trust?

The hall was deserted, as was the library. A low fire burned in the grate, casting warm light on the Turkey rug that graced the room. He lit the Argand lamp that sat in the center of the round library table.

"What do you think of our choice?" He wondered if she knew how her lavender scent tantalized him, or what effect the firelight had on her blond tresses, turning them to a burnished gold. He liked her simple gown of aqua-blue, reminding him of the sea on a summer day, with lace trim like foam. It was a far cry from the overembellished pink creation adorning Lady Felicia.

"I merely looked it over, but I think it will do." Dru glanced up at him, a question in her eyes.

"It has been some time since I read it, but it is a light farce with everyone misunderstanding everyone else."

"Very well." She didn't sound entirely convinced, but it was of no matter. After all, this was merely something to pass the time, to amuse them on a rainy day. "Now, as to the cast?"

"Sir Artifice will be Lord Ives, I believe," Adrian decided. "Lady Felicia will undoubtedly do well as Lady Fallacy. And Lord Humbug could be Gregory Vane. His ladylove, Miss Sham, could be Lydia Percy and Belinda Oaks could play Miss Fancy. What about if you do Miss Construe, and I shall take Lord Grasp?"

She had an adorably confused expression that he found enormously appealing. "You want me to take the part of Miss Construe? Why ever for?"

"You have a pleasant voice, and would be plausible in the part. Not that you misconstrue things. Do you?" He was close enough so he could sense her tension when he lightly touched her hand.

"There are moments when I wonder if I do. I should

think it wouldn't be all that difficult to find yourself living in a fool's paradise. It is easy, I suspect, to have the wrong idea about something or someone." She turned so she could look him in the eyes.

"You fear you have the wrong notion of someone?"

"I do." Her voice was a mere thread, a whisper. She searched his eyes, her own rich aqua-blue a liquid in which he might gladly drown.

He took a step, as he had earlier. Only this time there was no one around to interrupt. She didn't back away from him, and he took heart from her open expression. Her lips parted as though to speak. He silenced them the best way he knew how.

Her lips, when he touched them, were the softest of velvets; her skin put a rose petal to shame. The delicate scent of lavender haunted the very air around her. He gathered her close in his arms, and to his delight she responded wholeheartedly.

Her hands inched up to rest on his shoulders, and he was elated at their closeness. His hands learned the shape of her as she nestled against him. Such a delight was one that could be repeated forever, and he doubted he would ever tire of it—or her. He trailed a finger along her jaw, liking the tender line of it and reveling in her gasp of pleasure. He was about to repeat their kiss, longing to deepen it, when he heard sounds.

There were voices in the hall, drat it. Gently, he turned her so that she faced the table once again. And he took two steps away from her to be safe from her allure.

There was not a chance in the world that he would marry Lady Felicia now. He had tasted paradise, and he would never settle for nothingness.

"Dru . . ." he began.

The door burst open, and Lady Felicia marched in towing Lord Ives with her. "Well? You have been in here long enough to write an entire play!"

In a clear, composed voice Drusilla Herbert said, "We have assigned the various parts. Should you wish to join us in copying them out?"

"Write? Never! That would be far too tedious." She studied Dru first, then transferred her gaze to Adrian. Suspicion hung over her like a shroud.

"Perhaps Belinda and Lydia would assist? Lord Brentford, would you be a dear and ask them?" Only the expression in her eyes revealed a hint of what had passed between them. Fortunately, she did not look at Lady Felicia, who would have spotted that hint of sensuality immediately.

His mouth quirked up at one corner at her daring to call him a dear. Lady Felicia would pounce on that at once.

"I doubt he is your 'dear' anything, Miss Herbert." Lady Felicia abandoned Lord Ives to cling to Lord Brentford's arm. Lord Ives did not look pleased.

"I did not say that he was, precisely. But I appreciate his help. Is not that esteemed? Must we not admire a gentleman who is gracious and obliging? I do."

"Oh." Lady Felicia did not appear to know how to respond to the politely worded remark. The trouble with Dru was that she handled Felicia with such gentleness that the lady didn't know what to make of her. Adrian bit back a grin, exchanging a knowing look with Ives. After rummaging about in his desk drawer, Adrian found what he wanted.

"Here is a stack of paper for you, and I believe there are some pens somewhere around here."

"There are seven characters, but I believe Belinda and Lydia could share a copy of the play." Dru walked to the desk, taking the seat where Adrian usually sat when he wrote letters. She pulled a few pieces of paper to her, picked up a pen, and began to write.

The others stood silently, staring.

She glanced up absently. "Do fetch them for me, will you? Someone?"

Only Adrian likely noticed that her hand shook a trifle and that the color in her cheeks was a bit higher than usual. Good. It was comforting to know that he affected her as much as she did him!

"Well, I must say, Adrian, to order you about in your own home!" Lady Felicia sputtered.

"That was a request, and it is for our benefit. Come, let us fetch Miss Percy and Miss Oaks."

When they were gone, Dru let out a sigh and leaned against the back of the chair. Mercy! She had never believed a kiss could be like that, to so enthrall you that you scarce knew where you were. She was a wicked girl—she must be—for she would welcome another kiss just like it.

What a blessing that Lady Felicia had waited as long as she had before intruding on the library. Dru would have hated to miss one moment of that kiss.

Placing an elbow on the desktop, she leaned a cheek on her hand, sinking into a lovely reverie. She was falling into a delusion if she thought she was going to have a happy ending like Miss Construe in the play!

"Are we to help you?" Lydia caroled as she popped around the corner.

"Mama said I have a good hand," Belinda piped up as she came into the library on Lydia's heels.

"Here is paper and some pens. Perhaps we could put the play in the center of the library table, and all use it at once?" Dru reluctantly rose from the chair she knew belonged to Lord Brentford. The faintest hint of bay rum, along with fine leather, clung to it, reminding her of him.

"I had no idea it would be so exciting to come here," Lydia confided.

"Pay attention to the parts of the cousins. We decided you two could read the two cousins. I shall let you decide who will read which part." Dru was thankful for her inspired thought, eliminating any ill feeling between them.

Within minutes the three settled down to write. It was surprising how quickly they wrote, how fast the pages piled up.

"We shall be done this evening, I vow," Belinda said quietly.

"I believe you are right," Dru murmured. She could hear the sound of laughter coming from the other room. Lady Felicia would be pleased to have four men all to herself. She wondered what they did. A game, perhaps? Her mind strayed to possibilities, and her pen ceased to write.

"Is there a problem? Do you need the ink pot?" Lydia inquired earnestly.

Dru shook her head and returned to her pen and paper.

By the time Lady Brentford summoned the tea tray, the girls had completed six copies of the script. It was a blessedly short play, one of the farces put on late in the evening, following the main offering. People liked a comedy, to laugh and wink at a witty rejoinder.

They rose from the library table to join the others in the drawing room.

"Here we are with the copies for you. I shall let you assign them, Lord Brentford."

"I think you might well call me Adrian, being so close to the family and all," he grumbled, but low enough so the others couldn't tell what he said.

"I'll not take all the credit. I copied—as did Lydia and Belinda. Now you must do your share." She smiled at him, knowing he had something else in mind. She placed the copies into his hands, then slid away to pour tea for Lady Brentford and the others who preferred tea to wine.

"When will you read the play?" Lady Brentford inquired. "I declare, I do not know when I have been so vastly diverted. We must invite Lord and Lady Swithin and the Percys to hear it."

Lord Osman gave her a fond smile. "It is good to see you looking amused again."

"Indeed so," Miss Knight added. Binky had escaped from her room and crept into the drawing room on silent paws. He apparently recognized Dru, for he snarled at her before going on to plead with his mistress to pick him up.

Dru supposed the dog would never forgive her for ending his bid for freedom. When she thought of all that occurred that dreadful day, she rather hoped the little dog would succeed in his next attempt.

Miss Knight shot her a suspicious look, and Dru wondered if her thoughts were visible.

"I shall be Lady Fallacy? How quaint," Lady Felicia cried gaily. "It looks as though I have a fine role," she concluded with obvious satisfaction as she paged through the play.

"Ives, you read Sir Artifice and, Vane, you will be Lord Humburg." Adrian handed out scripts.

"I say, that sounds rather disagreeable," Gregory Vane declared with a laugh.

"It is no worse than being called Artifice!" Lord Ives insisted.

"Well, it is a comedy and titled *Delusion*. It isn't surprising that the names reflect that," Lord Brentford pointed out in a reasonable manner.

Dru put up a hand to cover the grin that longed to burst forth into laughter. As she touched her lips, her gaze chanced to meet that of Lord Brentford's—Adrian's. She hoped no one else observed the warm look he cast her. The fat would be in the fire for certain.

She thought one person did notice, but as she said nothing, Dru ceased to worry. Lady Brentford was not one to say anything that might embarrass a person, unlike Miss Knight or Lady Felicia.

When they all went up to their respective rooms later, Dru heard Harry Metcalf grumbling about not having a part to read. She would gladly have given him hers, had it not been a female part. She smiled, a feline sort of smile, for while Lady Felicia appeared to have the starring role, it was Dru that captured the heart of Lord Brentford in the role of Lord Grasp. How very, very nice.

With that silly thought, Dru changed into her night-dress and slipped between sheets that had been warmed against the damp of a rainy day. The embers of the fire that had heated her room cast a comforting glow over the interior. Within minutes she had drifted to sleep.

The following morning found it pouring rain outside Dru's window when Mary opened her draperies.

"A dreary day, miss."

"Perfect for reading a play, however. The men will not be tempted to wander off to do some manly sport."

"I heard Mr. Metcalf insisting that one of the men join in a game of billiards."

"None of them have bothered you, have they?" Dru wouldn't have put it past Harry Metcalf to attempt to seduce Mary, for she was a taking little slip of a girl. Big brown eyes surveyed the world with such assurance.

"No, miss. Mrs. Simpson gave me a long pin, such as might be used in a hat." She patted her bodice. "I keep it handy at all times. No man is going to persuade me between his sheets without a wedding!"

Dru nodded in relief. "Good. We will likely read the play this evening. If you like, you may sit in the back of the drawing room. I am certain the other maids would enjoy the play as well, for it is a comedy."

"Thank you!" Mary replied with surprise. "I know they all would, maybe the footmen, and Mrs. Simpson and Cook?"

"Goodness, we shall have quite an audience." It served to put Dru on her mettle. She tried to memorize the lines so not to be confused if someone forgot or something. She didn't trust Lady Felicia. She was not above trying to add to her lines to make her character more important. The only thing she couldn't do is change the ending of the play.

The practice went well, if one ignored Lydia's and Belinda's giggles, although they chimed in with their own lines perfectly on time. That they were amused might distract from their parts, for they were supposed to be serious. Dru had the feeling that they would sober up that evening when they came to read before the assembled parents and other lords and ladies.

Lady Felicia drifted over to survey's Dru's gown, a simple affair of blue India mull with pretty cream ribands tied in front.

"I must say I am surprised at your gowns. How is it that someone in the country can dress so *au courant*?"

"I know this will surprise you, but the post delivers magazines from London to our village. Amazing, is it not?" Dru smiled, but her eyes cautioned.

"Oh." Blinking at Dru's mild answer, her ladyship wandered off, as though in search of someone more unwary.

If she only knew, Dru mused. Her little darts often found an unguarded spot in Dru's heart, although she was careful not to let that lady know what hits she scored. But Lady Felicia did not have to proclaim Dru's background. It was known she was a simple country girl.

"I propose a run-through from start to finish." Lord Brentford waved his script in the air, motioning the various characters to take their places.

Out in the hallway Dru heard Lord Osman and Sir Bertram chatting with Harry Metcalf regarding a game of billiards. It was a relief to learn he was occupied. What a pity the pay didn't have more parts.

They did remarkably well, with only Lady Felicia muffing her lines a few times. Lord Brentford was charming and patient with her.

Dru studied the rug at her feet. Of course he would have patience with the woman his mother wanted him to marry. The wondrous kiss he had given Dru had been propinquity, nothing more. Why, he probably kissed every lady he could! She thought back to her original dislike for the man. He had ignored his dear mother before charging to Brentford Court to insist the party be canceled. Then, while he had reluctantly allowed that to go forth, he had planned to send Dru packing. Perhaps in the back of his mind, he still harbored a plan to eliminate her? Compel her to flee because of his attentions? She didn't like to think of his nurturing a scheme; it seemed beneath him. Yet, what did she really know of him?

She did not want to think it of him, indeed, she wished she could declare him her hero, just as in the play. But real life wasn't a theatrical production.

"If you are ready to join us, Miss Herbert?" His deep rich tones cut across her musings.

Dru's head shot up; her startled eyes met Lord Brentford's cool gaze with consternation. He had not spoken to her like that since they first met. So—that was the way it was to be? Perhaps her musings were not so far off the mark after all?

"Indeed, my lord. I shall endeavor to pay closer attention. So sorry." She flashed a look of antipathy in his direction. So he thought he could toy with her affections, did he? He would find her as elusive as an eel from now on. She read her lines with perfect intonation and coy sweetness when the end neared, and she was to fall into his arms—according to the play.

She edged away from him, not wishing to be near him when the conclusion was reached.

"Well-done, all of you." Lord Brentford nodded approval toward most of them, but Dru thought he deliberately did not look her way.

"Miss Herbert seems a bit absent," Lady Felicia said, her sugary tones falling clearly into the silence of the room. "Do you have the headache, my dear? Try a lavender-soaked cloth on your forehead. I always find it helpful."

"No, I am fine, my lady. Merely a slight problem that intruded." Dru slipped from the room while Lord Brentford was otherwise occupied with Lady Felicia on a question of one of her lines.

Perhaps a lavender cloth might help, after all. A headache seemed to be creeping up on her, in spite of her denial. She entered her bedroom in hopes of a retreat. "Mary, please find me the lavender oil."

Mary closed the draperies in Dru's room, then found the bottle of lavender oil.

Dru rubbed some of the oil on her forehead before she stretched out on her bed. Within a few minutes she could feel the lavender's beneficial effects.

Half an hour later she woke from a light doze in a much better frame of mind and without a trace of her headache. A glance at the clock warned her to dress for dinner and the ordeal ahead of her.

A rap on her door brought her from her dressing table.

Lady Brentford came in, a flurry of pretty draperies about her trim form. "How are you, my dear? Mary said you had the headache."

"I did as Lady Felicia suggested and put some lavender oil on my forehead. It was a splendid suggestion, for I am far better now."

"Good. I sent invitations to the Swithins and the Percys to join us for dinner and the evening. I depend on you to assist Mrs. Simpson, should she require help."

"Naturally I will. And may I say how pleased I am to see you looking so animated? Dare I wonder if a certain lord has put that twinkle back into your eyes?" Dru gave her employer a fond look, for she was indeed sparkling.

"How did you guess? Indeed, Lord Osman has me feeling like a girl again. I believe I shall marry him. I would rather be a Viscountess Osman than a Dowager Marchioness."

"You believe your son is to marry soon?" Dru's heart developed a sudden chill.

Her ladyship beamed a smile. "I believe so. He shows all the earmarks of a man in love."

Well, Dru thought it likely, given his extraordinary patience with Lady Felicia. He must indeed love her if he was willing to endure her flirting with other men.

Pink-and-white loveliness couldn't overcome everything.

"You feel well enough to oversee dinner and the reading of the play this evening?"

"Your son is directing the play, and I can cope with reading my few lines. I trust it will amuse your guests," Dru concluded with a smile at the lady who had been so very good to her. "I shall miss you dreadfully when I am gone." The words slipped out before she realized she said them rather than thought them. She was too outspoken at the wrong moments!

"I was unaware you intended to leave us. When, may I ask, do you plan to go?" Her ladyship suddenly grew aloof.

"I shall remain as long as you have need of me. But know that your son disapproves of my being here and may find a way to . . ." Dru hesitated to say more.

"Send you packing?" The lady sniffed with seeming amusement. "I doubt it. Carry on with him, my dear. I do."

Dru gave her words dubious consideration.

"Come with me. Let us look over the dining room. I believe we need more candles—although soft candle-light is kind to a lady, we should like to see what we eat!"

Laughing as no doubt intended, Dru walked to the main floor at her ladyship's side and into the dining room, where a footman inserted beeswax candles as needed.

Twenty chairs sat precisely at the table, now extended to the required length. A more elaborate epergne sat at the center with four elegant branches of candelabrum spaced the length. The rat-tail silver flatware gleamed with polishing, and nothing could have been more refined than the Wedgwood china with the Brentford crest centered on each plate or the delicate crystal finger bowls and glasses at each setting. Fine mustard pots were spaced between settings, with pepper pots and glass-lined salt dishes next to them.

"I think all is in readiness," Dru said after inspecting the epergne.

"Fine—let us assemble with the others now." Dinner was jovial. The Swithins and the Percys were happy additions to the party. Mrs. Simpson had organized the serving to perfection. Dru had not been required to help at all, save for placing the fruits on the epergne.

Avoiding Lord Brentford, Dru slipped in and out like the eel she had thought of earlier. If his glances in her direction seemed frustrated, she marked it to his annoyance with her.

The play was an enormous hit with everyone. The servants watched from the corridor and standing in the corners of the drawing room, while Lady Brentford and her friends, plus Harry Metcalf, observed the players from the comfort of their chairs and sofas.

"Kind sir," Dru read in ringing accents to Lord Brentford, "I will wed you and happily. 'Tis a comfort the misunderstanding and delusion is cleared at last."

She took her bow with the others, then glided from the room to supervise the serving of a light dessert to those present.

She was briskly marching toward the kitchen when Lord Brentford stepped in her path. She halted, giving him a wary look.

"Why do you disappear every time I want to speak with you?" He truly sounded put out.

"I am merely doing what I am paid to do, Lord Brentford." Her voice was stiff, her manner even stiffer.

"I thought we had gone beyond that. I see I am wrong."

"Adrian," Lady Felicia called, "do come and settle a dispute."

He gave Dru a searching look, then spun on his heel and left her alone.

Chapter Eleven

*T*he rain continued the next day. It wasn't a hard rain, but it was a persistent one, almost a mizzle.

Dru cast a discouraged look out of her window. Well, she was in the mood for rain. Actually, a deluge such as Noah faced would have been welcome. She could just step into a boat and float away!

Of course, running away never solved problems. She had promised Lady Brentford that she would remain as long as she was needed. That day had not yet arrived. At least, her ladyship had said nothing. What her son might do or say was something else.

Mary slipped into the room, holding something behind her, a look of expectation on her face. "This be for you, miss. And you'll be that surprised." She whipped the item from behind her to reveal the lilac sprigged gown, just as fresh and pretty as the day it was made.

"Mary! What a wonderful surprise! My dress—and it looks so fine. I shall wear it today, for I need cheering."

But when she went to slip it over her head, she noticed that the tear Binky made was not mended, it was entirely gone. A careful inspection caught several other tiny differences. "This is not the same dress, is it?"

"I never thought you would notice, really I didn't."

"What happened to the original?" Dru sank back

on the edge of her bed, still holding the sprigged muslin in her arms.

"Well, Mrs. Simpson did her best, but the print faded 'most completely away and the tears were hard to mend. Lord Brentford said to have the dress copied, so she did. Had it sewn by the local seamstress. I thought she did fine."

Dru studied Mary's anxious face before summoning a smile. "I agree. She did an excellent job." Dru allowed the little maid to assist her with the dress, fastening the tapes and adjusting the sleeves. It had been and now was a fetching thing. The trouble with it was that she owed Lord Brentford an apology . . . or something.

While Mary brushed and arranged her long blond tresses, Dru considered the matter. She didn't think she had anything to apologize for, but it was evident she had angered him by what she had said. This stylish re-creation was rubbing salt in her wounds for certain. She must do it, like it or not. Her father would scold her were he here, and his scolds were worse than a birching.

Once her hair was in shining order, Dru thanked Mary and left her room to wonder where she might locate the man she needed to see. While walking down the stairs, she debated on where to begin. She stood in the lower hall, undecided.

"Were you looking for someone?"

She knew that deep rich voice without even turning around to see who spoke. "Yes. You."

"I see. What may I do for you?" He executed a half bow, giving her an amused look.

"You already did. Do, that is. Oh, you have me all mixed up. What I mean to say is thank you for the new dress. It is so like my favorite, I could scarce tell them apart. Except this one does not have a tear from where Binky attacked it." Dru revolved so he might see how nicely the local seamstress had done.

"Very nice," he commented. "It was the least I

could do when you saved the little dog belonging to one of my mother's guests. You had a rotten time that day." He regarded her from a tired face that she would have sworn indicated a lack of sleep. Although what might keep him awake at night was beyond her. The house was as quiet as a tomb at night.

"I see. It was not necessary for you to repay my loss, but I thank you." She gave him a sad look before going to the kitchens to ask Cook if there was anything needed. She would have sought refuge in the gardens, but the rain prevented that.

Without considering the matter, Dru hunted out a waterproof cape and bundled it over her head. Before anyone was aware of her intent, she was out of the house and into the garden. She crunched along the gravel path, happy to be out. She picked a few flowers—just for herself.

"What in the world are you doing out in the rain?"

It had been exhilarating to feel the light rain on her face, to smell the damp earth and the primal scent of the flowers and growing things. "I just wanted a few blooms."

Lord Brentford tucked his hand under her elbow to march her back to the house. Once inside the back entry they stood, allowing the water to trickle down to the stone floor. He carefully lifted the waterproof cape from her head, shaking it out while shaking his head as well.

"You need a keeper."

"I do very well, thank you. Now, if you will excuse me?" Dru edged away from his tempting closeness. He thought she needed a keeper? What she needed was to be far away from him!

"Where do you arrange flowers?"

He ignored her obvious desire to have him gone. Really, the man had a thick head. He should know he wasn't to be found in this area.

"In here." She had walked on ahead of him and into the little room with the stone sink and wooden table.

"I will wait." He propped himself against the frame of the door, looking as though he had no plans to move in the foreseeable future.

"I do not see why." She permitted her eyes to rest on him for a few moments before turning her attention to the flowers. His hair was damp from the rain, plastered to his head in a dark swath. A few drops of water clung to his skin, and she knew the most absurd desire to lick them off, one at a time. And if that wasn't the most outrageous thought she had ever had, she didn't know what was. There were damp patches on the corbeau coat he wore, a coat that delineated his form to a spectacular degree. As did his biscuit-colored pantaloons. How he could ignore the drops of water on his fine black shoes was beyond her. His valet, Colyer, would have a raving fit.

"I want to talk with you, and you are slippery as an eel." His voice was plaintive, and she chuckled at the sound.

"I so intended. If you must know, I wished to avoid talking with you, considering the mood you were in yesterday." She paused a moment, taking a cautious glance at him before arranging her little cluster with care.

"You do that well," he commented while he watched.

"It was always my task at home." This time she refused to look at him, not wishing, yet wishing to feast her eyes on his fine form.

"Last night you said you would wed me and happily."

Dru spun around to give him a shocked stare. "But that was a play—words from a play! They were not meant to be taken seriously, and you must know it." She held a flower before her, unconsciously inhaling its delicate perfume, and gave him a hesitant smile. Surely he was making a very bad jest.

"You would not consider making it a reality?"

"No."

"That is it? No?"

"No, thank you," she said, still numb with shock. "It is not polite to tease."

"What makes you think I am teasing? Do you as a rule allow men to kiss you as you allowed me?" He shifted as though to move, yet remained where he was.

He hadn't stepped toward her, yet Dru felt as though he completely engulfed her, that he filled the little room with his presence. She froze, while not feeling threatened, certainly at risk. "Indeed, never! No one . . ." She fell silent.

"No one has kissed you at all in that manner, is that it?" One of his hands reached out to touch a strand of her hair that had escaped and now clung to the nape of her neck.

She knew he was aware that she trembled at his touch. Dru reluctantly nodded. What was the use of pretending otherwise when he obviously knew the answer?

"I suspected as much."

"Perhaps you know what you are talking about, but I do not." She glanced back at him. He had taken a step away from her, seeming ready to leave the tiny room.

"It will come to you in time. In the meanwhile, I shall leave you with this." One long step and he was beside her, a firm hand on her jaw tilting her face up to meet his. She met his gaze moments before his lips descended upon hers, and she forgot everything else except him.

The kiss before had been earthshaking; it had turned her world upside down. This was different: sweet, tantalizing, alluring, and very, very tempting. When his lips released hers, she felt lost, cold.

"Oh." If someone had demanded speech from her, she would have been incapable of it.

"As I said, think on it."

"Your mother wishes you to wed Lady Felicia" was the sum of what came to her scattered wits.

"Indeed? I would never permit another to dictate

my choice of wife. And that includes my mother." His face became austere, the ultimate aristocrat.

"It is a good thing I don't take you seriously, or you could be in dire trouble, sir. Now, be gone with you!" She shooed him on his way and hoped that she did not appear as shaken as she felt.

He shook his head and disappeared from her sight.

Dru leaned against the cold stone of the sink, wondering if she had taken leave of her senses. Had she actually allowed that man to kiss her again? And in such a manner! She was quite certain that her sanity had taken leave and might not return until she left this house.

She sent up her flowers with Mary, then headed for the drawing room.

She entered, expecting to find it empty. She was wrong. Lady Felicia sat at the pianoforte plunking out a melody. If she had hoped to escape without talking to the woman she heartily disliked, she failed.

"I see you have your lilac sprigged muslin back. I am amazed at how well Mrs. Simpson did with it." Lady Felicia sounded civil, yet with a superior hint in her voice.

Honesty compelled Dru to reply, "Actually, she didn't do anything to this. Lord Brentford paid a local seamstress to copy the original one. I am pleased with the results."

"I expect if you have few gowns and none from London, a village seamstress is well enough."

Dru gave Lady Felicia a level look. "You have no reason to sneer at my clothes. You wear the finest that your money can buy. I think it rag-mannered to make derogatory remarks about my gowns, as though I could afford better and don't know enough to buy them. I appreciate Lord Brentford arranging to have a favorite dress replaced. But I will not listen to your unkind remarks, nor must I." Dru turned to leave the room.

"You are too presumptuous, missy! If you think to

wed Lord Brentford, think again. *I* will wed him. His mother did not invite me here without good reason." Lady Felicia rose from the pianoforte to stand before Dru. Had she not been so petite, she might have been a challenge.

At first Dru felt chilled. Then reason returned. "Interesting. That is not my impression in the least. I have not had the feeling that his lordship permits someone else to dictate his path—least of all his mother." She almost added a remark about women who intend to marry one man while flirting madly with another, but didn't.

"That is all you know about it." Lady Felicia stamped her slippered foot before whirling about to pace across to the window. Here she stared out at the rain.

"Pity it rains," Dru commented as she left the room. She did think it would be nice to place Lady Felicia out in the downpour—perhaps it would wash away some of her powerful scent. The mental image of her haughty ladyship dripping with water, her artful curls in rat-tails about her face, and her flimsy gown clinging to her somewhat too-slender form was small comfort.

Around noon, Mrs. Simpson arranged a splendid buffet for anyone who wished a meal. Thinking to eat before the others, Dru went to the breakfast room, a pleasant little room in comparison to the grandeur of the dining room.

On the sideboard she found cold sliced meats, cold meat pasties, a selection of cheeses and breads, and even a handsome pudding for those who wanted a sweet.

The table had a dish cross in the center on which sat a dish of harico of venison. The flame from the spirit lamp set into the center of the dish cross burned steadily, and the harico, or strew, bubbled, sending forth a tempting aroma. Dru took a dainty helping of the venison, added bread and cheese to her plate, and found a chair situated so she might at once see anyone who ventured into the room.

Lord Ives paused in the doorway. "An indoor picnic?"

"I suppose you might call it that. Join me if you wish. I can recommend the harico of venison."

"Ah, a favorite of mine. I believe I will. Join you, that is." In short order he had filled his plate. He found a seat next to her and began a leisurely conversation as undemanding as he himself was.

He had Dru laughing over some absurdity when Lord Brentford entered the room. He strongly resembled the thundercloud that hung over the house.

"Well, I know the weather is nasty out, but surely, old fellow, it isn't that dire." Lord Ives winked at Dru, who had the temerity to giggle.

"Not you, too!" Lord Brentford frowned.

"And what is that supposed to mean, pray tell?" Dru shot back. "My imagination has limits, so I do not have the slightest notion what you mean."

"Too many people around who think they know what is in my head." He gave them a curious look.

"La, sir, and is there anything there?" Dru teased.

He glowered at her, but his dark eyes gleamed with suppressed mirth—at least she hoped it was that.

"You two enjoying an early luncheon?" Lord Brentford asked, a casual note in his voice. He now wore a look that seemed oddly suspicious. Surely not of them?

"I could not ask for better company," Lord Ives said with an intriguing smile. His gray gaze sought hers, warming her with his seeming admiration. "Miss Herbert is an excellent listener. That is such a refreshing trait. Do you not agree, Brentford?"

Before Lord Brentford could say a word, Dru responded to Lord Ives with an answering grin. She was not above enjoying a light flirtation. "You are a gallant gentleman, I vow. And I have found your conversation all that is agreeable."

"I think I hear my mother calling you," Lord Brentford said, sounding as though he had been eating sour

pickles. He helped himself to the venison and joined
them.

"Calling? Never! She would send Priddy or one of
the maids." Dru bit into her slice of bread and cheese,
a slow sensuous bite, savoring the rich texture and
delicate flavor. This flour was not some of the adulter-
ated stuff one heard about being sold in London. This
was far better—where one of the advantages of living
in the country, especially not far from a high-quality
mill.

"What shall we do this afternoon? Felicia has the
megrims, or something close to that. She is bored to
death, old chap." Lord Ives surveyed his friend as
though he expected him to magically summon a genie
to entertain her ladyship.

"Dru? Think of something," Lord Brentford
commanded.

"Dru? Aren't you being a bit familiar?" Lord Ives
inquired, his voice almost sounding ominous.

"Snip Snap Snorem," Dru mused. "That is a favorite card game. Or perhaps Diabolo."

"I haven't attempted that yet," Lord Ives said, now
sounding amused. "Can you manage that clever top?
Truly?"

"No," Dru confessed. "But I daresay someone
around here knows how."

"I do," Lord Brentford muttered. He took a bite of
his stew, staring at Dru as though she ought to know
what he was thinking.

"You must give lessons. Tell you what—you teach
Dru and she can teach me." Lord Ives bestowed a
warm, almost intimate smile on Dru that had her puzzled. But if he wanted to trifle with her, he would find
it hard going. She was not a girl to be trifled with. She
could tease. At least, a little bit. Nothing dangerous or
compromising.

"That depends on whether or not I manage to learn
how to balance that little top. It does not look simple
to do. I do not doubt it requires a special aptitude."

"La, what a silly girl you are," Lady Felicia said as

she sailed into the room. She selected a plate, dished up a taste of the venison, added a bit of bread, then slid onto a chair as close to Lord Brentford as possible. She tossed a saucy look at Lord Ives, then edged even closer to Lord Brentford.

"Do you know how to do the Diabolo, Felicia?" Lord Ives inquired. His manner was cool, almost indifferent. So . . . the saucy teasing had no effect on him?

"Naturally. Adrian taught me ages ago. They are not something new, you know."

Dru thought someone needed to take her down a peg or two.

"I shall teach Dru." Lord Brentford spooned a helping of pudding onto his plate and began to eat with every evidence of enjoyment. He behaved as though he had all the time in the world. Well, considering the rain, perhaps he did.

Lydia and Belinda popped around the corner, followed by Gregory Vane and Harry Metcalf.

"Um, something smells delicious. How clever—this is like an indoor picnic." Lydia beamed a smile on Harry, who gallantly offered her a plate, then pointed out the cheese he thought she might like.

Within a few minutes the group was chatting around the table.

"Adrian is going to teach Miss Herbert how to play Diabolo," Lady Felicia said slyly. "Do any of you know how to balance that funny top?"

"Oh, that is the game with a cord that is strung to two sticks and you must throw that double-headed top into the air and catch it again." Belinda gazed earnestly at the others. "My brother does it very well. Sad to say, I do not."

The laugher was general and not the least unkind.

"If we had several of them, we could have a contest to see which couple does the best," Mr. Vane suggested.

"It really isn't difficult to learn," Lord Brentford inserted. He placed his spoon in the empty dish. "Dru, if you are finished, help me sort out the various games in the cupboard. I feel certain we have at least one somewhere, perhaps two.

"Dru? You persist in being so casual, Adrian." Lady Felicia plainly thought she was the only one so entitled.

"I have decided we all may as well use Christian names while here. I know it is proper to be more formal, but it does become tedious."

"Here, here," Mr. Vane declared. "I agree. Belinda has a lovely sound, whereas Miss Oaks is forbidding. You are not at all forbidding, my dear girl."

Dru watched Belinda blush and made a mental note to tell the girl that London beaux had a tendency to flirt and there was nothing to their teasing. She'd not wish the girl to suffer hurt while here. And Gregory Vane was a handsome fellow.

She walked down the hall with Lord Brentford— never mind he suggested they dispense with formality, she could not.

"In here, I believe." Lord Brentford opened a door to a fair-sized room, outfitted with chairs and tables and others things to interest a young boy.

The room proved to be an ideal playroom for young people. While the nursery was on the upper floor where Nanny would reign supreme, this was a place where an older child might play and know there was supervision just around the corner. She watched Lord Brentford open a cupboard that overflowed with toys of all sorts.

"Goodness, you didn't lack for something to amuse you." She fingered wooden puzzles, a set of farm animals beautifully carved and painted, and in a neat box, she found a large collection of carefully packed soldiers.

"When one is alone, there needs to be ample toys for that amusement." He spoke without rancor, merely stating a fact.

"I was blessed to be part of a large family, with four sisters and a brother. Did you miss that?" She paused in her hunting to look up at him.

"I'd like to have more than one child, if that is what you wish to know." He gave her a curious look. "And you?"

"If possible, and if I do marry, I believe I should like several children. It seems more jolly for them, you see."

"And I require an heir, which doesn't always occur at the first try." His tone was dry, and he glanced at Dru with an unholy gleam in his eyes.

Dru knew she blushed. Never had she engaged in such intimate sort of conversation with a gentleman, especially one she liked.

"I think I found them. I could swear that I had two sets somewhere around here."

Grateful that the subject drastically changed, Dru took one set of sticks and the small double-headed top that went with them. He located and pulled out the other and carried it, nudging Dru ahead of him.

They strolled back to the breakfast room, pausing in the doorway to let the others know what had been found.

"We will be in the drawing room. The place is vast enough for two couples to try this." Lord Brentford held up one of the peculiar-looking tops, then nudged Dru to proceed.

She placed her set on the sofa table, then turned to study the man at her side. Why he had determined to teach her this foolish game she didn't know. She suspected it would not be as simple as he said.

"I believe the best way to do this is for me to stand behind you. You can hold the sticks, but I can guide if necessary. There is a certain skill in doing this."

Dru wondered if it was a trick of light that made his expression seem mischievous. She gave him a look that she was certain revealed her suspicions.

"Now, Dru, surely you would not imagine I would attempt anything improper with the door open and others about to join us at any moment?"

She hoped she didn't blush. "Of course not. How silly of me to think you might do something improper

merely because you have done so before." She turned
to face him only to be turned about so that her back
was to him once again.

Then she discovered precisely what his lordship intended to do—all with the utmost respectability, of
course. He literally wrapped his arms about her, drawing her against his lean form with shocking familiarity.

"Sir, I protest . . ." she began.

"Hush!" he said softly into her right ear. "Allow
me this. Now, take the two sticks in your hands."

Dru obeyed. If she leaned her head back, she would
be nestled against his strong shoulder. She didn't. But
she wanted to—very much.

He placed his hands under her forearms. When she
shot a look at him, he grinned. "Just to help you balance, dear girl."

"I believe I told you before that I am not your dear
girl, or dear anything, for that matter," she snapped
with quiet asperity.

"Mind me, now. The idea is to balance and spin
that top, throw it into the air and catch it again."

"Impossible," Dru retorted with a laugh. "It cannot
be done."

"Watch. I can do it. You can as well." He retrieved
the sticks from her, tossed the top into the air, caught
it on the cord, balancing it with a skill she knew at
once had taken some time to achieve.

When he had demonstrated just how to do the
game, he returned the sticks to her hands, then re-
sumed his position behind her. Only this time, Dru
would have sworn he stood just a trifle closer. She
wouldn't say a word. Let him tease all he pleased.
She would not rise to his bait. Let him wrap his arms
about her, enfold her in what amounted to an embrace. If it didn't bother him, she wouldn't let it
bother her. But of course it did. Bother her, that is.
And that is what he probably intended, the devious
rascal.

"It looks impossible," she murmured as she gave

the top a determined look, then made an attempt. It was an ignominious failure.

"No, no. You must do it like this." He wrapped himself even closer around her, guiding her arms to balance the sticks while tossing the top.

"It is no use," she whispered, turning her head until she could catch his eye. "You, sir, are far, far too distracting."

His slow smile should have warned her. It didn't. He captured a kiss before she could think.

"I believe you intended to do that all along," she mused.

"Well, you do tend to make it a mite difficult for a fellow to behave properly."

Voices chattering in the hall and drawing closer sent Lord Brentford to a more respectable distance from Dru.

"Let an expert have a go at it, will you?" Lord Ives inquired with a bright gaze glancing from Dru to Lord Brentford.

He did not wait for a reply, which was just as well as Dru didn't think she could have said a word.

"I do very well at this game," Lady Felicia said, sounding smug and overly confident.

"Please, challenge Lord Ives to a contest. I do not think I am cut out to be an expert at Diabolo," Dru said.

"Well, you can scarcely be an expert at everything, my dear," Lord Brentford murmured scandalously in her ear.

Chapter Twelve

$\mathcal{A}$drian studied the beautiful young woman standing so close to him. Why had he ever thought it necessary to send her away? She had done wonders for his mother in her recovery from the illness she had suffered this past winter. He must have been all about in his head to even consider such a thing as having Drusilla Herbert go home. He was sure his mother would have his head if he sent her away. She had become very attached to the young woman. He studied Dru without seeming to—quite enjoying the sight.

Her cheeks were still slightly flushed from their recent proximity, a proximity that he had found utterly delightful. She was wary of him, and rightly so. She probably thought him mad, given his somewhat outrageous proposal in the little room where she had arranged flowers. Well, perhaps he was. Mad, that is. He was not himself—the coolheaded, aloof peer that Society matrons tried to snare for hopeful daughters. In London, he kept a discreet distance from the young women making their bows to Society.

"Miss Herbert, how did you fare in your first attempt at playing Diabolo?" Gregory Vane strolled up to examine the sticks and top Dru held in her hand.

She glanced at Adrian before replying. What thoughts were racing through her mind? He would have liked to know what was behind the delicate blush that crept over her lovely skin.

"I fear I do not have a good sense of balance. I

could not seem to capture the top on the cord just right. That dratted top just kept falling to the floor." Her frustration rang clear in her voice.

"May I help you?" Vane requested, totally ignoring the narrow-eyed look from Adrian that promised retribution if he encroached on what Adrian considered his.

Apparently she was not averse to a bit of light flirtation with Vane, for she gave him one of her glorious smiles and handed him the sticks. He promptly returned them to her, then stood behind her, precisely as Adrian had done minutes ago. Adrian wondered what Vane hoped to achieve that Adrian had not.

He smoldered while Vane wrapped his arms about Dru, giving her hints on how best to toss the top into the air with a good chance of having it land on the cord.

"Move in anticipation of the top, then keep it balanced," he instructed, showing her how to more or less chase the top so when it fell, it would be where she wanted. "Watch it carefully."

Lady Felicia grabbed the other set of sticks and the top that went with them. Within minutes she had the top soaring into the air, then landing on the cord with the precise balance needed to keep it in place.

"Miss Herbert, this is how it is properly done. What a pity you had such a poor teacher!" She bestowed a dagger-sharp glare at Adrian, and he concealed a smile behind a hastily raised hand.

If her words indicated she had lost interest in Adrian as a husband, he could only be pleased. Had he wooed her in London, he might never have observed her temper. There was something to be said for a house party! Not to mention the competition of another beautiful young woman. Yet he was aware of all that was due Lady Felicia's station. And as a guest in his house, he must of necessity be polite and see she was agreeably entertained. He began to suspect she played a deep game. He hadn't been blind to her behavior with Ives.

Shifting his gaze back to where Dru took instructions from Vane, Adrian firmed his lips lest he say something best left unsaid. He did not wish to tip his hand before the others. It would be nice to woo his Drusilla in privacy rather than the bright inspection of the house party.

"I think I understand now, sir. How clever you are." Dru lightly tossed the top in the air, then managed to catch it on the cord, achieving a balance that kept it in place. She crowed with delight as again and again the top landed on the cord.

Lydia begged to try the game while Belinda laughingly refused, pointing out that her brothers had given up trying to teach her the intricacies of Diabolo.

"It is truly beyond me. I am all admiration for Lady Felicia's skill." Belinda smiled shyly. "It is easy to see how it is called the devil on two sticks. I do not think I have enough patience. I certainly cannot balance!"

Lady Felicia preened, then somehow missed the top when it next came down. She rather ungraciously handed the sticks to Lydia. "Well, it is not difficult. But not everyone has the necessary deftness. Keep your eyes on the top. Move the sticks so the cord will be where it is needed in order to catch the top when it comes down."

Dru watched, then handed her sticks to Belinda. "I think you should try again. Brothers are perhaps the worst teachers—they have so little patience." She spoke with the authority of one whose brother had tried her patience more than once.

Gregory Vane apparently was not averse to helping the pretty Belinda. He shifted his attentions to her, wrapping his arms about the blushing girl with a teasing smile.

"Your teacher has transferred his care to Miss Oaks. You do not mind?" Adrian asked Dru with a casualness he did not feel.

"Not in the least. Why should I? He is a charming gentleman and quite able to manage his affairs as he sees fit."

"Are you so certain of his admiration?" Adrian said

in what amounted to a snarl. He berated himself for allowing his pique to show.

"Not in the least. If you'll excuse me, I would see how your mother does. Recall I am not here as a guest and able to please myself. My purpose here is to comfort your mother, see that she does not become overly tired, and assist in entertaining her. She has vastly improved with the company to amuse her."

"Especially Lord Osman," Adrian muttered.

"Indeed, and you ought to thank your stars that he is so attentive to her every wish. What woman would not enjoy the attentions of such a gentleman." Dru regarded him as though he was an alien species of plant.

"But she is my mother," he grumbled, quite unable to comprehend why the affair bothered him so.

Dru gave him a pitying look, then swept from the room, leaving Gregory Vane to amuse the pretty Belinda while Harry Metcalf enthralled Lydia with his civility. Dru observed that Lady Felicia had turned her back on Lord Brentford and was flirting with Lord Ives. Well, perhaps a bit of competition would aid her cause to ensnare Adrian, Lord Brentford. Somehow Dru doubted it. He did not strike her as a fish ready to be reeled in, even by an expert "fisher" like her ladyship.

She found Lady Brentford, Lord Osman and the others in the little parlor. On the walls of this room hung magnificent tapestries depicting the various muses in classical garb. Above the hearth, where a small fire burned, was a fine mantel on which was carved exquisitely detailed musical instruments. The Turkey rug was of muted colors that harmonized beautifully with the tapestries. It was one of Dru's favorite rooms in the house.

Lady Brentford and Lord Osman with Mrs. Twywhitt and Miss Knight played whist, while Sir Bertram and Lord Somers were deep in a game of piquet. Candles augmented the light from the tall windows, admittedly poor on a rainy day.

"Is there something I might do for you? Perhaps you would enjoy wine and biscuits? Or would you prefer a light collation be set up for you?"

Her ladyship exchanged a look with Lord Osman. "Why not both? I think we deserve a respite from our efforts to win a fortune from each other."

"I shall see to it at once." Pleased there was something she might do for Lady Brentford, Dru hurried along to the kitchen, where she made her request known to Cook and Mrs. Simpson.

"Bless you, dear girl. I wondered if they might be wishing for some victuals about now." Mrs. Simpson began setting out trays upon which Cook proceeded to arrange dishes of cold food. They were attractively prepared and presented a colorful sight to tempt the most jaded palate.

Two pigeon pies and a galentine of chicken was supplemented by fresh breads, cold sliced ham, and a variety of cheeses. Her ladyship's favorite macaroons had pride of place on the larger tray.

"Will Priddy see to a table?"

"Don't worry your pretty head. Now that I know it is wanted, we can set about it at once."

She was thankful to be away from the other younger people for a time. She hadn't known what to think when Lord Brentford had wrapped his arms about her in such an intimate manner. Odd, it had not bothered her a bit when Gregory Vane copied him. It was Lord Brentford, Adrian, who had set her pulse racing, sent her feelings topsy-turvy. She scarce knew if she was on her head or feet!

It hadn't helped that he had teased her so. What evil spirit had prompted *that,* she couldn't imagine. But she thought it rather impertinent of him. Surely he must know that she was constrained from replying as she wished, since his mother employed her!

Pausing by a window that looked out to the rear gardens and the aspect beyond, she reflected that it would not be long before Lady Brentford decided she did not need Dru any longer. It would not be easy to leave this beautiful home—and home it was. While it had everything a palace might, it also was a lived-in place, comfortable and pleasant. There was not the formality and coldness Dru associated with a palace—not that she had ever been in such a place. It was an image from what her younger sister Tabitha had read aloud about the great homes as described in one of Father's magazines.

Mrs. Simpson caught up with her at that point. "I've set out a cold collation in the breakfast room, Miss Herbert. I thought you might be willing to suggest the young people enjoy a bite to eat. There is something about a rainy day that makes a body hungry."

"I will be happy to do that for you," Dru replied, reluctantly giving up her solitude for service she felt expected of her.

Lord Brentford joined Dru when she entered the drawing room.

"You look as though you have been given a commission."

Dru gave him a speculative look. "Mrs. Simpson has set out a cold collation in the breakfast room for our consumption. She asked if I would suggest they"— Dru nodded to the others in the room—"might enjoy a light meal of sorts."

Dru watched Lord Brentford engagingly summon the others to partake of a nuncheon to sustain them for the afternoon. She decided it would be difficult to think up entertainment for days on end, especially when the weather was so unkind as to rain.

"You look wonderful," he commented, breaking into her thoughts.

"I believe I will take a walk after we eat. It is tedious to remain in the house all the day."

"You could catch cold. It *is* raining."

"I am neither sugar nor salt—a bit of rain will not harm me." She thought his expression at her words amusing.

"But on the other hand, you might melt."

"I melt? Never." Dru turned away from her nemesis to coax Lydia and Belinda to join her in the breakfast room. Where they went the men followed, save for Lady Felicia and Lord Ives, who were deep in conversation. At least, he was. She was laughing and teasing and carrying on in a silly, affected manner Dru thought excessively stupid.

There was little doubt from the frequent glances in the direction of Lord Brentford that Lady Felicia attempted to make him jealous. Lord Ives seemed to censure her.

Dru was near the doorway when she heard sounds of arguing. Lady Felicia was in a rare tantrum. What was curious was that Lord Ives answered her back in no-nonsense terms. Dru couldn't make out the words and didn't intend to try. It was nothing to her if those two had a disagreement.

Angry steps were heard. Dru suspected Lady Felicia would storm up to her room in a fit of rage.

And then a bloodcurdling scream tore the air.

Dru dashed to the stairs. At the bottom of the steps, Lady Felicia was crumpled in a heap, unconscious, a purplish lump rising on her forehead.

"Fetch me a flannel and cold water," Dru ordered one of the maids who stood gawking. Dru gingerly straightened Lady Felicia's limbs, taking careful note that nothing appeared to be broken.

From behind her Lord Ives murmured, sounding most remorseful, "We argued. I never intended this to happen."

Dru wanted to ask what he *had* intended, but the maid hurried to her with a basin of cold water and a face flannel, and the thought slipped from her mind. Quickly, Dru dipped the flannel in the water, wrung it out, and then applied it to that nasty lump on her ladyship's forehead. A glance behind Dru revealed that not only Lord Brentford, but also everyone else attending the house party, had assembled to stare at the unfortunate victim of the stairs.

"How badly is she hurt?" Lady Brentford inquired anxiously.

"I do not know. Is there a doctor nearby?" Dru wondered aloud.

"The nearest one is several miles away. I'll fetch him." Lord Brentford stepped forward to gaze down at the pink-and-white beauty sprawled on the steps.

Dru barely caught his next words, and she doubted if anyone else heard them at all.

"It is the least I can do—I am her host." He turned away to head to the rear of the house.

Dru wanted to tell him that the beauty's temper probably had more to do with her fall than anything else.

Once Dru determined that the main injury to Lady Felicia had been the knock on her forehead, she enlisted the help of two stalwart footmen to carry the beauty to her bedroom. Dru followed immediately behind them. As she walked up the stairs, she could hear the others drifting back to the breakfast room and the small parlor to most likely discuss the dramatic turn of events.

In the appropriately pink-and-white bedroom, so fitting for the pink-and-white beauty, Dru turned down the covers of the large bed, motioning the footmen to place the woman there.

Her ladyship's abigail bustled in upon hearing the soft noises in a room that ought to have been silent. To her credit she didn't scream. She gave Dru a horrified stare, then approached the bed with cautious steps.

"What did she do this time?"

"I wasn't there, but I surmise she had an argument with someone, and when she turned to go up the staircase she fell, hitting her forehead against something—perhaps the banister? I am keeping a cold cloth on this rather nasty lump."

The little maid had followed with the basin of cold water, placing it on a bedside table at Dru's nod.

"Best undress my lady before she comes to," the abigail suggested with brisk capability.

Dru agreed. Between the two of them, they eased off the finery Lady Felicia wore.

Never before had Dru seen such a profusion of lace on a petticoat or stays so exquisitely crafted. The nightdress the abigail brought forth to put on her ladyship was without a doubt made of the finest cambric ever woven. Rows of tucks and lace enhanced the delicacy of the gown.

Studying the face now reposing on the fine linen-covered pillow, Dru could appreciate her beauty. No lines of discontent marred her expression. Indeed, that face was far too still for Dru's liking.

"I best find her a vinaigrette. I do not like her being out of the world like this," the abigail muttered before hunting through a drawer in the dresser by the window.

Several passes under Lady Felicia's nose resulted in a fretful twist of her head. But her eyelids remained shut, and she gave no other sign of rousing.

Dru went to wring out the cloth. She paused to stare out of the window at the rain-lashed scene beyond. Poor Lord Brentford was riding out in this weather. The maid reported in awed tones that the groom told her the master had dashed into the stables, saddled up his horse, and before anyone could argue him out of it, was gone.

And now he was tearing through the horrible rain to fetch a doctor. She hoped he wore not only his thick greatcoat but a waterproof cape as well. Otherwise she could have two patients on her hands. She had no illusion that anyone else would tend an invalid.

She turned from the window to survey the still figure on the bed. It was odd. True, the stairs could be dangerous if a body didn't pay attention. But each step was covered with a sensible piece of carpet. There had been no reason for Lady Felicia to trip—unless . . . Dru castigated herself for thinking ill of Lady Felicia when she was unconscious and flat on her back. One thing in favor of her being unconscious, the lady couldn't sting anyone with her sharp tongue.

"How does she do?" Lady Brentford inquired, coming into the room to stand at the foot of the bed. She surveyed the patient with a worried frown.

Dru shook her head. "She moved her head a bit when her abigail waved the vinaigrette under her nose. Otherwise she has been as you see her now." Dru glanced at the mantel clock, noting how slowly the time passed. It could be hours before the doctor would arrive.

"It is a puzzlement to me how she slipped and fell. All of the carpet pieces are firmly tacked down. Lord Osman checked them just to be certain."

Dru debated as to whether she ought to say anything, then cautiously said, "I believe she had been arguing. She does have a bit of a temper. Perhaps she spun around to go to her room and simply tripped?"

"I have indeed noticed she has a temper. One does not tend to observe that when in Society. A temper is always kept tightly under control. It would never do for the dragons of Society to see a young lady—no matter her rank—indulging in a tantrum."

"I imagine that would be ruinous," Dru agreed. At least that was one thing the rectory girls were not guilty of doing. None had nasty tempers. Father would have scolded them out of it in no time.

"Do you wish a maid to take over for you? I am sure you do not realize how long you have been up here." Lady Brentford stepped around to the side of the bed to study the unconscious woman who, in spite of the dark bruise on her forehead, still looked ravishing in her fragile nightdress, her dark curls clinging to her head in a beguiling manner.

Dru straightened her back, tired from bending over the bed. "I am quite fine, thank you. Since I was the one who came up with her, I should like to remain here—at least for the time being."

Brave words. The abigail had disappeared, and the room was far too silent.

The marchioness left the room, and all Dru could hear was the rain pelting the window and the ticking

of the clock. Even the fire made little sound. The
hands of the clock moved with exasperating lethargy,
crawling around the numbers with a pace a snail
could beat.

She persisted at her chosen task, methodically
wringing out the cloth when she refreshed it in the
cool water. While she performed this task she thought
about his lordship, wondering if he had reached the
doctor, when they would be here. Day had changed
to night.

It seemed as though she had stood by the bed forever when the door opened with an impatient thrust
and two men entered. One, she knew.

"Lord Brentford!"

"This is Doctor Jenkins. I caught him just as he was
returning from seeing a patient."

The abigail entered the room silently to stand by
Drusilla. Dru turned to her. "Perhaps you will stay
with the doctor while he examines our patient?" Dru
said nothing about the total absence of the abigail
from her mistress's bedside until now.

"Indeed, miss. You need some rest."

Dru left Lady Felicia in capable hands, walking
along the hall until she reached her room.

"Have you been with her all this time?" Adrian
asked, having joined her in leaving the room.

Weary to the point where she thought she might
fall asleep on her feet, Dru simply nodded.

"Best sleep for a bit."

Dru thought she might easily sleep around the
clock. She didn't object when he opened her door for
her, nudging her inside.

She paused, giving him an owlish look. "And you,
my lord, will you change from your damp clothing and
have a hot drink?"

"Do not worry about me. I am never ill."

Dru gave him a skeptical look but shut the door in
his face before flopping on her bed to bury her head
on her pillow. She would have slept more soundly had

she not heard a tremendous sneeze in the hallway as she closed her eyes.

Adrian sneezed again and cursed the rain, Lady Felicia, and the cold he feared he had caught as a result of his impetuous dash. The ride had been long, nasty, and extremely wet. His return in the damp chill of the doctor's carriage was little better.

"Hot mulled cider is what you need, my lord," Colyer intoned in his *I told you so* voice. The valet set about assisting Adrian from his sopping garments into dry things. He then urged him to sit before a blazing fire in his room. The valet tut-tutted under his breath as he considered the ruined garments. "These might be salvaged, but Weston would weep to see that coat."

"I can order another." Adrian gave a frightening sneeze, before subsiding against the comfort of a high-backed wing chair.

Colyer handed him an enormous white handkerchief before going out the door. "I shall return with your hot drink."

The implication to Adrian was to remain where he was, and no nonsense about it, either. He made a wry face, staring into the fire while he considered the consequences of this day.

A rap on his door disturbed his peace. Ives poked his face around it. When he observed Adrian stuffed onto his chair, a robe wrapped about him and a huge scrap of white cambric in hand, he entered the room. "Well? Have you learned anything regarding Lady Felicia?"

"Too soon to tell."

"Your dragon wouldn't let anyone near her while you were gone." Ives sauntered to the fireplace, hands in his pockets and a casual curiosity on his face.

"Most proper." Adrian sneezed, a satisfying sound at the mention of the woman who caused him such grief.

"You should have taken a carriage." This observation was met with another sneeze.

"I agree," Adrian replied with far more civility than he felt.

"You think Lady Felicia will recover without permanent damage?" This was uttered with a rush of words, quite as though Ives hated to express his fears. "I worry about her remaining unconscious for so long."

"We should be so fortunate," Adrian muttered. When Ives pinned him with a fierce glare, Adrian said more loudly, "We should hope for the fortunate. Did Dru say anything at all?"

"Not a word—other than to scold us for daring to make a sound."

"Well, one does not stampede through the bedroom of the wounded or ill. I doubt they will allow me back into the room. If you like, go find out what the doctor has to say." He waved his friend off.

The room was silent when Ives left. The gentle crackle of the fire, the rain still lashing at the window, and muted sounds from below were all that could be heard.

The door opened again to admit Colyer with the hot mulled cider. Adrian had to admit the drink felt good on his throat. It also made him feel sleepy, and he wondered what the valet had added to the drink.

Ives stepped into the room just at that moment. He approved the hot drink in hand with a nod.

"Well? What did you learn?" Adrian was beginning to feel a bit muzzy. Probably due to a drop of laudanum in the drink. He'd bet on it.

Ives shrugged, stalking across the room to stand before the fireplace once again. "He has bled her. Says she is resting comfortably. No reason why she shouldn't revive." Ives studied the toe of his highly polished black boot. "But she hasn't. At least to this point."

"Cheer up, my friend. A temper like hers isn't about to give up easily. She will recover to plague us all before you know it."

"I don't believe you care a jot for her." Ives stared

at Adrian with cold eyes. Well, Adrian couldn't blame him in one way. It would seem his friend gave more than a jot for the vixen.

"I suppose I best ask her to marry me," Adrian said, feeling as though he was pounding nails in his coffin. If her head was seriously injured, it would be the least he could do, or so his garbled brain was insisting. She fell in his home. His mother wanted the marriage. He truly was not thinking very clearly, but he suspected his reasoning was sound. Wasn't it?

Ives gave him a disgusted look. He strode from the room, the sharp clicks of his boots sending his disapproval of Adrian's scheme.

Well, Adrian decided as he began to sink into a muzzy-headed slumber, he hadn't proposed as yet. Perhaps there would be a miracle, and his proposal wouldn't be required.

And wouldn't *that* be the day!

Chapter Thirteen

Adrian was certain he was on fire. He couldn't recall being so hot in his life. He stirred, wishing he had a drink. His throat felt dryer than last week's toast. He tried to ask for water. All he heard was a squawking mumble. Did that croak belong to him?

His eyelids were too heavy to open. It was almost too much trouble to breathe. He inhaled the scent of lavender, thinking it brought healing with it—and memories of a gentle touch, a calm voice.

Blessedly cool hands raised his head. A glass touched his lips. It was wet and cold. Ah, water! He sipped as much as he could, feeling relief as the cooling liquid slipped down his throat. "Um." He couldn't talk, but he managed an appreciative sound.

A cool, damp cloth chilled his forehead. Oh, it felt so good. His throat eased by whatever was in that water and his body feeling just a little cooler, he sank back into welcome sleep.

"He is so terribly ill. What a foolish thing—to go haring off in the rain to fetch the doctor." Lady Brentford paused by her son's bedside, shaking her head in sorrow. "He has been like this for too long. Do you think that the fever will break soon?"

Dru glanced to the marchioness. "We can but hope, madam. He is a gallant gentleman to go for needed help. It is a shame he was so ill rewarded for his effort. You had best go to bed now, or you may take ill as

well. It would not do for you to have a relapse. I will
sit up for a while before turning your son's care over
to Colyer for the rest of the night. He won't be left
alone for a moment."

"I know I can trust you, dear girl."

"How does Lady Felicia do?" Dru asked out of
politeness. She didn't really care, for that haughty
beauty was in part responsible for the seriously ill
gentleman in Dru's temporary charge.

"Greatly improved. She is fussing over the lump on
her forehead, demanding her abigail do something
with her hair to cover the discoloration." Lady Brentford sounded contemptuous of such vanity. "I cannot
believe I thought she would make him a good wife.
A marriage between them would be a disaster!" On
that note she departed after another anxious perusal
of her son.

The room was utterly silent once her ladyship had
gone, save for the crackle of the fire and Lord Brentford's labored breathing. With a sinking heart Dru
studied the man she was coming to love. She suspected
she knew what was on his mind, behind his restlessness. He had called for Felicia in his delirium. He
might have jokingly asked Dru to marry him; it was
Felicia he intended to be his bride. Dru had to agree
with Lady Brentford, that marriage would be a
catastrophe.

What man could tolerate Lady Felicia's behavior for
long without acquiring a disgust of her? What she
needed was someone to give her the discipline that
she had not received the first time she put on one of
her histrionic displays. When Dru's eldest sister had
tried that approach, she had been given such a swat
that she had never tried it again. Her younger sisters
had learned from that example. However, it might be
too late for Felicia. And, anyway, Dru doubted that
Lord Brentford was the sort to inflict such a punish-
ment on a wife—even though she needed it.

She lifted the cloth, dropped it into the bowl of
lavender-scented water, rung it out, then replaced it

on his forehead. He was so terribly hot, the cloth dried out before she knew it.

She had little sympathy for Lady Felicia. She had suffered as a result of her own behavior. Poor Lord Brentford now ailed because he had dashed to her aid. It didn't explain why he thought he ought to marry her. Men were so stupid at times. It was taking noble conduct too far.

If only he had taken a carriage to summon the doctor. True, he had returned to the Court in the medic's carriage, but he was already soaked to the skin, and sitting in the cold vehicle had been little better than being in the rain.

The door opened and Lord Ives poked his head around. Seeing Dru, he entered to stand at her side. "How does he do? I must say, he looks feverish."

She shook her head. "Not well, I fear."

"Took a nasty soaking ride. What an idiot."

"You say such words, yet I think you are very fond of him." Dru dunked the cloth again. It dried so fearfully fast.

"Indeed, he is the best of friends. I'd not wish to lose him for such a reason."

Dru took a deep breath. "He will survive. He has a toughness of spirit that will pull him through. I feel it." She studied the man beneath the covers. He certainly did not look himself. "It is one time I wish he had done nothing."

Lord Ives frowned. "What?"

"I once, in a fit of righteousness, informed him that the trouble with doing nothing was that you never knew when you were done. Now I wish the words unsaid. He did too much."

"I imagine that happens to all of us at one time or another." He edged toward the door. "I'll attempt to keep his guests occupied. And I will be back to look in on him later. It is kind of you to take a turn at nursing him. I doubt there are many in the house who would do so."

"Some people are utterly worthless in a sickroom.

It takes patience." And a little love didn't hurt, either, she decided privately.

The room returned to the previous quiet once Lord Ives had gone. Dru continued with her routine of soaking the cloth in the tepid water, wringing it well, then replacing it on the forehead.

Mrs. Simpson slipped into the room, bearing the results of Dru's request. It was a poultice using ground mustard seed. Her father insisted it was the only way to cure a nasty cold.

The housekeeper handed the poultice to Dru, then helped roll the covers back to reveal Lord Brentford's broad chest. Dru heroically ignored the intriguing sight of dark brown curls on a finely muscled chest to gently drape the poultice where it would be beneficial. Within moments, the covers were back in place, up to his chin.

"He probably will not like this, but I feel it necessary to do everything I can think might help."

"Well, it's a blessing you are willing to take on his nursing. As though you hadn't enough with tending her ladyship what has a little bump on her head. Now you nurse his lordship. Of the two, he is by far the worse off." She paused on her way to the door to study the inert figure in the bed.

"But he will be better soon. We must think confidently. He will be better, given time."

Papa had one said that the ill could hear more than one thought. Dru resolved to speak positively in the unlikely event Lord Brentford could hear her. If he heard someone say he was likely to die, he might just do so.

Mrs. Simpson offered to bring up tea and toast for Dru, then quietly slipped from the room.

Dru listened to the crackling fire, the rain again beating against the windowpane . . . and his lordship's labored breathing. That, most of all, caught her ear.

A light tap on the door heralded the entrance of Lady Felicia with her abigail's assistance.

Dru held a finger to her lips, hoping that penetrating voice might be kept to a whisper.

"How is he?" Felicia studied the still form in the bed before turning to Dru. "You ought not be here. You are not even married, merely a spinster. You could find your reputation in shreds!"

"Even a spinster has her uses. It is Lady Brentford's express wish that I am here to take my turn at nursing—as I did with you, my lady." Dru offered a level stare at the beauty before returning her attention to the very ill gentleman in the bed.

That remark appeared to disconcert Lady Felicia a moment. "I must return to my bed. I will speak to you later. Let me know as soon as Adrian is conscious."

Dru watched the Beauty leave and wondered if it was necessary for her to lean quite so much on her abigail. Poor woman, Dru did not envy her in the least. No even the prospect of cast-off garments (with the hope that one would look well in pink and white) could make service to Felicia tolerable.

As to informing Lady Felicia about his lordship's consciousness, she would think about it. She hadn't missed his signs of agitation when Lady Felicia had been here.

When it came time for Colyer to take over, Dru left the room with reluctance. There was absolutely no sign of improvement.

She paused at Lady Felicia's room, convinced that *that* young woman needed no further care. All she wanted now was a willing slave to pander to her wants. Dru peeked around the door, first exchanging a look of sympathy with the abigail who opened the door to her.

"Why have you not summoned me to speak with Adrian?" Felicia demanded, albeit in a low voice.

"He remains unconscious. And how are you feeling?" Dru refused to say another word about Lord Brentford's condition; she truly had nothing to report.

"Well enough, save for this stupid bruise." Felicia poked at her hair, arranging and rearranging it over her forehead.

Dru might privately think it was no more than she

deserved, but she would never say so. "Such a pity things like this happen. How did you fall?"

"I suppose I lost my balance." Her gaze evaded Dru's.

"I trust you will feel better come morning." Dru backed from the room, thankful when the abigail closed the door against the complaining voice.

Colyer had listened to Dru's suggestions with every indication of respect. Still, Dru planned to waken in the night so as to check on his lordship. Colyer might be all well and good; he had not nursed as many patients at Dru.

Without a doctor in their village back home and the apothecary much in demand, it often fell to the lot of the rectory ladies to visit the sick and help the infirm.

Dru couldn't count the number of seriously ill she had nursed, most of them back to health. She knew grief for those she had lost, who were beyond her limited expertise. She had no intention of losing Lord Brentford.

Mentally telling herself that she needed to wake in three hours, she slipped from her gown and into her night wear, sadly lacking the fine-quality cambric or lace and tucks found on what Lady Felicia possessed.

There was no improvement during the night, nor the day that followed. Dru resolved to try something else to bring down his fever. The mustard plaster had not helped. She had tried cooling baths in the past, but mostly on children and infants. She didn't think it respectable for a spinster to do one for a gentleman patient.

She changed her mind that evening when it seemed to her that his fever had risen. It required drastic measures! Her maidenly modesty would be ignored. This was not the moment to be timorous.

The maid brought a fresh bowl of water, peeping at Dru with curious eyes. Once alone with her patient, Dru propped a chair against the door, not wishing any unexpected visitors, and set to work. First she measured in some lavender oil. Then she placed the cloth to soak.

With trembling hands she rolled back the covers so that only one side of his chest was exposed. Heart pounding, she began bathing him, carefully wringing the cloth each time to prevent soaking the bed. It was unlike anything she had done in the past. The firmly muscled body was intriguing, a part of her mind noted even as her hand brushed against his heated body, arranging the sheets for decency. She checked his skin to see if the bath helped to cool him, unable to admit she wanted to know the feel of him, touch the dark hair on his chest. His muscled torso was a far cry from that of a child.

What would it be like to be his wife, to know this man in the biblical sense? She was unlikely to find out. But she envied that woman, whoever she would be.

He would never know what she had done for him. She was not about to tell him, wishing to spare her own blushes as much as possible.

She washed his strong arms and hands, marveling at the beautiful muscles—if one called muscles beautiful. Unwrapping strong legs—one at a time—was enough to send her heart into palpitations. She tried not to think, not to be so aware of his body, but it wasn't easy.

Still, she persisted, rotating from one part of him to another, until she thought she knew *almost* every inch of him. After some time, when she was about ready to drop with fatigue, he stirred.

With proper haste, she dropped the cloth into the basin, rolled the bedcovers back over his body, then spoke.

"Lord Brentford? Can you hear me?"

"Water. I'm so thirsty."

Dru smiled, a thrill of excitement racing through her. Her anxious prayers had been answered. Unless she was much mistaken, his fever was down. Perhaps not much, but she believed it had broken. Whether

her drastic attack on him had served to help, she
didn't know. But she would do it again if needed! And
bother the question of propriety!

Offering him a drink of cool water required that
she raise his head. She propped him against her, then
let him drink. He sipped, then lolled against her
shoulder.

Before she could return him to his pillow, he looked
up into her face, his dark eyes studying her with curiosity. "Dru? What . . . you doin' here?"

"Keeping an eye on you." She smiled at his
expression.

"Shouldn't be here. Not proper." He frowned as
though it was a great effort to think, let alone talk.

"Your mother requested my assistance. Rest assured I shall take the very best care of you. Now, back
to sleep with you. You will feel better come morning."
She didn't know this, of course, but she suspected his
naturally strong constitution would help him to recover rapidly.

When Colyer came to relieve her, he commented
on how much better Lord Brentford's color was.

Dru fell into her bed exhausted, but satisfied she
had done her best. Now it was up to Lord Brentford.

Adrian shifted, untangling his legs from the sheets.
Egad, he felt as weak as a kitten. A movement off to
one side caught his eye. His valet quietly folded
clothing.

"Colyer?" The man nearly jumped out of his skin
at Adrian's words. Surely he didn't sound that bad?
"How long have I been in this bed?"

"Several days, my lord. You have had us that worried. Took a terrible cold, you did." The valet hurried
to the bedside to offer a soothing drink of barley
water, which his master swallowed with ill grace.

"Who was here—besides you?" Adrian recalled a
face, but it was so unlikely. He wanted to know for
certain.

"Your lady mother visited. And, of course, Miss Herbert tended you during the day. I stayed with you at night."

Adrian absorbed this information in silence. So Dru *had* been here. He hadn't imagined her voice.

"Why Miss Herbert?"

"She is skilled at nursing the sick. Seems she does it often at home." Colyer smoothed the coverlet, then took the pillow from behind Adrian to fluff it nicely before replacing it. "That was one reason your mother sent for her in the first place. Mrs. Herbert had mentioned the nursing that her daughter had done in the neighborhood. They have no doctor, and the apothecary is often not available."

"I see."

"I doubt it, sir. The young lady was at your bedside from morning to dark. At times she would be up in the night to check on you. If you are on the road to recovery, it is likely due to her effort, no one else." The valet nodded, then returned to his task of folding clothing.

Adrian subsided onto his pillow, wondering how in the world he could get out of the coil in which he now found himself! His mother expected him to marry Felicia—why else invite her to stay? He must ask her to marry him. She surely expected it. A true gentleman did not raise expectations in a lady.

His heart wouldn't be in such a future. He wanted only to be with Drusilla Herbert for the rest of his life, however long that might be. How he hated being noble and doing what was proper.

A rap on the door heralded the entrance of Lord Ives. "Well, I must say it is good to see you looking better. You have given us a bit of concern." Ives walked over to stand close to the bed, his gaze assessing.

"I feel like overcooked asparagus and twice as limp." Adrian studied his friend, wondering what was bothering him. Something appeared to be, that was certain.

"Miss Herbert likely saved your life, you know."

Adrian glanced to where Colyer remained on the far side of the room, then back to his friend. "I am told she spent her days at my bedside. I feel like someone poured a bottle of lavender oil over me."

"She is of the opinion that it has healing powers."

"Perhaps." He paused a few moments. "Have you, ah, seen Lady Felicia?" Adrian inquired with caution.

"Oh, yes. She is fluttering about the house like a wounded butterfly. She wants taming."

"I fancy you have the right of it, but how to handle the chit? Chastening her is not to *my* liking."

Ives turned away to stroll over to the fireplace, where he stood staring into the flames for a time. "The weather is improving. We have suffered a spell of nasty rain."

"I shall be up by tomorrow. We must think of something to entertain those here." Adrian eased himself up against the pillows, wondering if his bones had turned to jelly when he wasn't looking.

Ives turned again and shook his had. "I doubt you will feel like doing much."

"Mother's birthday. Perhaps a betrothal party?"

"Whose?"

"I imagine I must ask Lady Felicia to marry me. It seems Mother thinks it would be acceptable."

"You show more enthusiasm for buying a horse than picking a wife." Ives frowned, refusing to meet Adrian's eyes.

"And so I do." Adrian did not wish to get into a discussion of his forced choice.

"What about Miss Herbert?" Ives inquired.

"What about Miss Herbert?" Adrian shot back.

"Felicia was just remarking how insupportable it has been that she was not permitted to see you more than once whereas Dru Herbert was here all day, every day."

Cynically, Adrian wondered if Lady Felicia had tried to see him more than that. "You believe Lady Felicia will tattle once she is in Town?"

"Felicia is not so dreadful," Ives countered. "How can you think ill of the woman you contemplate marrying?" The expression in Ives's eyes gave Adrian pause. What was going on here? He'd swear it was a touch of jealousy.

"I will do what is right—by all concerned. I am well aware of what is due my title and name, not to mention my mother's expectations."

Ives gave him a troubled look before leaving the room.

Dru labored at pretending normalcy, while Lydia and Belinda, dear girls that they were, entertained Gregory Vane and Harry Metcalf. Why those two stayed on was more than Dru could understand. Harry scoffed at the touch of cold that kept Brentford from joining them.

Gregory Vane, perhaps a trifle more perceptive, commented on how little he had seen of Miss Herbert. "You have been like a pretty shadow around here, wafting here and drifting there. Bringing soothing drinks to the sickroom, were you?"

"You might say that." Dru thought of the hours spent cooling Lord Brentford's brow, the risky effort to cool his entire body. If anyone ever learned precisely what she had done, she would be ostracized forever!

"She was like a dragon," Lady Felicia complained. "I wished to see dear Lord Brentford, and she guarded his bed as though I might do him harm."

Dru turned aside, unwilling to look at the pretty face that spoke such a lie.

Gregory Vane took Dru's hand, walking with her to look out over the gardens from the rear windows. "Why do I have the feeling that Lady Felicia is not telling the entire story?"

Dru smiled at him, thankful she had one friend in this assortment of people. "Perhaps her memory is at fault?"

"You are gracious as well as kind."

Binky dashed into the room looking as though the little beast hunted for trouble. He spotted Dru and made for her at once. Before she could react, he had attacked her ankle.

"Next time I have the chance," she said in a low, threatening voice, "I shall make certain that you are free to roam as you please." She swatted the dog away, but not before he had chewed a hole in one of her best stockings. "Drat that dog," she murmured. "I rue the day I went chasing after it, thinking to restore a pet to a worried owner."

"Neither seem to be happy about it, do they?" he observed.

She grinned, thinking she could replace her stocking, but the friendship of this sympathetic gentleman was something she'd not wish to lose.

He leaned against the window surround, chatting about the flowers and the beauties of the area.

He straightened as someone entered the room. Dru turned away from the window as well.

"Lord Brentford!"

Adrian entered the room with less than his usual élan. The first thing he noticed was Dru having an intimate chat with Gregory Vane far across the room, away from all the others. And what might they have to say to one another?

Lady Felicia flounced up to his side, giving him a languishing look. "At last you join us. It has been dreadfully tedious with you holed up in your room. I vow, I had begun to wonder if Miss Herbert was keeping you captive up there." She gave Dru a sly glance before turning her attention to Adrian.

"She said you came to see me. Once."

"As to that, I was terribly weak. My brow, you know." Lady Felicia artfully brushed her hair back to reveal the remains of her swelling, now a magnificent yellow-and-purple blend of color.

"I see." And he did, in a way. He had been unconscious, unable to appreciate her heroic attempt. She far preferred an audience.

Miss Knight bustled into the room at that point, hunting around the room. "Has anyone seen my Binky?"

"He attacked Miss Herbert not long ago. Came dashing into the room and headed straight for her ankle." Gregory Vane made as though to lift up Dru's skirt, and she had to bat his hand away, chuckling at his words.

Miss Knight looked deeply offended. "Binky would never do harm to anyone."

"It is of no consequence, Miss Knight. Perhaps he thought my ankle bone would be tasty?" Dru teased.

Miss Knight was even more offended at this attempt to jest at Binky's expense. She sniffed, peering under several chairs before going off in the direction the dog had gone.

Adrian sought a chair, thinking it better to sit than try to stand. He was still weak and under no illusion that he could remain up for very long. Felicia trailed along behind him. He, in turn, watched as Dru Herbert flirted with Gregory Vane. There was no other word for it. The woman flirted, fluttering her long lashes, laughing in that charmingly husky way she had at some pleasantry Vane said for her ears alone.

"What is the problem, Adrian?' Lady Felicia inquired, frowning at the sight of Miss Herbert and Gregory Vane in happy dalliance. "You do not approve of a connection between those two?"

"No." Adrian knew he sounded too forceful in his denial. By Jove, he did not want Dru Herbert to take up with that fribble Gregory Vane. He doubted if Vane was ready to settle down as yet. He would flirt with Dru, break her heart, and leave her as he went on to some other, wealthier woman—someone with standing in Society as well as a fine dowry.

He happened to look up at Felicia at that moment and caught her studying Dru through narrowed eyes. As soon as she realized Adrian was watching her, she smiled, a halfhearted attempt.

He was tired, worn from the miserable effort to spend a little time with his guests. He took a deep breath and shut his eyes for a moment.

"Here, I think you could use this." He drank the glass of sherry someone handed him. He knew who it was without looking or considering the voice. Dru Herbert was the only one in the room who would be aware of how weak he was, that he needed a bit of restoring.

"Perhaps I shall go up to my room for a time?" He pushed himself up from the chair, praying he wouldn't sway or worse yet, collapse. He had been a fool to come down.

"Why not relax on the sofa?" Dru suggested dryly. "You could have us all at your beck and call. Even Binky might come to entertain you."

"Heaven forbid," Adrian muttered. He allowed Lady Felicia to assist him to the sofa. Dru offered a large shawl to Lady Felicia, who arranged it over Adrian with a show of concern. Why did he think it was a show and nothing genuine? Perhaps because of Ives's reaction to something Adrian had said earlier. It had set him to thinking.

Gregory Vane sauntered over to study Adrian. "I would say—just offhand, you know—that you could do with a bit of peace and quiet, old man. What say Harry and I take ourselves off tomorrow? Too late to go today, not with the distance we must cover. But first thing tomorrow."

"If you feel you must. But I feel much better this afternoon and sure to gain every day. I shouldn't like to put an end to our party."

"Rubbish," Vane replied with a grin.

Adrian could see why Dru might be taken with him. He was a pleasant chap with a handsome face and an engaging wit. He also seemed to be more perceptive than his chum, Harry. Harry wouldn't see a problem unless it jumped up and bit him.

"I say," Harry cried as he came into the drawing

room, "someone must do something about that nasty little beast." Harry was hobbling and looking as angry as a nest of disturbed hornets.

"Were you attacked by Binky, too?" Dru asked, grinning in spite of Harry's anger.

"You mean that beast attacked you first? Well, I fixed him." Harry looked rather smug.

Adrian exchanged a guarded look with Dru. He sighed. "And how did you do that?"

"He wanted to go out, so I opened the door and he was off in a shot. He may well be into the next county by now." Harry spoke with an enormous amount of satisfaction.

Dru burst out laughing.

Chapter Fourteen

*I*t was fortunate that Miss Knight did not hear the laughter that followed the announcement of her pet's dash to freedom. When she returned to the room, those present murmured words of sympathy, except for Lady Felicia. She eyed Dru, who wondered if the lady intended to tattle.

"Miss Herbert," Lady Felicia began, only to be interrupted by Lord Brentford.

"Miss Herbert," he repeated, "was attacked by your pet as was Harry Metcalf. I fear it is not popular around here at the moment."

"Never fear, Miss Knight," Dru said in a soothing manner to take some of the sting from Lord Brentford's words. "I fancy Binky will return before long."

The elderly spinster sniffed, wiped her nose and said to no one in particular, "He is all I have."

When she had trailed from the room, looking woebegone, Dru turned to Harry. "As much as I dislike that animal, I confess I feel sorry for her. A pet can be such comfort."

"What sort of pet do you plan to adopt? Spinsters usually have a cat, do they not?" Lady Felicia said.

Dru merely smiled. "I like both. What kind of pet do you intend to have?"

"I do not intend to be a spinster!" Lady Felicia's dark eyes flashed with annoyance.

Harry grinned and said most unforgivably, "But you are one now—leastwise until you marry."

"Which I shall!" She flashed Lord Ives a coy glance.

Lord Brentford looked uncomfortable, shifting about as though wishing he were elsewhere.

Lord Ives moved to his side and spoke in a quiet voice. He helped his friend to his feet and walked from the room with him, saying as they left, "Back to bed, I think."

Dru returned to the rear-facing window, followed by Gregory Vane. They stared at the deepening shadows that crossed the garden as the daylight faded.

"I suspect you care about your erstwhile patient more than you would like." He fingered the tassel of the drapery hanging to one side of the large window.

"Perhaps." She knew that what she had seen, had touched, would forever be etched in her memory. One did not forget the sight of such muscles, such a body easily. Thank heaven no one else knew. She wondered if anyone else was aware of the small birthmark on his lower thigh? It was shaped like an oak leaf. Curious thing.

"Once the four of us depart, you will remain? I imagine Lady Brentford will not willingly have you leave."

"As to that, I have come to care for her very much. She is the epitome of a gracious lady."

"She asked you to care for Brentford when he was ill?" Mr. Vane wore a pensive expression, quite as though he was pursuing a line of reasoning.

"Her Ladyship requested I do so since I have had experience tending the sick." Dru squarely met his gaze, wondering just how much he guessed. "Colyer was there much of the time and spent the nights watching him."

Mr. Vane nodded. "Ah, yes, Colyer. Good man." Pausing a few moments, Mr. Vane continued, "I shall miss you, you know. The other young ladies are fine, you are the jewel."

Dru could feel her face warming. Drat the blush. "I am certain you will find much to amuse you once in London."

Colyer entered the drawing room, coming immediately to Dru's side. "Would you be so kind as to assist me, Miss Herbert? A minor difficulty has arisen."

Dru tossed Mr. Vane an apologetic look before following the valet from the drawing room. She noted Lady Felicia watch her leave from where she stood close to Lord Ives, who had returned at once from helping Lord Brentford. What a good thing it was that there was someone who could keep the lady occupied.

Colyer said nothing as they trod the stairs to the upper floor. Dru followed him to Lord Brentford's door. She stopped, not wishing to enter. "What is the problem?"

"His lordship wishes to speak with you. That is all I know, miss." The valet opened the door, and Dru found herself escorted into the room whether she wished or not.

His lordship reclined in a chair by the fireplace, his feet propped on an ottoman. A tray with a teapot and all necessary for tea sat on a table at his side. She waited.

Adrian studied the young woman Colyer had brought up from the drawing room. He suspected she had been in conversation with Gregory Vane again. Her cheeks were still flushed, no doubt from his flattery!

"Will you join me in a cup of tea? Perhaps you would pour?" Adrian gestured to the tray.

Dru acquiesced, pouring out the milk and tea, sugaring it the way he liked before handing him his cup. She poured for herself, then perched on the edge of the chair as though awaiting a dreaded verdict. What did she anticipate?

He wondered just how close she had become to Vane. He was personable, wealthy, the sort of chap that a mother would like. Ah, but a father would see that restlessness in Vane's eyes, think he was perhaps too young to settle down.

"You will miss Vane when he departs tomorrow."

"Belinda Oaks and Lydia Percy go as well," she

reminded. "And Mr. Metcalf. He said you attended his sister's come-out ball. What was it like?"

She obviously did not wish to dwell on Gregory Vane. Well, he would oblige her for the moment. He sipped his tea before replying. He described what went on at a come-out ball: the flowers, the decorations, the kinds of gowns one saw.

"It sounds delightful. I hope my sister is able to attend a ball or two while in London. I have no idea how fashionable our aunt might be."

"Vane would know. He is very fashionable—moves in the highest circles. Would you like that?" He concentrated on her face to see if her thoughts might be revealed.

"I have no idea, not having been exposed to that sort of life. And why I should be the slightest interested in what Mr. Vane does or how he lives is beyond me. I doubt I will see him again once he leaves here." She gave Adrian a puzzled look before pouring more tea, sugaring it to her liking. She offered him more, which he accepted.

"Something very civilized about taking tea, is there not?" Adrian asked, peering at her over his cup.

"True." She looked about the room as though seeing it for the first time.

There was a tapestry on the far wall that had an oak tree featured on it, a little whim of his own. Leaves were delineated in fine detail. Not that anyone knew the significance of it. But with his odd little birthmark that no one, save his mother and nanny, knew about, it was a private fancy that he found amusing.

For some reason she also found it diverting.

"You admire the tapestry?" He wondered why. There was nothing really unusual about it.

She gave him an unguarded smile. Setting her teacup on the tray, she rose to walk over to study the weaving. "You have a fondness for oak leaves, I see." The look she gave him was far too knowing.

He frowned, wondering what prompted it.

She blushed at his frown, or he supposed his frown caused her to run the color of beetroot. Something had.

"You might say that." He watched and waited.

"I had better leave now. Thank you for the tea. I am glad you are feeling better, but perhaps you ought to take a nap?" She edged toward the door, looking guilty and wanting to flee.

He placed his teacup on the tray, rising to cross to her side. He had the strangest suspicion. A snatch of memory—a silken touch, a delicate scent, a cooling of skin—assailed him. "What happened when you were taking care of me that causes you to blush?"

"N-n-nothing. I gave you barley water to drink and tried to cool you with lavender water. You were extremely feverish."

And she was extremely nervous about something.

"How? Just my forehead?" He crossed his arms, casually standing between her and the door. Colyer was at the far end of the room and couldn't possibly overhear their softly spoken conversation.

"True," she answered eagerly, glancing at the door as though she wished she were on the other side of it.

"I dimly recall something more."

Her horrified expression brought to mind what he had forgotten. He had surfaced just long enough to be aware that someone was bathing him. Drusilla?

"It was you who bathed me."

She froze, looking so adorably guilty he almost laughed before the seriousness of the situation hit him. If she knew about his oak leaf birthmark, she had uncovered a great deal of him!

"This changes things." There was no way a gently bred young woman could be allowed to escape the consequences of her action.

"No, not at all," she insisted. "You forget that I am an experienced nurse. I have bathed patients before."

"Adult men?" Adrian fought the desire to exterminate every one of them.

She shook her head. "Only infants and children. But

it is the same procedure with the same aim in mind, to reduce the fever. It was successful, too."

Adrian relaxed a trifle, still standing guard against her escape. "It seemed to work well."

"Thank you," she replied uneasily, as though she wasn't certain what to say.

"I repeat that this changes things—for us." He watched as she stiffened, glaring at him as though he was at fault.

"Rubbish."

It was a succinct reply, but not too unexpected, given what he knew of her.

"We shall see." He glanced at the bed, wishing he had been a bit more conscious when she had bathed him. He could remember little of what could have been a delightful experience. "Perhaps I *will* rest for a bit before dinner."

In an instant she had whipped around him and had the door open. "I imagine I will see you then, my lord."

"Oh, yes, Miss Herbert. You will see me at dinner." And longer than that. He wondered what his mother would say if he revealed what had occurred. Somehow he doubted she would be horrified. She would, however, understand his reasoning on the matter. And he would be free of Felicia.

Dru paused in the hallway, burying her face in her hands. Never in her short life had she been so embarrassed. Oh, why had she stupidly studied that tapestry! And why must she blush at the slightest thing? For just a moment he had seemed amused. Then his reaction set in, causing a serious expression to settle on his handsome face.

He knew what she had done!

Hurrying to her room, she entered her refuge. "This is what happens to girls who are outspoken, who dare to take chances! It will be my downfall!" It was simple enough to scold herself. What her mother might say was beyond her.

"What will I do now? If I tell Lady Brentford I

wish to leave at once, she will demand to know why. What excuse could I offer? That her son has a strange notion that he ought to marry me?" It was what he would conclude.

Would that set well with the lady who . . . well . . . what did she want? At first she had said she would like Adrian to marry Lady Felicia. But then, only two nights ago, she had complained about her, saying marriage between Adrian and Lady Felicia would be a disaster. It would be, of course, but if that is what he truly desired—and Dru couldn't imagine why—he should have it.

What could she do to prevent his rash declaration? Then something he had quizzed her about returned. Mr. Vane. Lord Brentford had queried her about her feelings for Mr. Vane. Surely his lordship didn't imagine Dru cared twopence for the man? True, Mr. Vane was friendly, pleasant. Lord Ives spent more time looking after Lady Felicia than at Dru. Harry Metcalf paid no particular attention to anyone other than himself.

Tonight, in addition to celebrating Lady Brentford's birthday, it would be a farewell dinner for Mr. Vane and Harry Metcalf, Lydia, and Belinda as well. Perhaps Dru ought to muddy the water, as it were?

She walked to open her wardrobe. Mary entered with a freshly pressed gown in her arms.

"What do you think is my best gown? One likely to make an impression—a favorable one, of course."

Mary replaced the lilac sprigged muslin that had been carefully pressed, then pulled a silk gown from the wardrobe.

Dru smiled. It was one of that matched the unusual color of her eyes. Sea green, Tabitha called those eyes, and the dress was the same color. The neckline was lower than she usually wore, but the sleeves were pretty, being to her elbows and trimmed with lace. She nodded, exchanging a conspiratorial look with her maid.

"This is the last evening Mr. Vane and Mr. Metcalf

will be here. Belinda and Lydia will leave come morning, as well. When I depart, would you consider coming with me?" Dru asked this in a casual way, but she was serious. She had become attached to Mary while here.

"Yes, miss, I would." The maid assisted Dru into the sea green gown, tying tapes and straightening the skirt.

It was not easy to put the scene with Lord Brentford out of her mind. Her face grew warm just thinking about what he had guessed. Had she been more skilled at deception he would never have known, never have had the absurd but honorable notion that something had to be done. It would be like that fabled sword hanging over her head. Until then, she would avoid being alone with him or even near him.

Let him think she was enamored of Mr. Vane. She quite forgot what she had said earlier regarding the gentleman.

Mary handed her the long white gloves she would need, even if she took them off to dine. The dainty reticule came next, a simple gold mesh that looked splendid with the sea green silk.

Dru took a deep breath before leaving the safety of her room for the dangerous waters below.

"Meow." The small sound caught her attention.

"Kitty? Where have you been? Ever since that naughty Binky came, you have hidden from view. Poor kitty cat." She bent down to stroke the plump silver-striped tabby cat. It would probably be thankful to see the last of the guests, too. Particularly that dratted dog!

Well, she must face her censure. She was certain it would be that. No gently bred young lady *ever* viewed a gentleman less than fully clothed. Her downfall was so humiliating. What was even worse was that she would do it again if it were necessary!

"Miss Herbert." Mr. Vane stepped forth from the shadows to greet her at the bottom of the stairs. "You are in first looks."

"And good evening to you," Dru replied with a smile. It was nice to have at least one person of whom she need not be wary.

"Come, walk in with me. I always dislike entering a room by myself." He offered his arm, which she was glad to accept.

"That is a piece of nonsense, sir. A more polished gentleman I cannot imagine." Dru beamed up at him, thinking it was a pity he would never be more than a friend.

"Not even Brentford?"

"We shall not discuss our host." She gave him a searching glance before checking to see who had come down before them.

Belinda and Lydia chatted with Harry Metcalf. Bless his bachelor heart, he was being most agreeable to them.

Lord Ives spoke with Lady Felicia, a low-voiced conversation that seemed oddly earnest. Dru still felt there was something between those two.

A sound behind her alerted her senses. Lord Brentford had entered the room. How she knew this, she wasn't certain but she did. She gestured to the fireplace across the room. "A bit of warmth would be welcome this evening. There is a faint chill in the air."

Mr. Vane amiably escorted her to stand near the small fire. Like everything else in this house, it was neatly done. Once established there, she was able to turn to face Lord Brentford.

Would everyone else think his smile too intimate? Or was it her overactive imagination?

He was at her side at once. "I took your advice."

"A nap?" She tried to calm her heart. It kept wanting to race, to leap, to dance! He was standing much too close for her comfort.

"A rest. But sometimes a rest is sufficient. I needed to do a bit of thinking." The look he sent her might be considered as significant. She hoped it wasn't.

She was spared the results of his contemplation when his mother and her friends entered the room.

Kitty trotted along beside Lady Brentford, looking about with a saucy nose-in-the-air attitude. She was free of that dratted dog.

"Oh, I wonder if I shall ever see my Binky again," moaned Miss Knight at the sight of the cat.

"He will return," Dru assured her. "He is simply doing a bit of exploring."

Miss Knight sent Dru a grateful look. Lord Somers offered a consoling pat on Miss Knight's hand.

Dru chanced to glance to where Lady Felicia stood near Lord Ives. She was watching Lord Brentford. She must have observed that intimate smile he had given Dru. What had she made of it? Perhaps she had thought nothing of that slow, suggestive smile he had bestowed. And pigs might fly. Lady Felicia was nothing if not awake on all suits.

Surprisingly enough, Lady Felicia said nothing regarding the supposed intimacy between Dru and Lord Brentford. Perhaps it was no more than Dru's imagination?

However, Lady Felicia murmured often to Lord Ives, who escorted her to the dining room. Precedence was not strictly adhered to this evening. Lord Osman walked at Lady Brentford's side, chatting admirably. Lord Somers escorted Miss Knight, perhaps suggesting ways to retrieve the nasty little dog. Mrs. Twywhitt and Sir Bertram seemed to have much to discuss. Dru caught a word about some bird and decided those two had much in common.

Belinda and Lydia chatted happily with Mr. Vane and Harry Metcalf.

Dru found Lord Brentford at her side. She would have settled happily for Gregory Vane as a dinner partner. Lady Felicia and Lord Ives were opposite where Lord Brentford settled her next to him. It was all confusion. She ought not sit here, but here she was on his right, in a place of honor next to her host.

No one else appeared to notice anything amiss. Perhaps Dru was being overly sensitive? It was not going to be the most comfortable dinner she had endured. Nor was it.

Adrian almost smiled at the look of confusion on Dru Herbert's face as he led her to the bottom of the table and placed her at his right hand. This, by right, should have gone to the highest-ranking lady attending. He knew it and she knew it, and he could tell she was baffled. Adrian inwardly grinned.

When all were standing by the table, he nodded to the gentlemen to assist their partners to sit down. The general noise of scraping chairs and polite conservation covered Dru's hissed query.

"What is going on?"

"What do you suspect?"

Rather than tire the marchioness, the footman ladled out the cream of asparagus soup for each guest. At one ladle per bowl, it didn't take long to consume it.

Adrian lifted the lid from the platter of beautifully prepared salmon. The footman assisted in serving that as well, using the handsome silver fish slice to divide and serve the salmon. Adrian offered a dollop of sauce.

Dru nodded, still looking wary, as though she thought someone would come to tell her to move elsewhere.

Adrian didn't know when he had enjoyed himself so much.

The table had been set with the first course when they entered the dining room. It was surprising how the food could be shared, passed, and eaten as quickly as they did this evening. Except for Drusilla Herbert, who nibbled, frowned at her plate, then nibbled some more.

"It is not to your liking? Perhaps the next course is more to your preference?" Adrian said as he offered a tidbit of roast turkey.

She gave him a startled, anxious look. "Everything is delicious, my lord."

He wondered if she had tasted one bite of it.

During the lull when the first-course plates and serving dishes were removed and the second course brought in, the conversation became general.

Harry Metcalf spoke up. "We thought we could take Miss Oaks and Miss Percy home in the morning before we leave. If it is agreeable with you, of course."

Adrian glanced at the girls who were wide-eyed with the honor of having two London beaux attending them. "I should think that would be most agreeable. I am certain their parents will be pleased."

The conversation surged again as Lady Brentford's friends discussed the coming conclusion to the house party.

The second course was set on the table with the dishes arranged in perfect symmetry. Dru sampled a piece of fricandeau of veal, a bit of boiled ham with green peas, and a taste of the boiled chicken in celery sauce.

Finally it came time for the third course. The dishes and linen were removed.

Since they were celebrating Lady Brentford's birthday, Priddy entered, bearing a fine cake decorated with candied violets. There were exclamations of delight from the women present and praise for Cook, who had created the masterpiece.

Adrian made a toast to his mother, wishing her many more happy years. He had given her the sapphire pin earlier and was pleased to note she wore it. Lord Osman had given her an amethyst ring, but whether it had greater significance Adrian didn't know at this point. She wore it, and smiled often at the gentleman.

Priddy cut the cake and served it while such sweets as preserved oranges, olives, preserved peaches, and candied lemon slices on the little dishes from the epergne were passed around.

"This was a lovely thing to do for your mother. I believe her first name is Violet?" Dru gestured to the pretty candied violets that decorated the slices of cake.

"How appropriate, to have violets on the cake." Her hands fluttered before her, then she clasped a dessert fork with the air of one grasping at a straw.

"Don't be nervous. I will not upset you this evening. This is my mother's affair." He could see Dru visibly relax. "But this is where you belong for the nonce."

She flashed him a look of apprehension but made no reply.

"I, for one, would never countenance such a thing," Lady Felicia stated to Lord Ives, loud enough for others to hear her—and stare.

Adrian turned to her, wondering what it was that she would refuse.

At his look of inquiry, she said, "A forced marriage. Simply because someone decides that it should be done does not mean it must." She darted a look at Dru Herbert, then back to Adrian.

"I would agree with you," Dru inserted before Adrian could say a word.

"There are times when honor demands it, however," Adrian added in a reflective tone.

Lord Ives spoke up at this point. "I think it is more important that two parties know love and share many tastes."

Lady Felicia nodded in agreement. "There ought to be more than a melding of fortunes or a handing over of a dowry. Should women not have a bit of romance as well?"

"That would depend on the circumstances," Adrian said, hedging a little in the event she was going to try to pin him down. Although, from the way she had turned to Ives, it would seem that he was now in favor. If that was the case, Adrian could only give thanks and his blessing.

"What circumstances would compel two people to marry when they far from wished such a thing?" Dru asked quietly. "I think it utterly stupid."

"Ah—so you wish a bit of romance as well?" Lady Felicia asked, an odd smile tilting her lips.

"It would be pleasing." Dru stared down at her

plate. Adrian would have wagered that she was trying
not to blush.

"Oh, indeed. Perhaps a touch of mystery adds to
the whole. Wouldn't you agree, Miss Herbert?" He
toyed with his dessert fork, playing with a candied
violet.

She sought her wineglass, taking a gulp of the fine
champagne that deserved to be sipped and savored.

"Mystery?" she echoed, looking at him as though
he would be her undoing.

"Don't you think a bit of mystery is admirable in a
relationship, Lady Felicia? I should think it would add
a touch of spice to an otherwise bland relationship."

"What on earth are you talking about, Adrian?
Who has any mystery nowadays! Everyone knows
everything about everyone. Society is not that large,
and nothing can be kept secret for long." Lady Felicia
looked puzzled.

"Really?" Adrian slid his glance to Dru, who sat
quietly and considerably paler. It was cruel to tease
her so, but she deserved it.

At that fortuitous moment his mother tapped on
her glass, rising to escort the women to the drawing
room. Adrian compressed his lips when he assisted
Dru to her feet. "I will see you shortly," he murmured
to her obvious confusion.

Dru hurried after Lady Brentford, almost running
ahead to see if Priddy had brought in the tea urn
with the tray of china and a dish of the biscuits Lady
Brentford liked. They were delicate, crisp ginger.

Sighing with pleasure that all was in place, she assisted Lady Brentford to a comfortable chair, then
poured the tea that the footman handed around, along
with the crisp little biscuits.

What ever did Lord Brentford mean, going on as
he had? Dru didn't know if she was on her head or her
heels. Confused? Panicked, was more like it. Whatever
would come next!

Chapter Fifteen

When Dru came down to break her fast the next morning, she found the entry hall cluttered with cases and portmanteaus. Even as she hesitated by the bottom of the stairs, a traveling carriage drew up before the front door.

Priddy at his most stately summoned two footmen to begin stowing the various items, making a point that those belonging to Mr. Vane and Mr. Metcalf should be loaded first, with the things for Miss Oaks and Miss Percy to be placed in the very last.

"Last in, first out," he muttered as Dru hurried away in the direction of the breakfast room. She paused at the doorway to note the neighbor girls were there.

"I am so glad you are here," Belinda caroled. "I expect I shall see you at church on Sunday next, but I wanted to thank you now for making it possible for Lydia and me to enjoy such an agreeable visit here."

Lydia's eyes gleamed as she chimed in with her thanks. "I shall have a better idea of how to go on once we are in London for our Season. And we will have the advantage of knowing two nice gentlemen who are truly part of the *ton*," she added with a grin.

The girls were about done with their light meal when Gregory Vane and Harry Metcalf strolled into the room.

Dru offered what she hoped was a pleasant smile, but inwardly she was thankful they were about to depart. What a pity they couldn't spirit Lady Felicia along! Although, to be fair, that lady had been rather nice last evening. She had complimented Dru on the flowers, and had—after a look at Lord Ives—apologized when she had bumped into Dru.

The four who were about to depart engaged in cheerful chatter, allowing Dru to meditate about her own future. She would return to the rectory and resume her somewhat humdrum life. She hadn't known precisely how mundane it was until she had a chance to experience something else. Running a household like this had been a challenge, one she had found much to her liking. Her reaction to Lord Brentford she ignored. What one couldn't change, one left strictly alone.

She would miss this house—Mrs. Simpson and Priddy, and most of all Lady Brentford. At least Mary would come with her. Mrs. Simpson quite agreed. She rose from the table when she saw the others prepare to leave.

There was no sign of Lord Brentford in the entryway. Evidently he remained abed, still not entirely back to normal. Nor had Lord Ives deigned to come down. The men would see each other in London later on, no doubt.

The girls and the London beaux clattered down the front steps, made brief farewells to Dru, then straggled to the waiting carriage, laughing and joking.

Dru waved as they rolled down the avenue. With a fresh breeze it wasn't pleasant outside, so she hurried back.

"They have all left?"

At the sound of Lady Felicia's voice, Dru stopped. She glanced at the stairway where her ladyship posed. "Indeed."

"Good." She joined Dru in the walk to the rear of the house. She paused before going into the breakfast room. The used china had been whisked away, and all was pristine once more. "Keep me company . . . please?"

Wary, Dru slowly nodded. "Very well. Could I pour you some tea?" It was something to do, and a teacup was an item she could hide behind if necessary.

"That would be lovely." Lady Felicia dropped a roll and a bit of cheese on her plate, then seated herself with a grace that did her last governess credit.

Dru poured them each a cup of tea, and waited to hear why Lady Felicia wanted her company.

"I have been beastly to you, I know. Forgive me?"

Whatever Dru expected to hear, it wasn't this. "Naturally I forgive you anything you think ought to be forgiven." *That* was convoluted enough to be sufficiently vague. Now, *why* was her ladyship doing this?

Lady Felicia crumbled a bit of her roll before stiffening her spine. Her reply was not totally unexpected.

"You must know that when Lady Brentford invited me to this country house party, I thought it would produce a proposal of marriage from Lord Brentford. Needless to say, it did not." She grimaced after biting into the roll and cheese, then shrugged her elegantly clad shoulders. "Which is just as well. I found I was attracted to someone else who *does* want to marry me."

"Am I allowed to guess?" Dru said with a smile curving her lips. She had more than a little suspicion.

"Reginald, Lord Ives! Did you guess right?"

Dru chuckled lightly, almost overwhelmed by a peculiar feeling of relief. "Indeed, yes. I suspected there might be a growing attachment between you."

"And he made it clear what he would think of an attempt to trick anyone into a marriage. After all, a rich marquess is a better catch than a baron, no matter how wealthy he might be. I might be forgiven were I to make a dead set at the marquess . . . would I not?"

"The conversation at dinner?" Dru wondered. "He let you know how he felt about the matter?"

Lady Felicia nodded. She had no chance to say more as the object of her heart entered the room. He tarried by her chair a moment, resting his hand on her shoulder before he asked for coffee, along with eggs, gammon, toast, and anything else Cook might add for a hungry man. When he selected a chair, it was close to his chosen lady.

"May I offer my felicitations?" Dru said with genuine pleasure. It would appear that Lord Ives would be able to keep Lady Felicia in line.

"Of course!" Lord Ives sipped his coffee. He might be polite to Dru; he had eyes for no one but Lady Felicia.

"Has anyone seen a sign of my Binky?" Miss Knight demanded from the doorway. The lady looked as though she hadn't slept well—in fact, she seemed rather frazzled.

Dru was almost sorry for her until she recalled what a nasty little creature that dog could be. "I fear not."

Miss Knight availed herself of a soothing cup of tea, then wandered off, teacup in hand, to continue her search.

"Poor woman, but I cannot say I hope she finds her little dog. Such a nasty creature," Lady Felicia said.

"She cares for it. So . . . do you go to talk with your parents? What?" Dru knew she was being nosy, but it seemed that Lady Felicia was in an expansive mood.

"My mother is dead. Papa will be thrilled to have me off his hands. Dear Reginald, I will be so happy to move to your home as soon as may be!" Lady Felicia gave him a glowing look that rather surprised Dru. She hadn't thought her ladyship capable of genuine affection.

"A special license and a quiet wedding at St. George's, and we can be settled." Ives gave her a fond smile. "And you will have carte blanche in redoing the London house."

"Sounds like you have the right approach, Ives," Lord Brentford said as he joined them. "Congratulations are in order, I gather."

"I always like a happy ending," Dru observed.

This comment earned a quizzical look from Lord Brentford. "Do you, now?"

"Does not everyone?" Dru demanded to know, refusing to be flustered by his lordship. When she considered that she had bathed the man in his bed—even if he was unaware of her care at the time—she would *not* be intimidated by him. Especially since she knew the secret of the oak leaf birthmark. She'd wager few people were aware of it.

"May in inquire as to the direction of your thoughts?" her nemesis asked. "You have an ominously smug expression."

"I? Never." Dru rose from the table. "I had best see your mother. I fancy she will be delighted at the news. If I may?" Dru queried Lady Felicia, who nodded in reply.

Ignoring the odd look on Lord Brentford's face, Dru whisked herself around the corner of the room to dash up the stairs and along to Lady Brentford's room.

Upon hearing the news, that dear lady expressed fervent thanks. "It is not that she isn't of a good family. The Tait line is all that it should be. Perhaps had her mother lived, it might have been different for her. I suspect she terrified every governess she had."

"I would imagine she could do that," Dru agreed with a hastily suppressed grin.

"Well, her father, the Earl of Silchester, is wealthy, but a bit tight with money. Yet, I daresay he will come down handsomely for his only daughter when she weds—if for no reason than to be rid of the girl."

"Strange—that is what she said, more or less. She said he will be glad to be rid of her. How sad. I know my parents are happy when good things happen to any of us. I doubt they are glad to see us go, especially Mama."

"You will be returning home to your mama before too long. She will be happy to see you," the marchioness ventured to say. She turned aside to gather up a pretty painted fan and her reticule.

Dru's heart sank to her toes. "Your ladyship is doing so well now—quite recovered. I have a feeling that you have been energized by the friends who have been here?"

"That is true." The marchioness rose to leave her room with Kitty tagging along behind her.

It was amusing to see how the cat paraded down the hall now the dog was nowhere in evidence. "Kitty is happy with the house to herself again," Dru observed.

"Indeed. I am sorry that Cordelia's pet is gone missing, but I cannot say I miss the little beast."

Lord Osman left his room to join Lady Brentford, and Dru suddenly discovered a task in the opposite direction that simply must be done at once. She excused herself and marched off, as though there really was something to do.

Slipping down the servants' staircase proved simple. Dru found her way to the little room where the vases and urns were brought for her to refill or refresh. Priddy had brought three that drooped.

Once she found a cape to toss over her shoulders, Dru was off to the gardens. It was a soothing pastime, picking flowers and combining colors. Her trug was laden with blooms when she found she had company.

"Flowers again. About the only time I can find you alone is here in the gardens," Lord Brentford complained. He was muffled up against the spring breeze, but his head was bare and Dru looked askance at his carelessness.

"Cheer up. Your mother reminded me that I will not be here much longer." Dru paused, turning to face him. "I confess I like it here very much, as I like your lady mother. How blessed you are to have a mother as dear as she is." She urged him toward the house and out of the breeze. "Poor Lady Felicia—I gather her mother died some years ago. I daresay it accounts for a number of things."

She would always associate the scent of spring flowers with Adrian, Lord Brentford. All around her was the awakening of the world, with birds seeking mates, flowers springing forth to dress the garden with their finery. And she would soon be leaving him. It was a bittersweet time.

"Indeed," he agreed dryly. "Like how she came to be so spoiled and headstrong."

"Yet I believe that Lord Ives will manage her well."

"You think a woman can be managed?" He tilted his head to one side, studying her so her cheeks warmed from his perusal.

"I am not certain that I could be 'managed' in that way. Perhaps guided is a better word to use?" Dru succeeded in smiling at him, although she wasn't certain how good a smile it might be.

His smile was definitely roguish. It hinted to bold pirates and dashing bucks, of daring deeds and sensuous touches. It definitely had an effect on her heart!

"Let me help you with the flowers." He took the trug from her hands to carry it back to the house. "You sigh. Can it be that you are sorry to leave here? The gardens and the house? Or just my mother?"

Her heart turned over. Was he so looking forward to seeing the last of her? "I have mentioned once or twice that I have enjoyed my stay here with your mother."

"I will wager that you were handed more than you bargained for once you arrived. Mother tends to assume that because she is capable, everyone else is as well."

Dru walked ahead to open the gate, then took the trug from his hand. She looked down at the flowers for a moment, then shrugged. "I found it stimulating. While I do face challenges at home, I have nothing like this with which I must cope."

"I think Mother will have an interesting announcement this evening."

"A marriage to Lord Osman? I rather expect it. Are you unhappy about this change?"

"Not at all. At least the woman I marry will be the only Marchioness of Brentford. Mother will be Viscountess Osman, which ought to do her well enough."

Dru's mind focused on the part about his marriage. "You intend to marry before long, then?"

"Definitely. I think it would be a positive improvement in my life. I might even manage to persuade her to help me bathe." He gave Dru a lazy grin before leaving the room. His eyes had been alight with mischief, unless she very much mistook it.

She stared off into space, wondering how long it took a broken heart to heal.

But why did he think to have a wife who would help him bathe? She had admitted a little, true, but no one knew of her transgression. She refused to marry for such a stupid reason. That way was disaster! It would amount to a forced marriage, a situation she abhorred.

"Oh, I completely forgot. I wish to speak with you on the morrow. Would ten of the clock in the morning be agreeable with you?" He had popped back to stare at her in expectation of a reply.

He was going to send her home now. She knew it. How foolish if she thought for one moment that he would consider her for his marchioness! Why, she might be the great-niece of the Earl of Stanwell, but that scarce qualified her for such a rarified position as Marchioness of Brentford. Solid gentry was as good as her family might claim. She was satisfied with her position in life, she insisted. Of course she did not expect to marry the handsome peer who had captured her heart. It didn't mean that she couldn't long for that position.

"Of course. I will be there on the dot."

"Good. I knew I could count on you." He wandered into the room, kissed her on the cheek, then strolled out as though quite pleased with the world.

"Well, I never!" she whispered.

"I heard that. And you have so!"

He didn't enter the room, and judging by the steps that faded into the distance, he was soon gone.

Well, he had the right of it. He had kissed her and heaven help her, she had kissed him back.

She shortly took the first of her completed bouquets to the drawing room.

Mrs. Twywhitt and Sir Bertram were in the drawing

room, joined by Miss Knight and Lord Somers as Dru placed the flowers on the sofa table. She fluffed out some leaves. Adjusted a flower or two, then turned to leave the room.

"Will Lady Brentford be coming down soon, my dear?" Mrs. Twywhitt inquired.

"I should think so," Dru replied. "She was dressed and talking with Lord Osman when I last saw her in the upstairs hallway." Dru edged toward the doorway, thinking she preferred not to be included in any speculation.

Her news resulted in significant looks exchanged.

"I thought so," Mrs. Twywhitt said with satisfaction. "Violet is far too lovely a person to be left on the shelf for long. She and your mother were the closest of friends when in school, Miss Herbert. It is nice that you were able to come and assist Lady Brentford when she needed help."

Dru smiled and murmured faint words of agreement. It might be wise to pack her things at once. Her father's motto of "Be prepared, for you know not the hour of your departure" could be taken in more ways than one. With that in mind, she hurried up the stairs.

Lady Felicia left her room to intercept Dru. "I shall leave in the morning, along with Reginald. He convinced me to speak with Father at once. What point in waiting?"

"At least this party has been good for you—in that you found your heart's desire." Dru longed to be in her room, away from the ecstatic Lady Felicia. Happiness was not contagious when it applied to matters of the heart.

"And you? When will you leave?"

"Soon, I expect. Lady Brentford has made such an excellent recovery, I truly am not needed anymore."

"It seems to me that you perform a great number of services that her ladyship is glad to have done. Unless she goes shortly, I do not see how she can manage without you."

"With all the guests gone, there will be less to be done," Dru reminded. Mrs. Simpson and Priddy could take their ease, with maids and footmen to run errands for them.

"I must say," Lady Felicia continued with a thoughtful look at Dru, "I am astounded at the recovery Adrian made. He said something about lavender."

Dru swallowed with care. "I gave Colyer a bottle of lavender oil. I have seen it to be most effective in nasty colds." This was true as far as it went.

"Really? It is a good thing you were in the house, in that event. I have small knowledge of herbs and treatments. Adrian is fortunate you do." The pensive look deepened, but thankfully she said no more.

"I shall see you later." Dru sidled away, intent upon gaining her room.

"I understand we are to be given happy news from Lord Osman with our dinner this evening," Lady Felicia pirouetted, pausing as she reentered her room. "I wonder just who Adrian intends to wed?" Her look was searching.

Dru forced a polite smile. "I imagine we will learn in time." In her eyes time was her enemy. She hated to leave, for she loved the dratted man who lived here. How nonsensical could she be! Another downfall!

Once in her room she began to pack her belongings into her cases with Mary's help. Leaving only the gown to wear this evening and a sensible traveling dress out for the morrow—or whenever she was sent away.

"You may as well pack your things, Mary. I fancy that when I am dismissed, my departure will be prompt."

The young maid curtsied and went to the door. "I am thinking that her ladyship will not wish to part with you soon, miss. She has been dependent on you for some weeks now. Likely she will want you here for a while longer?"

"In that event I can always remove one of the practical dresses that we put on the top of that last case. It is difficult—not knowing precisely when I am to leave. His lordship requested I present myself at ten of the clock come tomorrow morning. I trust I shall learn more then."

Mary gave her a dubious look before leaving the room.

A sleepless night caught up with her, and Dru dozed off, waking when Mary came in to help her dress for dinner.

She wore the sea blue silk again, the one likened to the color of the sea and her eyes. It was a favorite, and besides they all knew her circumstances. She did not have the vast wardrobe Lady Felicia had brought with her. What her maid must be doing with all the packing to be done before morning boggled Dru's mind. But perhaps she had been forewarned and had begun this morning?

The drawing room was empty when she entered. The view to the rear of the house beckoned, so she walked to the far end of the room, where she stared off to the gardens. The late afternoon sun slanted golden rays across the various blooms, highlighting them in bright relief. It was a tranquil scene, one of which she could never tire, given the chance.

Lord Brentford came in then. She couldn't see him, but she sensed he was there. It was like an extra sense, this consciousness of him.

"I like that gown."

She rotated, turning her back on the gardens she loved. "Thank you. I am blessed to have a few I truly like."

He strolled across the room to face her, hands behind him. He looked splendid in a burgundy coat over a cream Marcella waistcoat and black pantaloons. Even his black patent slippers were perfect, as was the cravat tied in a complicated fashion.

"Mother and Osman intend to marry soon. She will be gone before long."

His charming grin did the most peculiar things to her breathing, not to mention her heart. "Why not? This is a lovely house, but I fancy life here could be very lonely without someone with whom to share it."

"I am coming to agree with you." He rocked gently back and forth, studying her with an intense gaze she found rather unsettling.

Dru took a deep breath. Was he perhaps going to share his personal news with her now? Or was she to be fobbed off with nothing more than a dismissal?

"Ah, you must be hungry." Lord Ives wandered into the room, closely followed by Sir Bertram and Lord Somers. Lord Brentford murmured an excuse so he might offer the gentlemen a drink.

Dru felt very ill at ease and wished that either she hadn't come down so early or the other women were here.

Her wish was granted. Lady Felicia swirled into the room, her cream gown trimmed with pink ribbons billowing about her ankles, Mrs. Twywhitt and Miss Knight right behind her.

Dru gave Lady Felicia a grateful look, going to meet her. If anyone had told her a few days ago that she would be in a charity with her, Dru would have pronounced him mad.

"I see Lady Brentford and Lord Osman are the last to join us. I can guess why." Lady Felicia sent a warm look to her betrothed gentleman.

"Priddy said they were in the library," Miss Knight offered. She still looked a bit lost without her dog.

"I fancy we shall know soon enough," Mrs. Twywhitt commented wisely as the happy couple appeared.

"I shall put all curiosity to rest at once," Lord Osman said immediately. "Lady Brentford has made me the happiest of men by consenting to be my wife."

Lady Brentford sought her son, obviously pleased that he appeared to be delighted by her news, if news it might be considered, given that so many were expecting this announcement.

The ladies all clustered about the marchioness, with Dru content to remain to the rear of the little group.

"You are pleased." Adrian came close to her.

"Did I not indicate so earlier?" Dru countered.

"This has been a successful party with two betrothals." He handed Dru a glass of champagne, and she took a grateful sip.

"True. I believe that when I return home, it is possible I may have similar news from my sisters. At least from Mama's last letter, she had great hopes."

"And what about you? What hopes do you nurture? Is there some worthy vicar to whom you have given your heart?"

"Hardly. My brother Adam is training to follow in Father's footsteps, but declares he will not settle for a curate post. The pay is abysmal, and often the living quarters are dreadful. A married vicar would have a better situation, but still, it is not an easy life." Growing up in the drafty rectory, Dru was well aware of this.

"It is the life he wants?"

Suddenly Dru wondered about Adam. Was the church what he wanted or was he being pushed into conforming to what her father wished him to do? "I am not sure."

"And what about you, then? If there isn't a worthy vicar waiting for you, what then?"

"Nothing, sir."

"Well, now, that ought to be changed."

And how could that be when her heart was given to the very man who didn't appear to want it?

Chapter Sixteen

An air of festivity marked the evening meal. Precedence again was forgotten as Lord Osman escorted in Lady Brentford to dinner while Lady Felicia went in on the arm of Lord Ives. Mrs. Twywhitt and Sir Bertram, deep in a discussion about a bird they were sure they had seen, happily walked together, while Lord Somers again consoled Miss Knight on her missing pet.

That left Drusilla and Lord Brentford.

She bestowed a wary glance on him before training her gaze on the floor. How difficult it was to place the tips of her fingers on his arm, as etiquette demanded. Of course with precedence out the window, surely she might omit this?

He foiled her plan by putting his hand over hers, quite as though he knew just what she was contemplating.

"I know the floor fascinates, but you could at least spare me a bit of conversation," he complained.

Startled, she flashed him a look of concern.

"That is better. Ives and Lady Felicia leave in the morning, and I believe all the others—save Osman—will as well."

"Pity about Miss Knight's dog." It was the polite thing to say, but Dru thought the spinster well rid of the little beast.

"Indeed." He continued the bland conversation while he escorted her to her place.

For Drusilla, there was the tantalizing knowledge that she knew him as no one else did. His arms, for instance—she knew precisely what those beautifully bare, muscled arms looked like. Her mind skittered away from the image of the rest of him. She had no desire to blush.

"I'd give a pony to know what is going on in your mind at the moment," he said as he again seated her next to him.

She had to smile. Really, it was too delicious not to smile. Her silence bothered him. She was so tempted to tease him about oak leaves, yet that would be asking for more trouble than she could handle.

"You enjoyed viewing the tapestry in my sitting room?" he murmured.

"Indeed. I have a distinct fondness for oak leaves— as depicted on the tapestry, of course." She watched as he seated himself next to her at the bottom of the table. Keeping her expression as bland as his conversation, she batted her lashes as she had seen Lady Felicia do.

His eyes promised retribution, but he said not a word.

Champagne of the finest quality was used to toast Lady Brentford and Lord Osman. Mrs. Simpson and Cook had excelled themselves in planning and preparing the dinner. The dinner proceeded precisely as it ought. The soup was delicious, as was the fish freshly caught in his lordship's fishpond.

She said nothing during the pause between the first and second courses, allowing the marquess to converse with Lady Felicia and Lord Ives. That didn't mean she wasn't conscious of everything he said or did.

It was when she was nibbling on an apple puff that he brought up the topic that had worried her.

"You will not forget to join me in the morning?"

"I said I would. In your library?"

"That appears to be as good a place as any." He gave her a speculative look she couldn't begin to interpret.

Dru's pleasure in the splendid dinner was ruined. The apple puff, usually a favorite, tasted like nothing. She picked at it, pushing bits around on her plate and hoping his lordship paid no attention to what she ate.

The marchioness indicated it was time for the ladies to leave the room. Thankful to escape, Dru edged back her chair and slipped away, heading toward the door.

She made the mistake of looking back at the bottom of the table, where Lord Brentford sat watching her. He winked. It was a very knowing wink, and she suspected her color rose as a result. Gracious, the man wasn't going to put her on the spot for her indelicacy of bathing him when he had that high fever was he?

She supposed she might have called Colyer to handle the task. Why it had not occurred to her at the time, she really couldn't say. Mama would have said she had matched her outspokenness with outrageous behavior, which led to her downfall. How had he guessed? Then she remembered her utterly stupid comment on the oak leaves. Why had she not learned to hold her tongue? Mama had declared it would get her into trouble someday. Dru had the bitter feeling that that day had arrived.

"Play for us, Drusilla, my dear."

The marchioness made her request so sweetly, Dru knew she must obey. Lady Felicia offered to turn the pages while Dru worked her way through a Mozart sonata. Since she had to concentrate on the music, there was no attempt at conversation. Dru wondered how early she might escape.

A footman entered the room, an air of excitement about him. In his arms a bundle of fur that made hoarse little yaps struggled. He made his way straight to Miss Knight.

"Your dog has returned, ma'am."

She shot up from her chair to hold out her arms to the scruffy little creature. "Binky, my precious doggy!" She clasped the animal tightly to her thin bosom.

"Well, she leaves tomorrow and so will that dratted dog," Lady Felicia murmured.

"Poor Kitty will have to go into hiding until they do," Dru added.

The little spaniel was dirty, although the footman explained they had made an effort to wipe him down.

"I shall have him bathed at once. Oh, I am so happy to have him back." She patted the matted head. "You naughty doggy. No more running away."

Lady Felicia exchanged a look with Dru. "What say this time of freedom gives it a taste for more?"

Dru returned to her music that had been interrupted when the footman made his dramatic entry.

"Well, Cordelia, if you want to see to your dog, by all means do so. I am glad he returned before it was time for you to depart." The marchioness waved the spinster on her way.

"What she means," whispered Lady Felicia, "is that she is thankful Miss Knight didn't insist upon remaining so she might look for that dratted animal."

"If she could break it of its habit of nibbling at ankles, that dog wouldn't be so bad," Dru replied.

"Nasty beast! Ives said I could have a poodle. They are far more intelligent dogs."

The men sauntered into the room at that point. Dru abandoned the pianoforte at once. She didn't think she could play with Lord Brentford's gaze upon her.

Only—he wasn't with the men. She looked to the marchioness, who wore a puzzled expression.

Lord Osman nodded. "Brentford was not feeling quite the thing, so begged to be excused. I suspect that nasty chill he took was harder on him than we realized."

The marchioness met Dru's concerned gaze. "Perhaps all he needs is a good night's sleep?"

No one offered any comment to that. Sir Bertram and Mrs. Twywhitt went off to the library to find a book on birds to settle a matter of identity. The remaining four of the older set chose to play a game of whist.

Lord Ives and Lady Felicia were polite, but Dru suspected they would far rather be in private conversation.

Dru waited for the right moment, then said, "I shall go to my room. It has been a long day, and I have some packing to finish."

Lady Felicia gave her a perplexed look. "I had no notion you were to leave tomorrow—as we do."

Dru shrugged. "I must depart soon, and I dislike being unprepared. I hate a last-minute scramble."

Since they were just as happy to be alone, no demur was made. Dru escaped with little more than a gentle query from Lady Brentford about refreshments. Since Dru had already discussed this with Mrs. Simpson, there was not the slightest trouble.

The problem with going to he room was that there was little to occupy her thoughts other than Lord Brentford and why he was feeling worse.

At long last she poked her head from her door, resolved to ask Colyer how his master did. There was no one in the hall, and she decided it as safe to go on. The only trouble with this scheme was that Colyer didn't answer the door when she lightly scratched on it.

Lord Brentford, arrayed in a navy dressing gown of some magnificence, opened the door to survey her, making her feel like a silly schoolgirl.

"I was concerned when you didn't join us after dinner. I was-er-going to inquire of Colyer how you are."

He leaned against the frame of the door to study her. "I was a bit tired. That chill I took was harder on me than I wanted to admit. No man likes to confess he feels as weak as a kitten."

Dru backed away from his tantalizing person. His cravat was gone, his shirt was open, and the three buttons undone. Enticing dark curls of hair teased her eye. She gulped at the sight and the memories it stirred. He seemed as fit as possible to her eyes. "I am glad you have the sense to rest." Turning, she made to go to her room.

"You will meet me in the morning." It wasn't a question much less an invitation. It was an order.

Dru bristled. "I do not see why whatever you have to say cannot be said here and now." She almost stamped her foot in exasperation.

"There is a time for everything." That was it. The discussion, if you might call it that, was closed.

Whirling about, she stormed back to her room, closing her door with a snap. She turned to her maid.

"Mary, help me please. I am retiring early. I have a fearful headache." She submitted to the maid's assistance in removing her gown and into her nightdress. Once changed, she dismissed Mary, advising she also take an early night.

Alone, she crept into her bed to contemplate what was going to be said on the morrow. Would he simply dismiss her? Would he castigate her for her stupidity in bathing him to reduce his high fever? Not that it was a stupid thing to do. It was merely foolhardy for *her* to do it.

She admitted it now—she ought to have summoned Colyer and handed him the lavender oil with instructions on how to proceed. Well, she hadn't and now she would have to live with the consequences. She doubted Lord Brentford would reveal her foolishness to anyone. Somehow she believed he was too private a person to do that. Still . . . with those uneasy thoughts milling about in her head, she finally drifted into a troubled sleep.

In the morning Adrian grinned at his image in the looking glass that hung in his dressing room. He admitted he hadn't *looked* ill last night, but he had been glad to sleep. He needed all his energy for today to cope with Drusilla Herbert and what must be done. He knew he had angered her last evening. Still weak, he was hardly in any position to discuss anything, let alone what he wanted.

Today, following a good night, he felt far more capable of arranging matters to suit him. He had seen his mother, advised her of his intentions. She had given him her blessing even as she looked curious; aware he wasn't telling her everything. But then, what son did?

He went down to breakfast to find Ives in the entryway instructing his valet and the footmen precisely how he wished the luggage to be stowed. Since Lord Silchester had sent Lady Felicia and her maid in a hired chaise, she had no carriage to fill. But it did present a problem of sorts.

It seemed to Adrian that a fourgon would be required for the mountain of luggage. When he suggested it to Ives, the man gave him a relieved smile. Adrian nodded to Priddy to see it done at once.

"I was hoping you would propose that. I can't believe all the cases and portmanteaus Felicia brought. I suppose I must accustom myself to such." He grinned at Adrian, then walked to the breakfast room with him.

"You think to leave early?" Adrian inquired when they found the room empty. If Ives had hoped to find Lady Felicia dressed and eating, he was disappointed.

"Felicia promised to have something in her room while she did last-minute packing." Both men knew that her ladyship would not lift a finger to stow away the remaining items, that her maid would take care of it all.

"Well, make a good meal now, for you never know what you will find on the road. Which way do you take?" Impatient for them to be gone, Adrian nevertheless played the gracious host, concerned for his guests' welfare.

When Dru hesitated at the doorway, Adrian beckoned her into the room. "Good morning, my dear." He'd made his voice and manner as warm as possible.

It was hard to say who looked more startled—Lord Ives or Dru.

Adrian smiled and said nothing to explain his greeting. He rose, pulled out a chair for her, then poured her a cup of tea, sugaring it as he knew she preferred. He set it before her chair—which was next to his.

She regarded him from enchantingly confused eyes. He must see to it that she went to the coast, so she could view the sea, discover how her eyes reflected all the hues found there. She had admitted there had been no money to travel, that she longed to explore the world. Adrian smiled at the thought.

"I see they are loading your carriage, Lord Ives. You plan to depart so early in the day?" She avoided looking at Adrian, which amused him.

"If Lady Felicia can be persuaded to leave betimes, yes. Thank heavens that Adrian is loaning me a fourgon. We would look like a traveling caravan otherwise, with luggage strapped to the top of the carriage as well as poking out from the boot."

Dru giggled. "That presents an amusing image, sir."

"It does, doesn't it? No doubt that fellow Rowlandson could do a clever caricature of such a scene."

"The sort of thing that appears in the London print shops? My sister mentioned seeing some. They are terribly naughty. Unkind, as well. I would be just as glad not to be the object of such," she declared with fervor.

"Indeed," Adrian agreed. "One has to live with care. It would be a pity to discover a weakness drawn for all to view. Funny, you'd think you have been discreet, and then someone you least expect threatens to reveal all the details of a happening you thought secret."

Ives gave him another surprised look, before narrowing his eyes into a regard of conjecture. "I doubt if that has ever applied to you, Adrian. You might have had a few wild moments, but no scandal has ever been heard about you."

"True, I have lived with a modicum of discretion. I am aware of what is due my name and position. Not all peers are." Adrian reflected on a few peers he knew who were a disgrace to the peerage, not to mention England.

"True," Ives murmured as he dug into a well-laden plate of food.

Lady Felicia entered the room just as Ives had finished eating. She looked fetching in her pink-and-white pelisse with pink plumes on her bonnet. Adrian wondered if Ives would persuade her to wear something other than pink and white? It was impossible to know what another person might do for love. And he was convinced that Lady Felicia had tumbled into love with his best friend in spite of her original intentions—his mother's as well.

Adrian watched Dru pretend to eat. She buttered a piece of toast, then nibbled at it. Sipping tea didn't count as eating, but she did sip at her tea. Adrian rose to fetch her a small bowl of hothouse berries, plunking them down before her to her obvious surprise. He motioned her to eat them.

It was a good sign that she obeyed, tasting one berry before continuing to eat more of them. The toast went as well. He didn't want a discussion if she was hungry.

"Miss Knight is quite happy to have her little dog restored to her," Lady Felicia said. "How strange people are to be so attached to such a nasty little animal."

"My mother's cat is another. I wonder what she will do since Osman is not all that fond of cats."

"Surely you could allow the pet to remain here, my lord," Dru chided.

"Someone would have to be responsible for it. Cats are peculiar creatures, or so my mother insists. They want to be loved and cared for, not left to servants."

"Who is to say a servant won't become attached to it? Perhaps Mrs. Simpson?" Dru gave him a challenging stare.

"She could take the cat into her retirement when I pension her off?" Adrian said, cocking a brow at the delightfully annoyed Dru Herbert.

"You never would! Pension her off, that is. She is still capable of running this house—at least most of the time. She could have help when there are guests."

Dru placed her fists on the table as though ready to do battle on behalf of his housekeeper.

"You have spent hours and hours helping her while we had all this company in the house. Would *you* take on the job of assistant to her?" Adrian deliberately spoke in a taunting manner, wanting to rouse Dru from her doldrums.

"Ahem," Lord Ives inserted into the argument. "Felicia and I will take off now before that rain begins. My coachman said he feels it in his bones that it will pour here before long." He left the table, offering his hand to Felicia, who joined him at once.

Adrian rose, extended his hand with sincere best wishes not only for a good trip, but also with the woman he intended to marry. Adrian didn't envy him at all.

Dru also rose from the table, leaving crumbs from her toast behind her as she walked with Lady Felicia.

"Excited?" Adrian heard her ask.

"A little. Papa will be pleased, I think. He thought I was daft to believe I could marry Adrian. It seems he was right. I will be happier with Reginald. He understands me and has wonderful patience. Adrian is not a patient man."

Adrian squelched a grin at that observation. He had to agree with her. He was not a patient man. If he wanted something, he wanted it now—not at some vague future date.

Mrs. Twywhitt and Sir Bertram came down the stairs, having decided to travel together in search of a bird he had described to her. Miss Knight descended as well, with Binky under her arm. At the top of the stairs, Adrian caught a glimpse of Kitty giving a narrow-eyed glare at the departing dog.

Lord Somers, after privately telling Adrian how much he detested that dratted animal, left the house alone, quite as though he couldn't wait to get away from Binky as well as Miss Knight.

Lady Brentford and Lord Osman said farewell to

their guests, then retreated to the drawing room once the entryway had been cleared.

Dru Herbert and Adrian were alone once Priddy left.

"It is nearly ten of the clock." Dru checked on the longcase clock that stood in the corner of the hall, then returned her attention to him. "The library, I believe you said?" She gave a brave tilt of her chin, flashing her eyes at him as though she expected the worst.

"I did." He walked along at her side. He might have thought her going to the scaffold, so reluctant was she. Did she fear him so much? Or was it possibly the thought of being dismissed that troubled her more?

They entered the room, now bathed in the morning sunlight. The clouds Ives's coachman insisted were coming had yet to appear. There were a few springlike white puffs in the sky. No rain, however. Now the sun warmed the earth, not to mention the room.

Adrian guided Dru to that side of the library. Her hair glistened in the sunshine as the purest of gold. Her eyes had darkened with whatever emotion she experienced, as she apparently perceived a confrontation coming between them.

"They are all gone." He watched her eyes, so very expressive.

"Yes."

"And we are alone—more or less what with Mother and Osman at the other end of the house."

"And now you are going to tell me that it is time I go as well." She glowered at him from those sea blue eyes he would swear had swirls of a storm in them.

"Am I, now? What brought you to that conclusion?" He rubbed his chin to keep from drawing her into his arms as he wished to do. Time enough later, he hoped. Strangely enough, he was not certain of the outcome of this meeting.

"Well, are you not?" she countered.

"As a matter of fact, I am not." He watched the conflicting emotions flit across her face. How rapidly they changed.

"Why? Your mother is much better. Mrs. Simpson will have less to do now. I fancy you will be returning to London. This is the longest you have stayed here in years according to Mrs. Simpson."

"All true," Adrian agreed. "You have no desire to go to London? You prefer to remain in Kent, deep in the countryside?"

"There is nothing wrong with the countryside," she countered.

"Did I say there is? I asked your preference, my dear." He took a step closer, and she held her ground, defying him with every inch of her slender form.

"What has that to do with your departure for London? And another thing . . . I am not your dear!"

Adrian decided the moment had come. Time was running out, as was his patience. He tenderly gathered Dru into his embrace, kissing her with all the considerable expertise he had accumulated over the years. Encouraged that she did not fight him, he deepened the kiss until they were both dizzy and breathless.

"You are indeed my dear. I wish you to marry me, my love."

"M-marry you? You can't marry me. Think of the gossip were you to wed an unknown, a country chit of little background and no wealth." She did not look resolute, rather as though she wanted convincing. At least that was what he told himself.

He did not argue. Instead, he simply kissed her again. He decided that it was the best way to settle a dispute. She couldn't talk if she was being kissed!

"Um, that isn't fair. I can't think when you kiss me. I still say it would never do." But Adrian could tell she was weakening. Her voice was less forceful, and her eyes refused to meet his gaze. She made not the slightest effort to escape his embrace, either.

"What if it were brought out that you had attended me in my illness? You know what a chatterbox Lady Felicia is. She might well let something slip. You and I could well end up in one of those Rowlandson caricatures in the London shopwindows. That would put paid to any chance you might have for a respectable marriage."

"So I should marry you to escape a possible scandal? No, thank you very much. I want more than that in my marriage."

"Like a husband who adores you, who loves the touch of your hand, admires your beauty and thoughtfulness, who will tolerate that outspoken tongue?"

"That isn't you . . . is it?" She searched his face, meeting his gaze with care.

Adrian rejoiced that she sounded hopeful rather than determined. "It is, my love. You are, are you not? Have I read you wrong? Can it be that you do not return my love?"

Dru nestled closer to him, turning up her face in a trusting move. "I do love you. Very much, as a matter of fact. Do you suppose you might convince me that I could love you even more?" she asked, her grin saucy.

Adrian did his best, which seemed to satisfy his beloved Drusilla very much.

"We shall marry soon," he murmured. "After all, I am not a patient man!"

A rustle at the door caught their attention. His mother and her betrothed stood hand in hand, looking curious.

"Adrian, Osman and I shall marry at once," his mother declared. "I shall leave here shortly. Are you to have an interesting announcement as well?" Lady Brentwood looked from Dru to Adrian with a tender smile.

"You must know we do. We will marry in her village, then have our honeymoon by the coast. I want Dru to see how the water matches her eyes."

While his mother and Lord Osman retreated to make their plans, Adrian returned his attention to his love, telling her of the delights in store for her.